SO-BCM-269

PENGUIN BOOKS

THE PENGUIN BOOK OF
NEW AMERICAN VOICES

Jay McInerney was born in 1955. He has written fiction for magazines such as *Esquire* and *Atlantic* and is the author of the novels *Ransom*; *Bright Lights, Big City*; *The Story of My Life*; and *Brightness Falls*. The last three of these are published by Penguin. He also wrote the screenplay for the film version of *Bright Lights, Big City*.

He lives in New York City.

COWBOYS, INDIANS AND COMMUTERS

THE PENGUIN BOOK OF NEW AMERICAN VOICES

EDITED BY JAY McINERNEY

PENGUIN BOOKS

PENGUIN BOOKS

Published by the Penguin Group
Penguin Books Ltd, 27 Wrights Lane, London W8 5TZ, England
Penguin Books USA Inc., 375 Hudson Street, New York, New York 10014, USA
Penguin Books Australia Ltd, Ringwood, Victoria, Australia
Penguin Books Canada Ltd, 10 Alcorn Avenue, Toronto, Ontario, Canada M4V 3B2
Penguin Books (NZ) Ltd, 182–190 Wairau Road, Auckland 10, New Zealand

Penguin Books Ltd, Registered Offices: Harmondsworth, Middlesex, England

First published by Viking 1994
Published in Penguin Books 1995
1 3 5 7 9 10 8 6 4 2

The Acknowledgements on pages ix–x constitute an extension of this copyright page

Illustrations by Hannah Tofts

Printed in England by Clays Ltd, St Ives plc

For Donald Barthelme and Raymond Carver

CONTENTS

ACKNOWLEDGEMENTS

Thanks are due to the copyright holders of the following stories for permission to reproduce them in this volume.

Sherman Alexie: "The Lone Ranger and Tonto Fistfight in Heaven", published by Atlantic Monthly Press, reprinted by permission of Grove/Atlantic, Inc., copyright © 1993.

Dorothy Allison: "River of Names", published in *Trash* by Firebrand Books, reprinted by permission of Dorothy Allison/ Firebrand Books, copyright © 1983, 1988.

Charles D'Ambrosio: "Her Real Name", published in *Paris Review*, reprinted by permission of Virginia Barber Literary Agency, Inc. Copyright © 1993 by Charles D'Ambrosio Jr.

Robert Antoni: "Granny Myna Tells of the Child", published in *Divina Trace* by The Overlook Press, reprinted by permission of Robert Antoni, copyright © 1991 by Robert Antoni.

Jennifer Egan: "The Stylist", published in *Emerald City* by Picador, reprinted by permission of Virginia Barber Literary Agency, Inc. Copyright © 1989 by Jennifer Egan.

Jeff Eugenides: "Capricious Gardens", published in the *Gettysburg Review*, reprinted by permission of Jeffrey Eugenides, copyright © 1989.

Pam Houston: "Cowboys are My Weakness", reprinted by

INTRODUCTION

A few years ago a young French novelist told me I was very lucky to be an American writer, to be free of the Academy and the big dragging dinosaur tail of a long literary tradition. I'm sure he's right, though just over a hundred years ago Henry James was complaining bitterly about the lack of a native tradition. It must be said that Europeans are a little too eager to value American fiction for what they imagine to be its childlike freedom, as if we were all cowboys scratching our names on the *tabula rasa* of the great American landscape. We do have a few minutes of history here, even if we frequently feel free to ignore it.

In terms of the short story, that history has a kind of false start with Edgar Allen Poe's tales and with his review of Nathaniel Hawthorne's *Twice Told Tales*, for *Graham's Magazine* in 1842, in which he argues for the superiority of the short prose narrative over the novel by virtue of its "unity of effect or impression," something that can only be sustained in the mind of the reader for one sitting. Poe's romances influenced the development of French Symbolism but had few progeny on his native soil. From the colloquial frontier tales of Mark Twain and Bret Harte, through the later stories of O Henry, Sherwood Anderson and Ernest Hemingway, the most influential story writer of the twentieth century, vernacular realism has been the dominant mode of our short-story tradition.

Donald Barthelme was the avatar of a movement away from the realistic short story in the nineteen sixties, his first collection appearing about the time that John F. Kennedy was shot and the Beatles first appeared on American shores. The well-crafted, character-driven short story was one of many institutions that came under fire during the sixties. Barthelme attempted to subvert conventional linear narrative with techniques borrowed from the visual arts – like collage and film – extending certain trends of continental modernism, influenced in part by the surrealists as well as the native improvisations of beat fiction. The "story" became a self-consciously artificial construct, often studded with heterogeneous and found materials, fragments of pop culture and art history; he delighted in juxtaposing what critics of the fifties, like Lionel Trilling, loftily dichotomized as high culture and low culture.

Barthelme was the Elvis of the American short story. *New Yorker* readers accustomed to John Cheever and John O'Hara didn't know what to make of these droll, discontinuous and sometimes illustrated narratives. His early fictions – story isn't really the right word – electrified the literary community, received wide circulation by virtue of being published in the *New Yorker*, and became part of a somewhat vaguely defined new literature in revolt against an equally nebulous literary tradition. The term "metafiction" came to characterise much of the new writing, which failed to take its artificial and "made" status for granted, or to allow the reader to do so.

Barthelme was one of our first postmodernists; it was partly his influence, amplified by foreigners like Borges and Calvino, that made so much of the fiction of the late sixties and seventies so self-conscious and tricky until writing about writing briefly came to seem the norm – Flann O'Brien-like fictions about writers attacked by their own characters became the staple of the better quarterlies and anthologies, though the very idea of characters was suspect. In fact, the idea of "fiction" came into question, not only under the scrutiny of literary Maoists; in the decade between Kennedy's assassination and Nixon's resignation short fiction became the testing ground of the new aesthetics; many of the big boys of the American novel turned to nonfiction on the somewhat dubious premise that contemporary reality had outstripped our ability to recollect it in tranquility. Norman Mailer and Truman Capote were among those who, for a time, abandoned the "fictional" novel.

The aesthetic battles of the sixties and seventies had perhaps their final shootout in a debate between John Gardner and William Gass in the mid seventies. In a series of essays and a book, Gardner attacked the metafictionists and numerous straw men of letters, arguing for the eternal verities, for character-based, naturalistic fiction which deals with moral issues. Gass elegantly sneered at this reactionary didacticism, and argued that literature was made of words, pure and simple, and had nothing to do with the world. Moral issues might be very important, Gass said, but they had nothing to do with the beautiful artifice and play of fiction.

Every Romantic revolution elicits its neo-classical reaction at about the moment when the old iconoclasm begins to look like the new formalism. When metafiction started to seem like an academic orthodoxy, baroque and safe, like the rock music of the seventies with its Moog synthesizers and elaborate light shows, various strands of reaction were unravelling. In the mid seventies, several publishing events helped shape the subsequent development and popularity of the American short story. In 1976, a short-story writer named Raymond Carver, who had developed a cult first among readers of small literary quarterlies and then in the pages of *Esquire* magazine, published his first collection, *Will You Please Be Quiet Please*. That same year, Ann Beattie began publishing in the *New Yorker*. And realism suddenly regained all its credibility.

I vividly remember the first time I picked up Carver. My

contemporary fictional diet at this time consisted of Barthelme and Thomas Pynchon and the delightfully baroque John Hawkes. I was staggered by the immediacy of Carver's narrative surface, the colloquial simplicity and concreteness of the language. The rhythms and the almost naive clarity reminded me of Hemingway's early stories. But in Hemingway's stories the realistic mode served a kind of romantic mood; Hemingway's alienated soldiers and sportsmen drifted through picturesque landscapes – the still-virgin forests of Michigan, or the history-drenched hills and piazzas of Europe, despair palliated with the temporary analgesic of a good *vin de pays* or a day on the trout stream. In Carver the stoic glamour of drinking is replaced by the dull grind of full-time alcoholism, the wine by cheap gin and vodka. Hunting and fishing also play a role in Carver's work, but the trout in his streams often turn out to be pollution-deformed mutants – as in his earliest published story, "Nobody Said Anything." The deer are ingloriously wounded by hunters who are then too lazy to track them down.

Carver came out of the great American West, but he wrote about a frontier that was dissipated and trashed, and he wrote about people who had never found a voice in fiction before, the grandsons and granddaughters of pioneers, who lived in trailer parks and worked, when they worked, in sawmills and gas stations and who were barely able to articulate their own needs and fears to themselves. One of the wonders of Carver's work is the way it seems to evoke the inchoate and inarticulate depths of its disenfranchised characters, the way in which, like Hemingway's best work, it suggests so much more than it states.

Even for someone like myself, who had never been inside a trailer park or a factory, there was something terribly liberating about a fiction which *seemed*, unlike so much intentional and unintentional artifice in our literature, to strip away the encrusted layers of received perception and academic filigree and to reflect such an unvarnished view of contemporary life. Carver wrote about a world in which the television was always on, the milk carton and the ketchup bottle sat on the kitchen table, cigarettes actually had ashes and people went to the laundromat with dirty socks and underwear. Before Carver, I don't believe there was any laundry in American fiction. Like all writers who break through the shell of previously received literary conventions for the rendering of "reality," Carver's fiction seemed in the mid seventies to be hyperreal. (So much so that some of the metafictionists tried to claim he wasn't really a realist at all, that his tongue was somehow in his cheek.)

Anne Beattie was, from a slightly different vantage, also recreating the realistic short story. Beattie's stories, first published in the *New Yorker*, shimmered with a fine tension between form and content. In distinction to Barthelme and Carver and Barth, her narrative strategies were almost traditional, seemingly descended from the domestic realism of earlier *New Yorker* writers like John Cheever and John Updike. Her characters were recognizably upper middle-class urbanites and suburbanites, who answered to the basic unities of cause and effect. Or did they? These people had somehow undergone a sea change from the martini-drinking, lawn-mowing commuters and housewives who had spawned them.

As its very least accomplishment, Beattie's fiction redecorated the realistic short story and repopulated it. Her characters had smoked pot, dropped acid, grown up with rock music and developed an extreme skepticism toward authority and most of the eternal verities. They had lived through the seeming quantum leap from the fifties to the seventies, through Kennedy's assassination and the Summer of Love and the Vietnam War and Woodstock and Watergate. If at first it seemed amazing how little they differed from their fictional predecessors, if it seemed almost a disappointment – *shit, did it all add up to just a few cool song lyrics and brand names and drug culture metaphors* – a retrenchment and retreat from aesthetic revolution and Cosmic consciousness (Bob Dylan's phrase), it was subtly but crucially different than pre-rock and roll, pre-Vietnam war fiction. Beattie's stories had a fresh narrative rhythm, a way of defying linear expectation of cumulative narrative development, and a habit of trailing off into thin air that seemed tremendously mimetic and apt to many young readers and writers but must have frustrated many *New Yorker* readers looking for epiphany.

Beattie and Carver helped inspire a great renaissance of interest in the short story in America, a genuine flowering of talent and accomplishment. At the same moment, or in their immediate wake, came such superb short-story writers as Joy Williams, Tobias Wolff, Mary Robison, Barry Hannah, Richard Ford, Bobbie Anne Mason and a dozen others creating an exciting new realism. Though the short-story publishing market was ostensibly small, their influence was amplified through the numerous creative writing programs which in the seventies became one of the few growth areas of American higher education. Both had a kind of deceptive transparency which made what they did look easy: *no exotic landscapes, no tedious erudition necessary, kids*. And the short story flourished by virtue of being far more *teachable* than the novel. At the same time, the university itself, and the thousands of trained readers/writers it was producing, became the primary market for this new product, a kind of literary perpetual-motion machine.

Somewhere along the way the term minimalism was applied to this revival of the realistic short story. The word has been repeated so often, in reference to such diverse work, that it has been almost entirely drained of meaning. Carver's second collection, *What We Talk about When We Talk about Love*, was probably intentionally minimalist, as was Mary Robison's first book, *Days*. Certainly some of these writers attempted to pare their work down to barest narrative essentials, to strip away all ornament and commentary and even exposition and to dispense with the baroque narrative high jinks of metafiction. To some extent this attitude seemed politically appropriate, mimetic of a kind of exhaustion and emotional shellshock in the wake of a failed social revolution and an unjust war. But this ultra-spare manner in the hands of its second-generation practitioners – the ones who hadn't lived through Woodstock and Vietnam – could easily seem mannerist.

In 1978 the publication of John Cheever's collected short stories gave another boost to the realistic short story by virtue of exhibiting some superb examples – many written in the forties and fifties – for a new audience, which found them remarkably fresh. And suddenly Cheever, who had suffered something of an eclipse in the fiercely egalitarian, levelling sixties, made middle-class life an acceptable subject of short fiction. Forget minimalism for a moment. If there was an orthodoxy for the short story in the eighties it was a regnant mode of deadpan domestic realism. Following Beattie and Carver, most young short-story writers in the eighties wrote meticulously crafted studies of (failed) personal and familial relationships, set as often as not in the Cheever country of the suburbs where the educated middle-class kids of the baby boom – and the creative writing boom – had been raised. À la Carver and Beattie, affectlessness of narrative voice was at a premium; outrageous as well as boring domestic incidents were related without fuss and fanfare. The American frontier seemed for a while to be located somewhere between the kitchen sink and the hibachi in the backyard. Nature was the lawn.

David Leavitt extended suburban domestic realism to include gay subject matter. Lorrie Moore amusingly subverted it with a metafictional wit. Amy Hempel miniaturized it to the max. A minority were working in different traditions. T. Corraghassen

Boyle's short fictions of the seventies and early eighties were in the subversive mold of Barthelme, wildly inventive and self-reflexive. But in the field of the short story, middle-class realists ruled.

If Frank O'Connor, the great Irish short-story writer, had looked at American fiction in the eighties, he might have been surprised to find the short story, as reflected by the current periodicals, firmly in the hands of the middle class. In his brilliant study of the short story, "The Lonely Voice," O'Connor had argued that while the novel usually told the story of an individual's eventual integration into the social order, the short story was the instrument of expression for "submerged population groups," the territory of outlaws, marginal characters, oppressed minorities. In fact, in the mid eighties, the American novel seemed to be far more likely to give voice to new and marginal cultures. One of the notable and welcome developments of the past few years – it would be a little too convenient to say the nineties – is the sudden emergence in the short-story marketplace of a rainbow of "submerged population groups."

If diversity reflects vitality, the American short story comes into the nineties in contentious good health. Experimentation and postmodern gamesmanship coexist with a new kind of colloquial realism. If Henry James and Washington Irving and Edgar Allan Poe struggled to forge an American identity, much recent fiction tends to deconstruct the idea of a single national literature. Identity is more narrowly parsed by those who may not feel "the American tradition" is exactly coextensive with their own. Academics and anthologists increasingly speak of gay fiction, Afro-American fiction, Chicano fiction, Western and Southern fiction, women's fiction, a situation reflected in a casual perusal of this anthology.

Until recently the burgeoning American underclass has been under-represented in fiction for obvious reasons – educational deprivation, lack of both power and role models. Toward the end of the eighties the rise of rap and hip-hop music and a new crop of black filmmakers brought urban black culture to a wider and whiter audience, and something similar may be happening in our literature. Jess Mowry, a short-story writer whose stories, set in the streets and housing projects of Oakland California, were first published in small literary magazines like ZYZZYVA, drew wide attention with the publication in 1990 of his novel *Way Past Cool*. Like Mowry, Abraham Rodriguez Jr. writes in the fierce vernacular of the ghetto – in his case the black and Hispanic communities of New York's South Bronx.

Sherman Alexie is a Spokane/Coeur D'Alene Indian who also began his publishing career in the small literary magazines and whose story collection, *The Lone Ranger and Tonto Fistfight in Heaven*, shuttles back and forth between the rural ghetto of a Western Indian Reservation and the city of Seattle. Pam Houston, in "Cowboys are My Weakness," playfully celebrates and undermines the myths of the American West; Alexie's stories dissect the same myths with sharp instruments. But beneath their skeptical, naturalistic surfaces we catch shimmering glimpses of the mythology and "magic" of a native American heritage which the narrator can neither accept as a modern American in Nike sneakers, nor entirely reject as someone for whom being a modern American has failed.

William Vollmann's *Rainbow Stories*, published in 1989, present a rogues' gallery of skinheads, whores, sexual fetishists, terrorists. Something of a documentary realist on the one hand, Vollmann nevertheless fractures his narratives with bold headlines and metafictional footnotes. He writes at the farthest remove from the genteel tradition, which is to say it's hard to imagine him in the *New Yorker*. (Though the *New Yorker* is becoming far more catholic and less predictable under new management.) Also a novelist, Vollmann seems unafraid of not making sense, of boring or disgusting his reader, and uninterested in the finely wrought art object.

Vollmann is in many ways almost a throwback to the sixties and seventies, an experimental postmodernist, as is the furiously inventive David Foster Wallace, who, in his 1990 *Girl With Curious Hair*, published a hilariously self-conscious 150-page "story" about a postmodern creative writing seminar which seems to be taught by the metafictional master John Barth. (Like Vollmann, Foster Wallace is obviously not worrying about his audience's attention span.) Foster Wallace's settings and narrative strategies are wildly diverse and relentlessly contemporary – another story purports to be an intimate and exhaustive look behind the scenes of an actual television game show. Foster Wallace has also co-written a fairly scholarly study of rap music, and some of his work experiments with the "sampling" technique of rap in which soundtracks are assembled out of snippets of tape from pre-existing songs.

Another new postmodernist, Gail Donohue Storey, was a student of Donald Barthelme's, whose adventurous spirit I find beneath the hypnotic poetry of her story "Totally Nude Live Girls." Mark Leyner also seems to have ignored or rejected the domestic realism of the eighties and found his literary inspiration, if anywhere, in the anti-fiction and metafiction of the sixties. Leyner's fiction has something of the quality of Barthelme's early work – wry, self-conscious and often discontinuous narratives, which branch out into other narratives, studded with pop culture allusions. But Leyner's sense of narrative doesn't come from the visual arts but from new computer technology; his narratives seem to mimic the random access memory of the computer disk: he performs a kind of digital sampling technique, grazing on the data banks of history, appropriating the dialects of high technology, literature, pop culture and advertising.

Leyner's fiction is relentlessly of the moment; Donna Tartt's 1992 "Sleepytown," with its wonderful evocation of the Southern literary tradition, seems as if it might have been written anytime in the last fifty years. We might take these as two poles, and feel grateful for the distance between them. One of the best things we can say about the Great American Short Story toward the end of the century is that anything goes – even that there is no such beast.

EDITOR'S NOTE

The rules are these: I have tried to limit this anthology to short stories by writers whose publishing careers have begun in the nineties. I was not seeking a politically correct diversity, nor trying to make the case for multiculturalism – if so, there would be a better balance between men and women. On the other hand, as I consulted my memory, the literary periodicals, and various editors, agents and writers, I was struck by a sense of demographic and aesthetic variety in the short fiction being published in America in the past few years. I tried to seek out and include work that seemed fresh and provocative, and in doing so probably discriminated against the clean, well-behaved short story with impeccable table manners. The final criterion for selection was simply the personal taste of a professional writer and amateur reader.

THE LONE RANGER AND TONTO FISTFIGHT IN HEAVEN

Sherman Alexie

Sherman Alexie, a Spokane/Coeur d'Alene Indian, is a writer and poet born in 1966. A contributor to various publications such as the *New York Quarterly, Beloit Poetry Journal, Kenyon Review* and ZYZZYVA, his already published books of poetry, *I Would Steal Horses* (1992) and *Old Shirts & New Skins* (1993), and his book of stories and poems, *The Business of Fancydancing* (1992), are soon to be followed by another book of poems, another story collection, and a novel on which he is currently working.

THE LONE RANGER AND TONTO FISTFIGHT IN HEAVEN

Too hot to sleep so I walked down to the Third Avenue 7–11 for a creamsicle and the company of a graveyard shift cashier. I know that game. I worked graveyard for a Seattle 7–11 and got robbed once too often. The last time the bastard locked me in the cooler. He even took my wallet and basketball shoes.

The graveyard shift worker in the Third Avenue 7–11 looked like they all do. Acne scars and a bad haircut, work pants that showed off his white socks, and those cheap black shoes that have no support. My arches still ache from my year at the Seattle 7–11.

"Hello," he asked when I walked into his store. "How you doing?"

I gave him a half-wave as I headed back to the freezer. He looked me over so he could describe me to the police later. I knew the look. One of my old girlfriends said I started to look at her that way, too. She left me not long after that. No, I left her and don't blame her for anything. That's how it happened. When one person starts to look at another like a criminal, then the love is over. It's logical.

"I don't trust you," she said to me. "You get too angry."

She was white and I lived with her in Seattle. Some nights, we fought so bad that I would just get in my car and drive all

3

night, only stop to fill up on gas. In fact, I worked the graveyard shift to spend as much time away from her as possible. But I learned all about Seattle that way, driving its back ways and dirty alleys.

Sometimes, though, I would forget where I was and get lost. I'd drive for hours, searching for something familiar. Seems like I'd spent my whole life that way, looking for anything I recognized. Once, I ended up in a nice residential neighborhood and somebody must have been worried because the police showed up and pulled me over.

"What are you doing out here?" the police officer asked me as he looked over my license and registration.

"I'm lost."

"Well, where are you supposed to be?" he asked me and I knew there were plenty of places I wanted to be, but none where I was supposed to be.

"I got in a fight with my girlfriend," I said. "I was just driving around, blowing off steam, you know?"

"Well, you should be more careful where you drive," the officer said. "You're making people nervous. You don't fit the profile of the neighborhood."

I wanted to tell him that I didn't really fit the profile of the country but I knew it would just get me into trouble.

"Can I help you?" the 7–11 clerk asked me loudly, searching for some response that would reassure him that I wasn't an armed robber. He knew this dark skin and long, black hair of mine was dangerous. I had potential.

"Just getting a creamsicle," I said after a long interval. It was a sick twist to pull on the guy but it was late and I was bored. I grabbed my creamsicle and walked back to the counter slowly, scanned the aisles for effect. I wanted to whistle low and menacingly but I never learned to whistle.

"Pretty hot out tonight?" he asked, that old rhetorical

weather bullshit question designed to put us both at ease.

"Hot enough to make you go crazy," I said and smiled. He swallowed hard like a white man does in those situations. I looked him over. Same old green, red, and white 7-11 jacket and thick glasses. But he wasn't ugly, just misplaced and marked by loneliness. If he wasn't working there that night, he'd be at home alone, flipping through channels and wishing he could afford HBO or Showtime.

"Will this be all?" he asked me, in that company effort to make me do some impulse shopping. Like adding a clause onto a treaty. *We'll take Washington and Oregon and you get six pine trees and a brand-new Chrysler Cordoba.* I knew how to make and break promises.

"No," I said and paused. "Give me a Cherry Slushie, too."

"What size?" he asked, relieved.

"Large," I said and he turned his back to me to make the drink. He realized his mistake but it was too late. He stiffened, ready for the gunshot or the blow behind the ear. When it didn't come, he turned back to me.

"I'm sorry," he said. "What size did you say?"

"Small," I said and changed the story.

"But I thought you said large."

"If you knew I wanted a large, then why did you ask me again?" I asked him and laughed. He looked at me, couldn't decide if I was giving him serious shit or just goofing. There was something about him I liked, even if it was three in the morning and he was white.

"Hey," I said. "Forget the Slushie. What I want to know is if you know all the words to the theme from *The Brady Bunch*?"

He looked at me, confused at first, then laughed.

"Shit," he said. "I was hoping you weren't crazy. You were scaring me."

"Well, I'm going to get crazy if you don't know the words."

5

He laughed loudly then, told me to take the creamsicle for free. He was the graveyard shift manager and those little demonstrations of power tickled him. All 75¢ of it. I knew how much everything cost.

"Thanks," I said to him and walked out the door. I took my time walking home, let the heat of the night melt the creamsicle all over my hand. At three in the morning I could act just as young as I want to act. There was no one around to ask me to grow up.

In Seattle, I broke lamps. She and I would argue and I'd break a lamp, just pick it up and throw it down. At first, she'd buy replacement lamps, expensive and beautiful. But after a while, she'd buy lamps from Goodwill or garage sales. Then, she just gave up the idea entirely and we'd argue in the dark.

"You're just like your brother," she'd yell. "Drunk all the time and stupid."

"My brother don't drink that much."

She and I never tried to hurt each other physically. I did love her, after all, and she loved me. But those arguments were just as damaging as a fist. Words can be like that, you know? Whenever I get into arguments now, I remember her and I also remember Mohammed Ali. He knew the power of his fists but more importantly, he knew the power of his words, too. Even though he only had an IQ of 80 or so, Ali was a genius. And she was a genius, too. She knew exactly what to say to cause me the most pain.

But don't get me wrong. I walked through that relationship with an executioner's hood. Or more appropriately, with war paint and sharp arrows. She was a kindergarten teacher and I continually insulted her for that.

"Hey, school marm," I asked. "Did your kids teach you anything new today?"

And I always had crazy dreams. I always have had them but it seemed they became nightmares more often in Seattle.

In one dream, she was a missionary's wife and I was a minor war chief. We fell in love and tried to keep it secret. But the missionary caught us fucking in the barn and shot me. As I lay dying, my tribe learned of the shooting and attacked the whites all across the reservation. I died and my soul drifted above the reservation.

Disembodied, I could see everything that was happening. Whites killing Indians and Indians killing whites. At first, it was small, just my tribe and the few whites who lived there. But, my dream grew, intensified. Other tribes arrived on horseback to continue the slaughter of whites and the United States Cavalry rode into battle.

The most vivid image of that dream stays with me. Three mounted soldiers played polo with a dead Indian woman's head. When I first dreamed it, I thought it was just a product of my anger and imagination. But since then, I've read similar accounts of that kind of evil in the old West. Even more terrifying, though, is the fact that those kind of brutal things are happening today in places like El Salvador.

All I know for sure, though, is that I woke from that dream in terror, packed up all my possessions, and left Seattle in the middle of the night.

"I love you," she said as I left her. "And don't ever come back."

I drove through the night, over the Cascades, down into the plains of Central Washington, and back home to the Spokane Indian Reservation.

When I finished the creamsicle that the 7–11 clerk gave me, I held the wooden stick up into the air and shouted out very loudly. A couple lights flashed on in windows and a police car cruised by me a few minutes later. I waved to the men in blue and they waved back accidentally. When I got home it was still too hot to sleep so I picked up a week-old newspaper from the floor and read.

There was another civil war, another terrorist bomb exploded, and one more plane crashed and all aboard were presumed dead. The crime rate was rising in every city with populations larger than 100,000 and a farmer in Iowa shot his banker after foreclosure on his 1,000 acres.

A kid from Spokane won the local spelling bee by spelling out the word *rhinoceros*.

When I got back to the reservation, my family wasn't surprised to see me. They'd been expecting me back since the day I left for Seattle. There's an old Indian poet who said that Indians can reside in the city, but they can never live there. That's as close to truth as any of us can get.

Mostly, I watched television. For weeks, I flipped through channels, searched for answers in the game shows and soap operas. My mother would circle the want ads in red and hand the paper to me.

"What are you going to do with the rest of your life?" she asked.

"Don't know," I said and normally, for almost any other Indian in the country, that would have been a perfectly fine answer. But I was special, a former college student, a smart kid. I was one of those Indians who was supposed to make it, to rise above the rest of the reservation like a fucking eagle or something. I was the new kind of warrior.

For a few months, I didn't even look at the want ads my mother circled, just left the newspaper where she had set it down. After a while, though, I got tired of the television and started to play basketball again. I'd been a good player in high school, nearly great, and almost played at the college I attended for a couple years. But I'd been too out of shape from drinking and sadness to ever be good again. Still, I liked the way the ball felt in my hands and the way my feet felt inside my shoes.

At first, I just shot baskets all by myself. It was selfish and I also wanted to learn the game again before I played against anybody else. Since I had been good before and embarrassed fellow tribal members, I knew they would want to take revenge on me. Forget about the cowboys versus Indians business. The most intense competition on any reservation is Indians versus Indians.

But on the night I was ready to play for real, there was this white guy at the gym, playing with all the Indians.

"Who is that?" I asked Jimmy Seyler.

"He's the new BIA chief's kid."

"Can he play?"

"Oh, yeah."

And he could play. He played Indian ball, fast and loose, better than all the Indians there.

"How long he's been playing here?" I asked.

"Long enough."

I stretched my muscles and everybody watched me. All these Indians watched one of their old and dusty heroes. Even though I had played most of my ball at the white high school I went to, I was still all Indian, you know? I was Indian when it counted and this BIA kid needed to be beaten by an Indian, any Indian.

I jumped into the game and played well for a little while. It felt good. I hit a few shots, grabbed a rebound or two, played enough defense to keep the other team honest. Then, that white kid took over the game. He was too good. Later, he'd play college ball back East and nearly made the Knicks team a couple years back. But we didn't know any of that would happen. We just knew he was better that day and every other day.

The next morning, I woke up tired and hungry, so I grabbed the want ads, found a job I wanted, and drove to Spokane to get it. I've been working at the high school exchange program ever since, typing and answering phones. Sometimes, I wonder if the people on the other end of the line know that I'm Indian and if their voices would change if they did know.

One day, I picked up the phone and it was her, calling from Seattle.

"I got your number from your mom," she said. "I'm glad you're working."

"Yeah, nothing like a regular paycheck."

"Are you drinking?"

"No, I've been on the wagon for almost a year."

"Good."

The connection was good. I could hear her breathing in the spaces between our words. How do you talk to the real person whose ghost has haunted you? How do you tell the difference between the two?

"Listen," I said. "I'm sorry for everything."

"Me, too."

"What's going to happen to us?" I asked her and wished I had the answer for myself.

"I don't know," she said. "I want to change the world."

These days, living alone in Spokane, I wish I lived closer to the river, to the falls where ghosts of salmon jump. I wish I could sleep. I put down my paper or book and turn off all the lights, lay quietly in the dark. It may take hours, even years, for me to sleep again. There's nothing surprising or disappointing in that.

I know how all my dreams end anyway.

RIVER OF NAMES

Dorothy Allison

Dorothy Allison, born in Greenville, South Carolina, is a writer and poet who has contributed to various publications and collections. Her already published works – the novel, *Bastard out of Carolina* (1992), the book of short stories, *Trash* (1988) and the book of poetry, *The Women Who Hate Me* (1990) – are soon to be followed by her next novel, *Cavedweller*.

RIVER OF NAMES

At a picnic at my aunt's farm, the only time the whole family ever gathered, my sister Billie and I chased chickens into the barn. Billie ran right through the open doors and out again, but I stopped, caught by a shadow moving over me. My cousin, Tommy, eight years old as I was, swung in the sunlight with his face as black as his shoes – the rope around his neck pulled up into the sunlit heights of the barn, fascinating, horrible. Wasn't he running ahead of us? Someone came up behind me. Someone began to scream. My mama took my head in her hands and turned my eyes away.

Jesse and I have been lovers for a year now. She tells me stories about her childhood, about her father going off each day to the university, her mother who made all her dresses, her grandmother who always smelled of dill bread and vanilla. I listen with my mouth open, not believing but wanting, aching for the fairy tale she thinks is everyone's life.

"What did your grandmother smell like?"

I lie to her the way I always do, a lie stolen from a book. "Like lavender", stomach churning over the memory of sour sweat and snuff.

I realize I do not really know what lavender smells like, and I am for a moment afraid she will ask something else, some

13

question that will betray me. But Jesse slides over to hug me, to press her face against my ear, to whisper, "How wonderful to be part of such a large family."

I hug her back and close my eyes. I cannot say a word.

I was born between the older cousins and the younger, born in a pause of babies and therefore outside, always watching. Once, way before Tommy died, I was pushed out on the steps while everyone stood listening to my Cousin Barbara. Her screams went up and down in the back of the house. Cousin Cora brought buckets of bloody rags out to be burned. The other cousins all ran off to catch the sparks or poke the fire with dogwood sticks. I waited on the porch making up words to the shouts around me. I did not understand what was happening. Some of the older cousins obviously did, their strange expressions broken by stranger laughs. I had seen them helping her up the stairs while the thick blood ran down her legs. After a while the blood on the rags was thin, watery, almost pink. Cora threw them on the fire and stood motionless in the stinking smoke.

Randall went by and said there'd be a baby, a hatched egg to throw out with the rags, but there wasn't. I watched to see and there wasn't; nothing but the blood, thinning out desperately while the house slowed down and grew quiet, hours of cries growing soft and low, moaning under the smoke. My Aunt Raylene came out on the porch and almost fell on me, not seeing me, not seeing anything at all. She beat on the post until there were knuckle-sized dents in the peeling paint, beat on that post like it could feel, cursing it and herself and every child in the yard, singing up and down, "Goddamn, goddamn, that girl . . . no sense . . . goddamn!"

I've these pictures my mama gave me – stained sepia prints of bare dirt yards, plank porches, and step after step of children –

cousins, uncles, aunts; mysteries. The mystery is how many no one remembers. I show them to Jesse, not saying who they are, and when she laughs at the broken teeth, torn overalls, the dirt, I set my teeth at what I do not want to remember and cannot forget.

We were so many we were without number and, like tadpoles, if there was one less from time to time, who counted? My maternal great-grandmother had eleven daughters, seven sons; my grandmother, six sons, five daughters. Each one made at least six. Some made nine. Six times six, eleven times nine. They went on like multiplication tables. They died and were not missed. I come of an enormous family and I cannot tell half their stories. Somehow it was always made to seem they killed themselves: car wrecks, shotguns, dusty ropes, screaming, falling out of windows, things inside them. I am the point of a pyramid, sliding back under the weight of the ones who came after, and it does not matter that I am the lesbian, the one who will not have children.

I tell the stories and it comes out funny. I drink bourbon and make myself drawl, tell all those old funny stories. Someone always seems to ask me, which one was that? I show the pictures and she says, "Wasn't she the one in the story about the bridge?" I put the pictures away, drink more, and someone always finds them, then says, "Goddamn! How many of you were there anyway?"

I don't answer.

Jesse used to say, "You've got such a fascination with violence. You've got so many terrible stories."

She said it with her smooth mouth, that chin nobody ever slapped, and I love that chin, but when Jesse spoke then, my hands shook and I wanted nothing so much as to tell her terrible stories.

So I made a list. I told her: that one went insane – got her little brother with a tire iron; the three of them slit their arms, not the wrists but the bigger veins up near the elbow; she, now *she* strangled the boy she was sleeping with and got sent away; that one drank lye and died laughing soundlessly. In one year I lost eight cousins. It was the year everybody ran away. Four disappeared and were never found. One fell in the river and was drowned. One was run down hitchhiking north. One was shot running through the woods, while Grace, the last one, tried to walk from Greenville to Greer for some reason nobody knew. She fell off the overpass a mile down from the Sears, Roebuck warehouse and lay there for hunger and heat and dying.

Later, sleeping, but not sleeping, I found that my hands were up under Jesse's chin. I rolled away, but I didn't cry. I almost never let myself cry.

Almost always, we were raped, my cousins and I. That was some kind of joke, too.

> *What's a South Carolina virgin?*
> *'At's a ten-year-old can run fast.*

It wasn't funny for me in my mama's bed with my stepfather, not for my cousin, Billie, in the attic with my uncle, not for Lucille in the woods with another cousin, for Danny with four strangers in a parking lot, or for Pammie who made the papers. Cora read it out loud: "Repeatedly by persons unknown." They stayed unknown since Pammie never spoke again. Perforations, lacerations, contusions and bruises. I heard all the words, big words, little words, words too terrible to understand. DEAD BY AN ACT OF MAN. With the prick still in them, the broom handle, the tree branch, the grease gun . . . objects, things not to be believed . . . whiskey bottles, can openers, grass shears, glass, metal, vegetables . . . not to be believed, not to be believed.

Jesse says, "You've got a gift for words."

"Don't talk," I beg her, "don't talk." And this once, she just holds me, blessedly silent.

I dig out the pictures, stare into the faces. Which one was I? Survivors do hate themselves, I know, over the core of fierce self-love, never understanding, always asking, "Why me and not her, not him?" There is such mystery in it, and I have hated myself as much as I have loved others, hated the simple fact of my own survival. Having survived, am I supposed to say something, do something, be something?

I loved my Cousin Butch. He had this big old head, pale thin hair, and enormous, watery eyes. All the cousins did, though Butch's head was the largest, his hair the palest. I was the dark-headed one. All the rest of the family seemed pale carbons of each other in shades of blond, though later on everybody's hair went brown or red and I didn't stand out so. Butch and I stood out then – I because I was so dark and fast, and he because of that big head and the crazy things he did. Butch used to climb on the back of my Uncle Lucius's truck, open the gas tank and hang his head over, breathe deeply, strangle, gag, vomit, and breathe again. It went so deep, it tingled in your toes. I climbed up after him and tried it myself, but I was too young to hang on long, and I fell heavily to the ground, dizzy and giggling. Butch could hang on, put his hand down into the tank and pull up a cupped palm of gas, breathe deep and laugh. He would climb down roughly, swinging down from the door handle, laughing, staggering, and stinking of gasoline. Someone caught him at it. Someone threw a match. "I'll teach you."

Just like that, gone before you understand.

I wake up in the night screaming, "No, no, I won't!" Dirty water rises in the back of my throat, the liquid language of my own terror and rage. "Hold me. Hold me." Jesse rolls over on me; her hands grip my hipbones tightly.

"I love you. I love you. I'm here," she repeats.

I stare up into her dark eyes, puzzled, afraid. I draw a breath in deeply, smile my bland smile. "Did I fool you?" I laugh, rolling away from her. Jesse punches me playfully, and I catch her hand in the air.

"My love," she whispers, and cups her body against my hip, closes her eyes. I bring my hand up in front of my face and watch the knuckles, the nails as they tremble, tremble. I watch for a long time while she sleeps, warm and still against me.

James went blind. One of the uncles got him in the face with home-brewed alcohol.

Lucille climbed out the front window of Aunt Raylene's house and jumped. They said she jumped. No one said why.

My Uncle Matthew used to beat my Aunt Raylene. The twins, Mark and Luke, swore to stop him, pulled him out in the yard one time, throwing him between them like a loose bag of grain. Uncle Matthew screamed like a pig coming up for slaughter. I got both my sisters in the tool shed for safety, but I hung back to watch. Little Bo came running out of the house, off the porch, feet first into his daddy's arms. Uncle Matthew started swinging him like a scythe, going after the bigger boys, Bo's head thudding their shoulders, their hips. Afterward, Bo crawled around in the dirt, the blood running out of his ears and his tongue hanging out of his mouth, while Mark and Luke finally got their daddy down. It was a long time before I realized that they never told anybody else what had happened to Bo.

Randall tried to teach Lucille and me to wrestle. "Put your hands up." His legs were wide apart, his torso bobbing up and down, his head moving constantly. Then his hand flashed at my face. I threw myself back into the dirt, lay still. He turned to Lucille, not noticing that I didn't get up. He punched at her, laughing. She wrapped her hands around her head, curled over so her knees were up against her throat.

"No, no," he yelled. "Move like her." He turned to me. "Move." He kicked at me. I rocked into a ball, froze.

"No, no!" He kicked me. I grunted, didn't move. He turned to Lucille. "You." Her teeth were chattering but she held herself still, wrapped up tighter than bacon slices.

"You move!" he shouted. Lucille just hugged her head tighter and started to sob.

"Son of a bitch," Randall grumbled, "you two will never be any good."

He walked away. Very slowly we stood up, embarrassed, looked at each other. We knew.

If you fight back, they kill you.

My sister was seven. She was screaming. My stepfather picked her up by her left arm, swung her forward and back. It gave. The arm went around loosely. She just kept screaming. I didn't know you could break it like that.

I was running up the hall. He was right behind me. "Mama! Mama!" His left hand – he was left-handed – closed around my throat, pushed me against the wall, and then he lifted me that way. I kicked, but I couldn't reach him. He was yelling, but there was so much noise in my ears I couldn't hear him.

"Please, Daddy. Please, Daddy. I'll do anything, I promise. Daddy, anything you want. Please, Daddy."

I couldn't have said that. I couldn't talk around that fist at my throat, couldn't breathe. I woke up when I hit the floor. I looked up at him.

"If I live long enough, I'll fucking kill you."

He picked me up by my throat again.

What's wrong with her?
Why's she always following you around?
Nobody really wanted answers.

A full bottle of vodka will kill you when you're nine and the bottle is a quart. It was a third cousin proved that. We learned what that and other things could do. Every year there was something new.

You're growing up.
My big girl.

There was codeine in the cabinet, paregoric for the baby's teeth, whiskey, beer, and wine in the house. Jeanne brought home MDA, PCP, acid; Randall, grass, speed, and mescaline. It all worked to dull things down, to pass the time.

Stealing was a way to pass the time. Things we needed, things we didn't, for the nerve of it, the anger, the need. *You're growing up*, we told each other. But sooner or later, we all got caught. Then it was, *When are you going to learn?*

Caught, nightmares happened. *Razorback desperate*, was the conclusion of the man down at the county farm where Mark and Luke were sent at fifteen. They both got their heads shaved, their earlobes sliced.

What's the matter, kid? Can't you take it?

Caught at sixteen, June was sent to Jessup County Girls' Home where the baby was adopted out and she slashed her wrists on the bedsprings.

Lou got caught at seventeen and held in the station downtown, raped on the floor of the holding tank.

Are you a boy or are you a girl?
On your knees, kid, can you take it?

Caught at eighteen and sent to prison, Jack came back seven years later blank-faced, understanding nothing. He married a quiet girl from out of town, had three babies in four years. Then Jack came home one night from the textile mill, carrying one of those big handles off the high-speed spindle machine. He used it to beat them all to death and went back to work in the morning.

Cousin Melvina married at fourteen, had three kids in two and a half years, and welfare took them all away. She ran off with a carnival mechanic, had three more babies before he left her for a motorcycle acrobat. Welfare took those, too. But the next baby was hydrocephalic, a little waterhead they left with her, and the three that followed, even the one she used to hate so – the one she had after she fell off the porch and couldn't remember whose child it was.

"How many children do you have?" I asked her.

"You mean the ones I have, or the ones I had? Four," she told me, "or eleven."

My aunt, the one I was named for, tried to take off for Oklahoma. That was after she'd lost the youngest girl and they told her Bo would never be "right". She packed up biscuits, cold chicken, and Coca-Cola, a lot of loose clothes, Cora and her new baby, Cy, and the four youngest girls. They set off from Greenville in the afternoon, hoping to make Oklahoma by the weekend, but they only got as far as Augusta. The bridge there went out under them.

"An Act of God," my uncle said.

My aunt and Cora crawled out down river, and two of the girls turned up in the weeds, screaming loud enough to be found in the dark. But one of the girls never came up out of that dark water, and Nancy, who had been holding Cy, was found still wrapped around the baby, in the water, under the car.

"An Act of God," my aunt said. "God's got one damn sense of humor."

My sister had her baby in a bad year. Before he was born we had talked about it. "Are you afraid?" I asked.

"He'll be fine," she'd replied, not understanding, speaking instead to the other fear. "Don't we have a tradition of bastards?"

He was fine, a classically ugly healthy little boy with that shock of white hair that marked so many of us. But afterward, it was that bad year with my sister down with pleurisy, then cystitis, and no work, no money, having to move back home with my cold-eyed stepfather. I would come home to see her, from the woman I could not admit I'd been with, and take my infinitely fragile nephew and hold him, rocking him, rocking myself.

One night I came home to screaming – the baby, my sister, no one else there. She was standing by the crib, bent over, screaming red-faced, "Shut up! Shut up!" With each word her fist slammed the mattress fanning the baby's ear.

"Don't!" I grabbed her, pulling her back, doing it as gently as I could so I wouldn't break the stitches from her operation. She had her other arm clamped across her abdomen and couldn't fight me at all. She just kept shrieking.

"That little bastard just screams and screams. That little bastard. I'll kill him."

Then the words seeped in and she looked at me while her son kept crying and kicking his feet. By his head the mattress still showed the impact of her fist.

"Oh no," she moaned, "I wasn't going to be like that. I always promised myself." She started to cry, holding her belly and sobbing. "We an't no different. We an't no different."

Jesse wraps her arm around my stomach, presses her belly into my back. I relax against her. "You sure you can't have children?" she asks. "I sure would like to see what your kids would turn out to be like."

I stiffen, say, "I can't have children. I've never wanted children."

"Still," she says, "you're so good with children, so gentle."

I think of all the times my hands have curled into fists, when I have just barely held on. I open my mouth, close it, can't speak. What could I say now? All the times I have not spoken before, all the things I just could not tell her, the shame, the self-hatred, the fear; all of that hangs between us now – a wall I cannot tear down.

I would like to turn around and talk to her, tell her . . . "I've got a dust river in my head, a river of names endlessly repeating. That dirty water rises in me, all those children screaming out their lives in my memory, and I become someone else, someone I have tried so hard not to be."

But I don't say anything, and I know, as surely as I know I will never have a child, that by not speaking I am condemning us, that I cannot go on loving you and hating you for your fairy-tale life, for not asking about what you have no reason to imagine, for that soft-chinned innocence I love.

Jesse puts her hands behind my neck, smiles and says, "You tell the funniest stories."

I put my hands behind her back, feeling the ridges of my knuckles pulsing.

"Yeah," I tell her. "But I lie."

HER REAL NAME

Charles D'Ambrosio

Charles D'Ambrosio's stories have appeared in the *New Yorker, Paris Review* and *Story*. His story "Her Real Name" won the *Paris Review*'s Aga Khan Prize. He is currently completing a collection of stories to be published by Little, Brown and Co.

HER REAL NAME

for PLA

I

The girl's scalp looked as though it had been singed by fire –
strands of thatchy red hair snaked away from her face, then
settled against her skin, pasted there by sweat and sunscreen
and the blown grit and dust of travel. For a while her thin hair
had remained as light and clean as the down of a newborn
chick, but it was getting hotter as they drove west, heading
into a summer-long drought that scorched the landscape, that
withered the grass and melted the black tar between expansion
joints in the road and bloated like balloons the bodies of
raccoon and deer and dog and made everything on the highway
ahead ripple like a mirage through waves of rising heat. Since
leaving Fargo, it had been too hot to wear the wig, and it now
lay on the seat between them, still holding within its webbing
the shape of her head. Next to it, a bag of orange candy –
smiles, she called them – spilled across the vinyl. Sugar crystals
ran into the dirty stitching and stuck to her thigh. Gum
wrappers and greasy white bags littered the floor, and on the
dash, amid a flotsam of plastic cups, pennies and matchbooks,
a bumper-sticker curled in the heat. "Expect a Miracle," it
read. The man and the girl had been living in his car for the
past month. Neither of them had bathed in days.

The girl cradled a black Bible in her lap, the leather covers
as worn and ragged as old tennis shoes. The inner leaf

27

contained a family tree dating back to 1827, names tightly scrawled in black against yellowing parchment, a genealogy as ponderous as those kept in Genesis, the book of the generations of Adam. The list of ancestors on the inner leaf was meaningless ancient history to the man, whose name was Jones, but the girl said her family had carried that same Bible with them wherever they went, for one hundred and fifty years, and that she wanted it with her too. "That's me," the girl had said, showing Jones her name, the newest of all, penned in generous loops of Bic blue. She's written it in herself along the margin of the page. *b. 1960–*. The girl read different passages aloud as they drove, invoking a mix of epic beauty and bad memories, the Exodus and the leather belt her stepfather used to beat her when she broke a commandment – one of the original ten or one of his additions. Jones wasn't sure what faith she placed in the austere Christianity of her forefathers, but reading aloud seemed to cast a spell over her. She had a beautiful church-trained voice that lifted each verse into a soothing melody, a song whose tune of succor rose and fell somewhere beyond the harsh demands of faith. Only minutes before she'd read herself to sleep with a passage from Jeremiah.

Now, as if she felt Jones staring, the girl stirred.

"You were looking at me," she said. "You were thinking something."

Her face was shapeless, soft and pale as warm putty.

"I could feel it," she said. "Where are we?"

They hadn't gone more than a mile since she'd dozed off. She reached for the candy on the seat.

"You hungry? You want a smile, Jones?"

"No, none for me," Jones said.

"A Life Saver?" She held the unraveled package out.

"Nothing, thanks."

"Me eating candy, and my teeth falling out." The girl licked the sugar off a smile and asked, "How far to Las Vegas?"

Jones jammed a tape in the eight-track. He was driving a 1967 Belvedere he'd bought for seven hundred dollars cash in Newport News, and it had come with a bulky eight-track, like an atavistic organ, bolted beneath the glove box. He'd found two tapes in the trunk, and now, after fifteen thousand miles, he was fairly sick of both Tom Jones and Steppenwolf. But he preferred the low-fidelity noise of either tape to the sound of himself lying.

"Why don't you come with me little girl," he sang along, in a high, mocking falsetto, "on a magic carpet ride."

"How far?" the girl asked.

Jones adjusted his grip on the steering wheel. "Another day, maybe."

She seemed to fall asleep again, her dry-lidded eyes shut like a lizard's, her parched, flaking lips parted, her frail body given over to the car's gentle rocking. Jones turned his attention back to the road, a hypnotic black line snaking through waves of yellow grass. It seemed to Jones that they'd been traveling through eastern Montana forever, that the same two or three trees, the same two or three farmhouses and grain silos were rushing past like scenery in an old movie, only suggesting movement. Endless fields, afire in the bright sun, were occasionally broken by stands of dark cottonwood or the gutted chassis of a rusting car. Collapsing barns leaned over in the grass, giving into the hot wind and the insistent flatness, as if passively accepting the laws of a world whose only landmark, as far as Jones could see, was the level horizon.

"He's out there," the girl said. "I can feel him out there when I close my eyes. He knows where we are." *This introduces Fenrize*

"I doubt that very much," Jones said.

The girl struggled to turn, gripping the headrest; she looked through the rear window at the warp of the road as it narrowed to a pinprick on the pale edge of the world they'd left behind; it was out of the vanishing point that her father would come.

"I expect he'll be caught up soon," she said. "He's got a sense. One time he predicted an earthquake."

"It's a big country," Jones said. "We could've gone a million other ways. Maybe if you think real hard about Florida that'll foul up his super-duper predicting equipment."

"Prayer," the girl said. "He prays. Nothing fancy. We're like Jonah sneaking on that boat in Tarshish; they found him out."

The girl closed her eyes; she splashed water on face and chest.

"It's so hot," she said. "Tell me some more about the Eskimos."

"I'm running out of things to say about Eskimos," Jones said. "I only read that one book."

"Say old stuff, I don't care."

He searched his memory for what he remembered of Knud Rasmussen.

"Nothing's wasted," Jones said. "They use everything. The Inuit can make a sled out of a slain dog. They kill the dog and skin it, then cut the hide into two strips."

"I'm burning alive," the girl said.

"They roll up the hide and freeze the strips in water to make the runners. Then they join the runners together with the dog's rib bones." Jones nibbled the corner of an orange smile. "One minute the dog's pulling the sled, the next minute he is the sled." He saw that the girl was asleep. "That's irony," he said, and then repeated the word. "Irony." It sounded weak, inadequate; it described nothing; he drove silently on. Out through the windshield he saw a landscape too wide for the eye to measure – the crushing breadth of the burnt fields and the thin black thread of road vanishing into a vast blue sky as if the clouds massed on the horizon were distant cities and they were going to them.

She'd been working the pumps and the register at a crossroads station in southern Illinois, a rail-thin girl with stiff red hair the color of rust, worried, chipped nails and green eyes without luster. She wore gray coveralls that ballooned over her body like a clown's outfit, the long legs and sleeves rolled into thick cuffs. "I've never seen the ocean," she'd said, pointing to the remains of a peeling bumper sticker on Jones's car. ". . . be sailing," it read. She stood on the pump island while Jones filled his tank. The hooded blue lights above them pulsed in sync to the hovering sound of cicadas and both were a comforting close presence in the black land spreading out around the station. Jones wanted to tell the girl to look around her, right now: this flat patch of nothing was as good as an ocean. Instead, making conversation, Jones said, "I just got out of the Navy."

"You from around here?" she asked.

"Nope," Jones said.

He topped off his tank and reached into the car where he kept his money clipped to the sunvisor.

"I knew that," she said. "I seen your plates."

Jones handed her a twenty from his roll of muster pay. The money represented for him his final six months in the Navy, half a year in which he hadn't once set foot on land. Tired of the sea, knowing he'd never make a career out of it, on his last tour Jones had refused the temptations of shore leave, hoping to hit land with enough of a stake to last him a year. Now, as he looked at the dwindling roll, he was torn between exhaustion and a renewed desire to move on before he went broke.

"Where in Virginia you from?"

"I'm not," Jones said. "I bought the car in Newport News. Those are just old plates."

"That's too bad," the girl said. "I like the name. Virginia. Don't you?"

"I guess it's not special to me one way or the other," Jones said.

The girl folded the twenty in half and ran her thin fingers back and forth over the crease. That she worked in a gas station in the middle of nowhere struck Jones as sexy, and now he looked at her closely, trying to decide whether or not he wanted to stop a night or two in Carbondale. Except for the strange texture and tint of her red hair, he thought she looked good, and the huge coveralls, rippling in the breeze, made her seem sweet and lost, somehow innocent and alone in a way that gave Jones the sudden confidence that he could pick her up without much trouble.

"You gonna break that?" Jones asked, nodding at the bill.

Her arm vanished entirely as she reached into the deep pocket of her coveralls and pulled out a roll of bills stained black with grease and oil. Jones took the change, then looked off, around the station. In the east a dome of light rose above Carbondale, a pale yellow pressing out against the night sky. The road running in front of the station was empty except for a spotlight that shone on a green dinosaur and a Sinclair sign that spun on a pole above it.

"Don't get scared, working out here?" he asked.

"Nah," she said. "Hardly anyone comes out this way, 'less they're like you, 'less they're going somewhere. Had a man from Vernal gas here the other night. That's in Utah."

"Still —"

"Some nights I wouldn't care if I got robbed."

Jones took his toilet kit — a plastic sack that contained a thin, curved bone-like bar of soap, a dull razor and a balding toothbrush — out of the glove box. "You mind if I wash up?"

"Washroom's around back," she said. "By the propane tanks."

In the bathroom, he took off his T-shirt and washed himself with a wetted towel, watching his reflection in the mirror above the sink as though it were someone else, someone from his past. Gray eyes, a sharp sculpted jaw, ears that jutted

32

absurdly from his close-cropped head: a Navy face. Six months of shipboard isolation had left him with little sense of himself outside of his duties as an officer. In that time, held in the chrysalis of his berth, he'd forgotten not only what he looked like, but what other people might see when they looked at him. Now he was a civilian. He decided to shave, lathering up with the bar of soap. The mustache came off in four or five painful strokes.

For a moment the warm breeze was bracing against his cleanly shaven face. He stood in the lot, a little stiff, at attention, and when the girl waved to him from the cashier's widow, Jones saluted.

"See you later," he said.

"Okay," she said.

Jones drove away, stopping at a convenience store about a mile down the road. He grabbed two six-packs, a cheap Styrofoam cooler and a bag of ice and wandered down the aisle where the toys were kept. He selected a pink gun that fired rubber suction darts. He returned to the station and parked his car in the shadow of the dinosaur. He waited. The girl sat in the glass booth behind a rack of road atlases, suddenly the sweetheart of every town he'd traveled through in the last few months. To be with someone who knew his name, to hear another voice would be enough for tonight. Jones twisted open a beer and loaded the dart gun. He licked the suction tip, took aim and fired.

"Hey," the girl shouted.

"Wanna go somewhere?" Jones asked.

They'd crossed the Mississippi three weeks ago and driven north though Iowa, staying in motels and eating in diners, enjoying high times until his money began to run out. Then they started sleeping in the car, parked at rest stops or in empty lots, arms and legs braided together in the back seat of the Belvedere. One morning Jones had gone to a bakeshop and bought a loaf of day-old sourdough bread for thirty-five cents. It was the cool blue hour before dawn, but already, as he crossed the parking lot, the sky was growing pale, and the patches of tar were softening beneath his shoes, and in the sultry air the last weak light of the streetlamps threw off dull coronas of yellow and pink. Only one other car was parked in the empty lot, and its windows had been smashed out, a spray of glass scattered like seeds across the asphalt. As Jones approached the Belvedere, he saw the girl slowly lift the hair away from her head. It was as if he were witness to some miracle of revelation set in reverse, as if the rising sun and the new day had not bestowed but instead stripped the world of vision, exposed and left it bare. Her skull was blue, a hidden thing not meant for the light. Jones opened her door. She held the wig of curly red hair in her lap.

"Damn," he said. He paced off a small circle in the parking lot.

The girl combed her fingers calmly through the hair on her lap. She'd understood when she removed the wig that revealing herself to Jones would tip fate irrevocably. She felt that in this moment she would know Jones, and know him forever. She waited for Jones to spend his shock and anger, afraid that when he cooled down she might be on her way back to Carbondale, to the gas station and her stepfather and the church and the prayers for miraculous intercession. When Jones asked what was wrong with her, and she told him, he punted the loaf of sourdough across the empty lot.

"Why haven't you said anything?"

"What was I supposed to say, Jones?"

"The truth might've made a good start."

"Seems to me you've been having yourself a fine time without it," she said. "Hasn't been all that crucial so far."

"Jesus Christ."

"Besides, I wouldn't be here now if I'd told you. You'd have been long gone."

Jones denied it. "You don't know me from Adam," he said.

"Maybe not," she said. She set the wig on her head. "I'll keep it on if you think I'm ugly." The girl swung her legs out of the car and walked across the lot. She picked up the bread and brought it back. "These things drag out," she said.

She brushed pebbles and dirt and splinters of grass from the crust and then cracked the loaf in half.

"You didn't get any orange juice, did you?" she asked. "This old bread needs orange juice."

She reached inside and tore a hunk of clean white bread from the core and passed the loaf to Jones. He ate a piece and calmed down.

"Who knows how long I've got?" she said.

When they headed out again that morning, going west seemed inevitable – driving into the sun was too much to bear, and having it at their backs in the quiet and vacant dawn gave them the feeling, however brief, that they could outrace it. It was 1977, it was August, it was the season when the rolling fields were feverish with sunflowers turning on withered stalks to reach the light, facing them in the east as they drove off at dawn, gazing after them in the west as the sun set, and they searched the highway ahead for the softly glowing neon strip, for the revolving signs and lighted windows and the melancholy trickle of small-town traffic that would bloom brightly on the horizon and mean food and a place to stop for the night. If Jones wasn't too tired, he pushed on, preferring the solitude of night driving, when actual distances collapsed unseen, and the car seemed to float unmoored through limitless space, the reassuring hum of tires rolling beneath him, the lights of towns hovering across the darkened land like constellations in a warm universe. By day, he stopped only when the girl wanted to see a natural wonder, a landmark, a point of historical interest. Early this morning they'd visited the valley of Little Big Horn. Silence held sway over the sight, a silence that touched the history of a century ago and then reached beyond it, running back to the burnt ridges and bluffs and to a time when the flat golden plain in the West had not yet felt the weight of footprints. Jones watched the girl search among the huddled white markers, looking for the blackened stone where Custer fell. She'd climbed over the wrought-iron fence to stand beside the stone and a bull snake cooling in the shadow slithered off through the yellow grass. She seemed okay, not really sick, only a little odd and alien when she took off the wig. Now and then Jones would look at the girl and think, *you're dying*, but the unvarying heat hammered the days into a dull sameness, and driving induced a kind of amnesia, and for the most part Jones had shoved the idea out of his mind until this morning when they'd discussed their next move.

"We could drive to Nevada," she'd said. "Seems we're headed that direction, anyhow."

"Maybe," Jones had said.

"It only takes an hour to get married," the girl said, "and they rent you the works. A veil, flowers. We'll gamble. I've never done that. Have you? Roulette – what do you think, Jones?"

"I said maybe."

"Jones," she said. "I'm not into maybe."

"I don't know," Jones said. "I haven't thought it out."

"What's to think?" the girl said. "You'd be a widower in no time."

Jones squeezed the girl's knee, knobby and hard like a foal's. "Jesus," he said.

"It's not a big commitment I'm asking for."

"Okay, all right," Jones had said. "Don't get morbid."

Night fell, and the highway rose into the mountains. With the continental divide coming up, Jones couldn't decide whether or not to wake the girl. She didn't like to miss a landmark or border or any attraction advertised on a billboard. They'd stopped for the Parade of Presidents, "America's Heritage in Wax," and to see alligators and prairie dogs and an ostrich and the bleached white bones of dinosaurs, and by now the back of the car was covered with bumper stickers and decals, and the trunk was full of souvenirs she'd bought, snow-filled baubles, bolo ties, beaded Indian belts, engraved bracelets, pennants. Wall Drug, Mt. Rushmore, The Little Big Horn and a bare rutted patch of dirt in the sweetgrass that, according to a bullet-riddled placard, was the Lewis and Clark Trail – she'd stocked up on hokey junk and sentimental trinkets, and the stuff now commemorated a wandering path across state lines, over rivers, up mountains, into empty fields where battles had been fought and decided and down the streets of dirty, forgotten towns where once, long ago, something important had happened.

Jones gave her a shake, and said, "Now all the rivers flow west."

"Jones?" She was disoriented, a child spooked on waking in unfamiliar surroundings. "I'm not feeling too good."

"You want to lie down?"

"I could use a beer," the girl said. "Something to kill this."

Jones eased the car over the breakdown line. The mountains cut a crown of darkness out of the night sky, and a row of telephone poles, silhouetted in the starlight, seemed like crosses planted along the highway. He arranged the back seat, shoving his duffle to the floor and unrolling the sleeping bag. The car shook as a semi passed, spraying a phalanx of gravel in its wake.

"Let's get there soon," the girl said.

"Get in back," Jones said.

"I'm praying," she said.

37

"That's good," he said. Jones ran his hand over the girl's head. Wispy strands of hair pulled loose and stuck to his palm. "We'll stop in the next town."

Back on the road, the wind dried his T-shirt, and the sweat-soaked cotton turned stiff as cardboard. Beneath him the worn tires rolled over the warm asphalt like the murmur of a river. On the move once more, he felt only relief, a sense of his body freed from its strict place in time, drifting through the huddled blue lights of towns named after Indians and cavalrymen and battles, after blind expectations and the comforts of the known past, after the sustaining beliefs and fears of pioneers. Outlook, Savage, Plentywood. Going west, names changed, became deposits of utopian history, places named Hope and Endwell, Wisdom and Independence and Loveland. Whenever the roadsigns flashed by, luminous for an instant, Jones felt as though he were journeying through a forgotten allegory.

The girl asked, "When do you think we'll be there?"

"We're not going to Las Vegas," Jones said. He had not known his decision until he spoke and heard the words aloud.

"Why not?"

"I'm taking you to a hospital."

"They'll send me home," the girl said.

"They might."

"Dad'll say you abducted me."

"You know that's not the deal."

"Don't matter," the girl said. "He'll say you're working for Satan and his demonic forces, even if you don't know it. He says just about everybody is."

"Well, I'm not," Jones said.

"You might be without you knowing it," the girl said.

They were crossing the Bitterroot. Jones lost radio reception, and so he listened to the girl's prayers, words coming to him in fragments, *Jesus* and *savior* and *amen*, the music of her voice carried away by the wind, choked off whenever she dry-heaved in the seat behind him. Somewhere in western Idaho she fell asleep, and for the next few hours Jones listened to the car tires sing. Outside Spokane, on an illuminated billboard set back in a wheatfield, a figure of Jesus walked on water, holding a staff. Jones considered the odd concession to realism: a man walking on water would hardly need to support himself with a crutch. The thought was gone as soon as the billboard vanished behind him. No others took its place. Bored, he searched the radio dial for voices but for long empty stretches pulled in nothing but the sizzle of static, a strange surging cackle filling the car as if suddenly he'd lost contact with earth.

A red neon vacancy sign sputtered ambiguously, the *no* weakly charged and half-lit. Behind the motel and across the railroad tracks, the Columbia River snaked through Wenatchee, flowing wide and quiet, a serene blue vein dividing the town from the apple orchards. The low brown hills were splotched with squares of green, patches of garden carved out of burnt land, and beyond them to the west, rising up, etched into the blue sky, a snowcapped mountain range rimmed the horizon like teeth set in some huge jaw.

"We're here," Jones said.

"Where?"

"Wen-a-tchee," he said.

"Wena-tchee," he tried again.

"Just a place," he said, finally. "Let's get upstairs."

In their room, Jones set the girl on the bed. He spritzed the sheets with tap water, cooling them, and opened the window. A hot breeze pushed the brown burlap curtains into the room. The gray, dusty leaves of an apple tree spread outside the window and beneath the tree the unnatural blue of a swimming pool shimmered without revealing any depth in the morning sun. A slight breeze rippled the water, and an inflated lifesaver floated aimlessly across the surface.

The girl was kneeling at the foot of the bed, her hands folded and her head bowed in prayer. She was naked, her body a dull, white votary candle, and snuffed flame of her hair a dying red ember.

"Kneel here with me," she said.

"You go ahead," Jones said. He sat on the edge of the bed and pulled off his boots.

"It wouldn't hurt you," she said, "to get on your knees."

"We had this discussion before," he said.

"I believe it was a miracle," the girl said. She was referring to the remission of her cancer, the answered prayers. Her stepfather belonged to an evangelical sect that believed the literal rapture of Judgement Day was near at hand. Several dates he'd predicted for the end of time had already come and gone. Two months ago, he'd taken her out of medical treatment, refusing science in favor of prayer. Her illness bloomed with metaphoric possibilities and large portents for the congregation of the Church of the Redeemer in Carbondale, and was used as a kind of augury, variously read as a sign of God's covenant, or as proof of Man's fallenness, his wickedness and sin. For a while she'd been in remission, and news of her cure had brought a host of desperate seekers to the church.

At a display in South Dakota, against the evidence of bones before them, the girl had said dinosaurs didn't die sixty million years ago. "It was about ten thousand years ago," she had insisted. Her stepfather believed they'd been on the boat with Noah.

"Some big ass boat," Jones had said. Jones no longer had any interest in arguing. But he said, "And now that you're sick again, what's that?"

"It's what the Lord wants."

"There's no talking to you," Jones said.

"We're all just here to bear witness," she said.

"Have your prayers ever been answered?"

"The night you came by the station, I asked for that. I prayed and you came."

"I was hungry. I wanted a candy bar."

"That's what you think," the girl said. "But you don't know. You don't really know why you stopped or what the plan is or anything. Who made you hungry? Huh? Think about that." The rush of words seemed to exhaust her. She wrapped a corner of the sheet around her finger and repeated, "Who made you hungry?"

"So you prayed for me, and I came," Jones said. "Me, in particular? or just someone, anyone?" He stripped off his shirt, wadded it up and wiped the sweat from his armpits. "Your illness doesn't mean anything. You're just sick, that's all."

Jones cranked the hot water and stayed in the shower, his first in days, until it scalded his skin a splotchy pink. Finished, he toweled off, standing over the girl. She was choking down cries.

"Why don't you take a shower?" Jones said.

"Maybe I should go back home."

"Maybe you should just stand out there on the road and let your old dad's radar find you." Then Jones said, "If that's what you want, I'll get you a bus ticket. You can be on your way tomorrow."

The girl shook her head. "It's no place to me," she said.

"The Eskimos don't have homes, either," Jones said. "They don't have a word for it. They can't even ask each other, Hey, where do you live?"

II

Dr. McKillop sat on an apple crate and pulled a flask from his coat pocket. The afternoon heat was bad, but the harsh light was worse; he squinted up hill, vaguely wishing he were sober.

It was too late, though, and with a sense of anticipation, of happy fatality, he drank, and the sun-warmed scotch bit hard at the back of his throat. McKillop felt the alcoholic's secret pleasure at submitting to something greater than himself, a realignment with destiny: he took another drink. Swimming in the reflection of the silver flask, he noticed a young white man. He was tall and thin, his cheekbones sharp and high, and in the glare his deep eye sockets seemed empty, pools of cool blue shadow. When the man finally approached, McKillop offered him the flask.

"I was told in town I could find you here," Jones said.

McKillop nodded. "You must be desperate."

The doctor wiped dust and sweat from his neck with a sunbleached bandana. One of the day pickers had fallen from a tree and broken his arm, and McKillop had been called to reset it. He was no longer a doctor, not legally, not since six months ago when he'd been caught prescribing cocaine to himself. The probationary status of his medical license didn't matter to the migrants who worked the apple orchards, and McKillop was glad for the work. It kept trouble at a distance.

"Let me guess," McKillop said. "You don't have any money? Or you're looking for pharmaceuticals?"

"The bartender at Yakima Suzie's gave me your name," Jones said.

"You can get drunk, you can smoke cigars and gamble in a bar. You can find plenty in a bar. I know I have." McKillop pressed a dry brown apple blossom between his fingers, then sniffed beneath his nails. "But a doctor, a doctor you probably shouldn't find in a bar." He looked up at Jones, and said, "I've been defrocked."

"I'm not looking for a priest," Jones said. The doctor's stentorian voice and overblown statements were starting to annoy him. The doctor wore huraches with tire-tread soles, and his toes were caked with dirt, and the long curled nails looked yellow and unhealthy. He knotted his long raggedy hair in a ponytail.

Jones remained silent while a flatbed full of migrants rumbled by, jouncing over a worn two-track of gray dust and chuckholes. The green of the garden, of the orchards he'd seen from the valley, was an illusion; the trail of rising dust blew through the trees and settled and bleached the branches and leaves bone gray. A grasshopper spit brown juice on Jones' hand; he flicked it away and said, "I've got a girl in pain."

"Well, a girl in pain." McKillop capped his flask and wiped his forehead again. He spat in the dust, a dry glob rolling up thick and hard at his feet. He crushed it away with the rubber heel of his sandal. He looked up into the lattice of leaves, the sun filtered through; many of the apples with a western exposure were still green on the branch. McKillop stood and plucked one of the unripe apples and put it in his pocket. "For later," he said.

The room smelled like rotting mayonnaise. Her body glistened with a yellow liquid. She'd vomited on herself, on the pillows, on the floor. Face down, she clutched the sheets and tore them from the bed. She rolled over on her back, kicking the mattress and arching herself off the bed, lifting her body, twisting as though she were a wrestler attempting to escape a hold.

Jones pinned her arms against the bed while she bucked, trying to free herself. Her teeth were clenched, then she gasped, gulping for air. Her upper lip held a delicate dew of sweat in a mustache of faint blonde hair. She made fists of her thin, skeletal hands, and then opened them, clawing Jones with her yellowed nails.

McKillop drew morphine from a glass vial and found a blue vein running in the girl's arm. A drop of blood beaded where the needle punctured her skin. McKillop dabbed the blood away with the bedsheet and pressed a Band-aid over the spot.

43

The girl's body relaxed, as if she were suddenly without skeleton.

Windblown dust clouded the window. Jones slid it open along runners clogged with dirt and desiccated flies and looked down into the motel pool. Lit by underwater lights, it glowed like a jewel. A lawn chair lay on its side near the bottom, gently wavering in an invisible current.

"She needs a doctor," McKillop said.

"That's you," Jones said. "You're the doctor."

McKillop shook his head.

"Don't leave," the girl said. Only her index finger flickered, lifting slightly off the bed, as if all her struggle had been reduced to a tiny spasm.

"Wait outside," Jones said to the doctor.

When he'd gone, Jones turned on the television, a broken color set that bathed the room in a blue glow; he searched for a clear channel, but the screen remained a sea of pulsing static behind which vague figures swam in surreal distortion, auras without source. He stripped the bed and wetted a thin, rough towel with warm water and began to wipe the vomit off the girl's face, off her hard, shallow chest, off her stomach as it rose and fell with each breath. "Feels good," she said. Jones rinsed the towel and continued the ablution, working down her stick-thin legs and then turning her on to her stomach, massaging the tepid towel over her back and buttocks, along her thighs. The curtains fluttered, parting like wings and rising into the room. It was early, but the sun was setting in the valley, the brown rim of hills holding a halo of bright light, an emphatic, contoured seam of gold, and different sounds – the screeching of tires, the jangling of keys, a dog barking – began to carry clearly, sounds so ordinary and near they seemed to have a source, not within the room, not out in the world, but in memory.

When the girl sank into sleep, Jones slipped out into the hallway.

"Your wife?" McKillop asked.

"Just a girl I picked up."

"Jesus, man." With forced jocularity, the doctor slapped Jones on the back. "You know how to pick them."

Out on the street dusk settled, a moment of suspension. The sky was still deep blue with a weak edge of white draining away in the west. An Indian crouched on the curb outside the motel, his face brown and puckered like a windfall apple in autumn.

Jones and McKillop entered a bar next door.

"I'm taking her to a hospital," Jones said.

"There's precious little a hospital can do," the doctor said.

"Let's have a drink here," he called out. "They'll start a morphine drip. It'll keep her euphoric until she dies."

"Then I'll send her home," Jones said. In the Navy he'd learned one thing, and for Jones it amounted to a philosophy: there was no real reason to go forward, but enormous penalties were paid by those who refused. He'd learned this lesson rubbing Brasso into his belt buckle and spit shining his boots for inspections that never came. "I could leave right now," he said. "I could drive away."

"Why don't you?" the doctor said. "Turn tail, that's what I'd do." He ordered boilermakers and drank his by dumping the shot of bourbon into the schooner of beer. He polished off his first drink and called for another round.

"Deep down," McKillop said, "I'm really shallow."

Jones said, "I had this feeling if I kept driving everything would be okay."

"The healing, recuperative powers of the West," the doctor said. "Teddy Roosevelt, and all that. The West was a necessary invention of the Civil War, a place of harmony and union. From the body politic to the body —"

Jones only half-listened. He found himself resisting the doctor's glib reductions.

"I'd like to hit the road," McKillop was saying. The phrase had an antiquated sound. Even in the cool of the bar, McKillop was sweating. He pressed a fat finger down on a bread crumb, then flicked it away.

"You looked bad when you saw her," Jones said.

"I'll be alright," McKillop said. He downed his drink. "I'm feeling better now. You'll need help, but I'm not your doctor."

McKillop bought a roll of quarters and made a few sloppy calls to friends in Seattle, waking them, demanding favors for the sake of old times, invoking old obligations, twice being told to fuck off, and finally getting through to an old resident friend at Mercy Hospital, who said he'd look at the girl if nothing else could be done.

"We'll take care of her," McKillop said to Jones. They walked down to the section of windowless warehouses and blank-faced cold storage buildings, walked along cobbled streets softly pearled with blue lamplight, apple crates stacked up twenty, thirty feet high against the brick. Beyond the train tracks, the Columbia flowed quietly; a path of cold moonlight stretched across the water like a bridge in a dream, the first step always there, at Jones's feet. Through crate slats Jones saw eyes staring, men slumped in the boxes for the night, out of the wind, behind a chinking of newspaper, cardboard, fluttering plastic. Jones stopped. A canvas awning above a loading dock snapped in the breeze like a doused jib sail.

"Don't you worry, Jonesy boy," the doctor said. "We'll get her squared away. Tomorrow, in Seattle." He reached into his bag and handed Jones a vial and a syringe. "If it gets too much, the pain, you know, give her this. Only half, four or five milligrams. You can do it, right? Just find a vein."

A fire burned on the banks of the river. A circle of light breathed out and the shadows of stone-still men danced hilariously. A woman walked through the grass outside the circle; her legs were shackled by her own pants, blue jeans dropped down around her ankles, stumbling, standing, stumbling, struggling. "I know what you want," she shouted back at the circle of men. "I know what you want." She fell, laughing hideously.

The doctor was clutching Jones' hand, squeezing and shaking it, and Jones got the idea that the doctor might never let go.

Outside the motel, the same wrecked Indian stood and approached Jones. His left cowboy boot was so worn down around the heel that the bare shoe tacks gave a sharp metallic click on the cement with each crippled step. He blinked, and thrust a hand at Jones.

"My eyes hurt when I open 'em," he said. "And they hurt when I close 'em. All night I don't know what to do. I keep opening and closing my eyes."

Jones reached into his pocket and pulled a rumpled dollar loose from his wad of muster pay.

"I swear," the Indian said. "Somebody's making my eyes go black."

Jones gave him the bone. He tried to see in the man the facial lines of an Eskimo, but his skin was weathered, the lines eroded.

"SoHappy," he said.

"Me too," Jones said.

"No," the Indian said, thumping his chest. "SoHappy. Johnny SoHappy, that's me. Fucking me."

He blinked and backed away, wandering off alone, shoe tacks roughly clawing the sidewalk.

The girl was awake, shrouded in white sheets, staring at the ceiling, her breathing shallow but regular. Jones lay in the bed beside her, suffering a mild case of the spins. The walls turned, soft and summery, like the last revolution of a carousel wobbling to a stop. He looked out the window. Under the moonlight each leaf on the apple tree was a spoonful of milk.

Jones felt the girl's dry, thin fingers wrap around his wrist like a bird clutching at a perch.

47

"I love you," she whispered. Her voice was hoarse and frightening.

Jones shut his eyes against the spinning room. The spinning of the room crept beneath his closed lids, and Jones opened his eyes, to no effect. The room continued to spin.

"Howabout you, Jones? You could just say it, I wouldn't care if it wasn't the truth. Not anymore."

Jones pressed her hand lightly.

"Where are we, Jones?" she asked. "I mean, really. What's the name of this place?"

They were a long way from Carbondale, from the home he'd seen the night they left. An oak tree hiding the collapsing remains of a childhood fort, a frayed rope with knotted footholds dangling from the hatch, a sprinkler turned slowly over the grass, a lounge chair beneath a sun shade, a paper plate weighted against the wind by an empty cocktail glass.

"I'm hot," she said.

Jones lifted her out of bed. She was hot, but she wasn't sweating. Against his fingers, her skin felt dry and powdery, friable, as if the next breeze might blow it all away, and he'd be left holding a skeleton. He wrapped her in a white sheet. She hooked her arms around his neck, and Jones carried her, airy as balsa, into the aqueous green light of the hallway and down the steps.

"Where we going?" she asked.

The surface of the pool shimmered, smooth as a turquoise stone. Jones unwrapped the sheet and let it fall. The girl was naked underneath.

"Hold on," Jones said.

He walked down the steps at the shallow end, the water washing up around his ankles, his knees, his waist, and then he gently lowered the girl until her back floated on the surface.

"Don't let go," she said, flinching as she touched water. In panic, she gasped for air.

"I won't," Jones said. "Just relax."

Her skin seemed to soak in water, drink it up like a dehydrated sponge, and she felt heavier, more substantial. Her arms and legs grew supple, rising and falling in rhythm to the water. He steered her around the shallow end.

"Except in songs on the radio," she said, "nobody's ever said they love me."

Her eyes were wide and vacant, staring up through the leaves of the apple tree, out past them into the night sky, the moon, the vault of stars.

"You think anybody's watching us?" the girl asked.

Jones looked up at the rows of darkened rooms surrounding the pool. Here and there a nightlight glowed. Air conditioners droned.

"I doubt it," he said.

She let her arms spread wide and float on the surface as Jones eased her toward the edge of the pool. He lifted her out and set her down on the sheet. At the deep end of the pool, below the diving board, he saw the lounge chair, its yellow webbing and chrome arms shining in the beams of underwater light. He took a deep breath and dove in. The water was as warm as the air, easing the descent from one element to the next. Jones crept along the bottom until he found the chair. Pressure rang in his ears, and a dizziness spread through him as he dragged it along the length of the pool. For a moment he wanted to stop, to stay on the bottom and let everything go black; he held himself until every cell in his blood screamed and the involuntary instincts of his body craving air drove him back up and he surfaced, his last breath exploding out of him. He set the chair against the apple tree.

They sat beneath the tree while Jones caught his breath. A hot wind dried their skin.

"I liked Little Big Horn the best," the girl said.

"It was okay." Jones watched a leaf float across the pool. "You really think he's looking for you?"

49

"I know he is," she said. "He's got all his buddies on the police force that are saved – you know, born again."

"You want to go back there?"

The girl was quiet, then she said, "Weekends Dad and them hunt around under bridges by rivers, looking for graffiti with satanic messages. For devil worship you need the four elements. You need earth, wind, fire and water. That's what he says. So they look by rivers, and maybe they see some graffiti, or they find an old chicken bone, and they think they really got themselves something."

It seemed an answer, wired through biblical circuitry.

"Tomorrow you're going to a hospital," Jones said. "The doctor arranged it. Everything's set."

He carried the girl upstairs and placed her on the bed. In five weeks she'd gone from a girl he'd picked up in the heartland to an old woman, her body retreating from the world, shrunken and curled and lighter by the hour, it seemed. Her hair had never grown back, and the ulcerations from early chemo treatments had so weakened her gums that a tooth had come loose, falling out, leaving a black gap in a smile that should have been seductive to the young boys back in Carbondale. The whites of her eyes had turned scarlet red. Her limbs were skeletal, fleshless and starved. She'd said she was eighteen, but now she could have passed for eighty.

"You think I'll go to hell?"

"Probably."

"Jones –"

"Well, why do you talk like that?"

"I don't know." She clutched the sheet around her neck. "When I open my mouth these things just come out. They're the only words I have."

"One of my tours," Jones said, "we were on maneuvers in the Mediterranean." A boiler exploded, he said, and a man caught fire in a pool of burning oil. Crazed, aflame, engulfed, the man ran in erratic circles on the deck, a bright, whirling light in the darkness, shooting back and forth like an errant roman candle, while other men chased him, half-afraid to tackle the man and catch fire themselves. Finally, beyond all hope, out of his mind, the man jumped over the deck railing, into the sea. "You could hear the flames whipping in the wind as he fell," Jones said. "Then he was gone. It was the sorriest thing I ever witnessed." Afterwards, he'd helped extinguish the fire, and for doing his duty he'd been awarded a dime-sized decoration for heroism.

"Everywhere we go," she said, and there was a long pause as her breath gurgled up through lungs full of fluid, "there's never any air-conditioning."

Jones held her hand, a bone. He thought she coughed this time, but again she was only trying to breathe. Suddenly he did not want to be in bed beside her. But he couldn't move.

"The Eskimos live in ice huts," he said.

"Sounds nice right now."

"It's very cold," Jones continued.

"I wish we were going there."

The girl coughed, and then curled into a fetal ball. "It's like hot knives stabbing me from inside." she said.

Jones lifted himself from the bed. He turned on the bedside lamp and took the morphine and the syringe from his shirt pocket. "The first explorers thought Eskimos roamed from place to place because they were poor," he said. "They thought the Eskimos were bums." He ripped the cellophane wrapper from the syringe, and pushed the needle into the vial, slowly drawing the plunger back until half the clear liquid had been sucked into the barrel. "They were always on the move," he said. The girl bit into the pillow until her gums bled and left an imprint of her mouth on the case. Her body had an alertness, a tension that Jones sensed in the tortured angles she held her arms at, the faint weak flex of her atrophied muscles.

She raised her head and opened her mouth wide, her startled red eyes searching the room as if to see where all the air had gone. "But when you think about it, you understand that it's efficient." Jones pushed the air bubbles out of the syringe until a drop of morphine beaded like dew at the tip of the needle. "Movement is the only way for them to survive in the cold. Even their morality is based on the cold, on movement." Jones now continued speaking only to dispel the silence and the lone sound of the girl's labored breathing. He unclenched her hand from the sheets and bent her arm back, flat against the bed. "They don't have police," he said, "and they don't have lawyers or judges. The worst punishment for an Eskimo is to be left behind, to be left in the cold." Inspecting her arm, he found the widest vein possible and imagined it flowing all the way to her heart and drove the needle in.

McKillop had taken the girl's purse and dumped the contents on the bed. He rummaged through it, and found a blue gumball, safety pins, pennies, a shopping list and several pamphlets from which he read. "Listen," he said. "For centuries lovers of God and of righteousness have been praying: Let your kingdom come. But what is that kingdom that Jesus Christ taught us to pray for? Use your Bible to learn the who, what, when, why and where of the Kingdom." He laughed. "Ironic, huh?"

"We don't know, do we?" Jones said.

"Oh come on," the doctor said. He took up a scrap of notepaper. "Blush. Lipstick-Toffee, Ruby Red. Two pair white cotton socks. Call Carolyn."

"Stay out of her stuff," Jones said.

"I was looking for ID," he said. "What's her name?"

Jones thought for a moment, and then said, "It's better that you don't know."

"You didn't OD her, did you?"

"No," Jones said. Once last night he'd woken to the sound of the girl's voice, calling out. She spoke to someone who was not in the room and began to pick invisible things out of the air. Watching her struggle with these phantoms had made Jones feel horribly alone. Delirious, she ended by singing the refrain of a hymn. He said to the doctor, "I thought about it though."

"You could tell the truth. It's rather unsavory, but it's always an option."

Jones looked at the doctor. "It's too late," he said. "I've tried the truth myself, and it doesn't work that well anyway. Half the time, maybe, but no more. What good is that? The world's a broke-dick operation."

"The big question is," McKillop said, "who's going to care?"

"Her family," Jones said. "Born-again Christians."

"I was raised a Catholic." McKillop pulled a silver chain from around his neck and showed Jones a tarnished cross. "It was my mother's religion. I don't believe, but it still spooks me."

"This is against the law."

"If you sent her home, there'd be questions."

"There'll be questions anyway," Jones said. "Her stepdad's a fanatic. He'll be looking for me. He believes in what he's doing, you know?"

"I vaguely remember believing –"

"Not everything has to do with you," Jones said. He felt the sadness of language, the solitude of it. The doctor had no faith beyond a system of small ironies; it was like trying to keep the rain off by calling to mind the memory of an umbrella.

The doctor had dispensed with the nicety of a flask and now drank straight from the bottle.

"Never made it home last night," McKillop said.

"You look it," Jones said.

"I got lucky," McKillop said. "Sort of." He wiped his lips and said, "I wish I had a doughnut." He pulled the green apple from his pocket, buffing it on the lapel of his wrinkled jacket. He offered the bottle to Jones. Jones shook his head. "I'd watched this woman for a long time, desired her from afar, and then suddenly there I was, in bed with her, touching her, smelling her, tasting her. But I couldn't get it up."

"Maybe you should stop drinking."

"I like drinking."

"It's not practical," Jones said.

"Quitting's a drastic measure," McKillop said. He took a bite of the apple. "For a man who gets lucky as little as I do."

"I'll see you," Jones said.

III

The peaks no longer appeared as teeth set in a jaw, but loomed large and then vanished as mountains, becoming sheered-off walls, slopes of crushed stone, of scree and talus, outcroppings of wind-stunted trees clinging to striated rock. Reaching the pass, the air was cooler, with patches of pure white snow surviving the intense summer heat in pockets of shadow. The odometer approached one hundred thousand for what Jones guessed was the second time in the Belvedere's life. He watched the numbers slowly circle around and return to zero. Briefly the ledger seemed balanced, wiped clean, and then the moment was gone. The numbers changed, and mile one was history.

By afternoon he had crossed the bridge at Deception Pass and driven south and caught a ferry to Port Townsend. He drove west along 101 and then veered north, hugging the shoreline of the Strait of Juan de Fuca, passing through Pysht and Sekiu, driving until he hit Neah Bay and the Makah Reservation, when finally there was no more road. It had remained hot all the way west, and now a wildfire burned across the crown of a mountain rising against the western verge of the reservation. The sky turned yellow under a pall of black smoke. Flecks of ash sifted like snow through the air. White shacks lined either side of the street, staggering forward on legs of leaning cinder block, and a few barefoot children played in the dirt yards, chasing dust devils. Several girls in dresses as sheer and delicate as cobwebs stood shielding their eyes and staring at the fire. Sunlight spread through the thin fabric, skirts flickering in the wind, so that each of the young girls seemed to be going up in flames.

Jones moved slowly through town, raising a trail of white dust, which mingled with the black ash and settled over the children. The shacks, a scattering of wrecked cars, and then along the foot of the mountain he followed an eroded logging road until it too vanished. A yellow mobile home sat on a bluff, and behind it, hidden by a brake of wind-crippled cedar, was the ocean. Jones heard the surf and caught the smell of rough-churned sea. A man in overalls came out of the mobile home – to Jones, he looked like an Eskimo. Jones switched off the ignition. The car rocked dead, but for a moment he felt the pressure of the entire country he'd crossed at his back, the vibration of the road still working up through the steering column, into his hands and along his arms, becoming an ache in his shoulders, a numbness traveling down his spine. Then the vibrations stopped and he felt his body settle into the present.

Jones got out of the car. The man hooked a thumb in his breast pocket, the ghost habit of a smoker. Behind cracked lips, his teeth were rotten. He watched a retrofit bomber sweep out over the ocean, bank high and round and circle back over the hill, spraying clouds of retardant. The chemicals fell away in a rust red curtain that closed over the line of fire.

"How'd it start?" Jones asked.

"Tiny bit of broken bottle will start a fire, sun hits it right." The man lit a cigarette. "Been a dry summer. They logged that hill off mostly, and don't nobody burn the slash. Where you headed?"

Jones said he was just driving.

"Used to be a love colony down there," the man said. He pointed vaguely toward the ocean. "You get the hippies coming back now and again, looking for the old path down. But the trails all growed over." The man ran his tongue over the black gum between missing front teeth. "I thought maybe you was one of them."

"No," Jones said. "Never been here before."

"You can park, you want," he said. "There's a game trail runs partways down."

"Thanks."

"You'll see the old Zellerbach mill."

He found the abandoned mill in ruin, a twisted heap of metal. He sat on a rusted flume and pulled a patch of burnt weeds from the foundation. With a stick he chipped at the hard, dry ground, and dug out three scoops of loose dirt, wrapping them in one of the girl's shirts. When he finished, he sat against a stump, counting the growth rings with his finger until near heartwood he'd numbered 200 years.

A clam-shell chime chattered like cold teeth beneath the awning of a bait shop. Inside the breakwater, boats pulled at their moorings. Jones walked up and down the docks of the marina until he found a Livingston slung by davits to the deck of a cabin cruiser. The windows of the cruiser were all dark, canvas had been stretched across the wheelhouse, and the home port stenciled across the stern was Akutan. He lowered the lifeboat into the water, pushed off, and let himself drift quietly away from the marina.

When he'd rowed out into the shipping lane, Jones pull-started the twenty-horse Evinrude, and followed a flashing red beacon out around the tip of Cape Flattery to the ocean. He kept just outside the line of breaking waves, hugging the shore, the boat tossed high enough at times along the crest of a swell to see a beach wracked with bone-gray driftwood. Jones pulled the motor and rode the surf until the hull scraped sand. He loaded the girl into the boat, up front for ballast.

He poled himself off the sand with the oar and then rowed. Each incoming wave rejected his effort, angling the bow high and pushing the boat back in a froth of crushed white foam. Finally he managed to cradle the boat in the trough between breaking waves. The motor kicked out of the water with a high-rev whine, and Jones steered for open sea, heading due west. Beyond the edge of the shelf, the rough surface chop gave way to rolling swells, and Jones knew he was in deep water. He'd forgotten how black a night at sea was, how even the coldest, dying star seemed near and bright in the dark. He became afraid and drew the world in like a timid child, trembling with unreasonable fears – the terrible life below him, the girl's stepfather and his fanatic pursuit, his own fugitive life in flight from this moment. If it became history he would be judged and found guilty. Spindrift raked over the bow, splashing his face. The sea heaved in a sleepy rhythm. He crossed the black stern of a container ship at anchor, four or five stories of high wall, and when he throttled back to a dead drift he heard voices from the deck top, human voices speaking in a language he did not understand.

He ran another mile and cut the engine. The round world was seamless with the night sky, undivided, the horizon liquid and invisible except for a spray of stars that flashed like phosphorescence, rising out of the water. A cool breeze whispered over the surface. August was over. He'd piled the sleeping bag with beach rocks, and then he'd cleaned the car of evidence, collected the souvenirs, the trinkets, the orange smiles, the wig, and stuffed them down into the foot of the bag, knotting it shut with nylon rope. He'd taken the Bible, opened it to the genealogy, and scratched the month and year into the margins. Jones considered the possibility, as he rocked in the trough of a swell, that all this would one day break free from its deep hold in the sea, wash to the surface, the bumper stickers from Indian battles, and decals commemorating the footpaths and wagon trails of explorers and pioneers, the resting places of men and women who'd left their names to towns and maps. And then the girl herself, identified by her remains, a story told by teeth and bones, interpreted.

Jones looped a rope tether around the handle of his flashlight and tied the other end to the sleeping bag. He checked the beam, which shone solidly in the darkness, a wide swath of white light carved out of the air. He unpackaged the soil he'd collected from the collapsed mill, and sprinkled it across the sleeping bag, spreading earth from head to foot. It seemed a paltry ritual – the dirt, the light – but he was determined to observe ceremony. With his tongue he licked away a coating of salt from the rim of his lips. His hands were growing cold and stiff. He hoisted the head end of the bag over the port side and then pivoted the girl's feet around until the whole bag pitched overboard. Jones held it up a final instant, clutching the flashlight, allowing the air bubbles to escape, and then let go. Down she swirled, a trail of light spinning through a sea that showed green in the weakening beam and then went black. In silence Jones let himself drift until, borne away by the current, he could no longer know for certain where she'd gone down.

Back within the breakwater, Jones tied the lifeboat with a slack line to a wooden cleat. The mountain had vanished from view, swallowed by darkness, but a prevailing westerly had blown the wildfire across its crown, and a flare of red-yellow flame swept into the sky. An old Makah trudged up the road, dragging a stick through the dust, leaning on it when he stopped to watch the hieroglyphic write itself in fire on the edge of the reservation. Jones sat on the dock, dangling his legs. Flakes of feathery black ash drifted through the air and fanned lightly against his face. Spume crusted and stung his lips, and he was thirsty. He listened to the rhythm of the water as it played an icy cool music in the cadenced clinking of ropes and pulleys and bell buoys. Out beyond the breakwater the red and green running lights of a sailboat appeared, straggling into port. The wind lifted the voices of the sailors and carried them across the water like a song. One of the sailors shouted, "There it is." He stood on the foredeck and pointed toward the banner of flames rising in the sky.

GRANNY MYNA
TELLS OF THE CHILD

Robert Antoni

Robert Antoni won The Commonwealth Writer's Prize for Best First Book for *Divina Trace* (1991). In addition to being published in numerous periodicals including the *Paris Review* and *Conjunctions*, he is currently a professor in Creative Writing at the University of Miami, and is completing his second novel.

GRANNY MYNA
TELLS OF THE CHILD

The bottle was big and obzockee. I was having a hard time toting it. It was the day before my thirteenth birthday, seventy-seven years ago: tomorrow I will be ninety years of age. I am still a practising physician, and as I sit here in this library, at this desk of my father's, of my father's father – lugged as a trunk of purpleheart wood by six Warrahoon Indians out of the misty jungles of Venezuela, floated down the Orinoco and towed across the Caribbean behind three rowing pirogues, my grandfather calling the cadence stroke by stroke in a language nearly forgotten – I can still hear him, sitting behind this desk, looking out of this window at this moon above the same black, glistening sea. I can still hear him. I know my grandfather's voice, even though he died ages before I was born. Even though I could not remember who told the story or when I'd heard it, nor did I know what those words meant or whether they were words at all, as I carried the huge glassbottle my steps suddenly fell into the rhythm of his voice: *Na-me-na-na-ha! Na-me-na-na-ha! Na-me-na-na-ha!*

I was bareback, wearing only my baggy school shortpants and my old jesusboots, so skinny my navel stuck out in a tight knot. I held the bottle against my chest. My arms were wrapped around it, my fingers cupped into the hollow of the bottom, the top butting up my chin with every step. I couldn't look

63

down, so I didn't have to see what I knew was inside. It was a very old bottle, the kind used to preserve fruit, made of thick glass with wire clamps to hold down its glass lid. I was sweating. My stomach kept sticking to the bottle. My bung navel rubbed against the glass, sometimes pinching and sending a shock down my legs to my toes. I sucked in my belly as I walked.

The sun was already rising behind me, rising with the dust stirred up by my hurrying feet. I was thinking: *Maraval must be ten mile from Domingo Cemetery at least. How you could foot it there and back in time?* Thinking: *Ten mile from Domingo Cemetery to Maraval Swamp fa the least. Daddy ga box you ears fa true if you don't get back in time. This bottle heavy like a boulderstone. And these arms only crying to drop off. But how you could stop to put it down?*

There were no people yet on the trace, only some potcakes curled up among the weeds pushing out in the middle, and a few old billies on their way to pasture, lengths of twisted rotten cord dragging behind them. They were as tall as I was, and they came at me snuffling, pressing their bearded faces into mine, staring at me through silver eyes from another world. I kicked them away, thinking: *How she could be dead if she eyes aren't closed? But if she isn't dead, and you are home in you bed dreaming all this, then how you could be tired toting this bottle?* Thinking: *You know they ga start with the funeral first thing as she was so hurry hurry. So you best just keep on walking, and don't even bother templating bout stopping to put it down to waste no time, and anyway you don't want to have to look at he face neither.*

There were small villages along Divina Trace, the footpath which began behind the convent, weaving its way through tenements in the outskirts of St Maggy, and passing behind the graveyard. Then it stretched out through cocoa and coconut estates in the country, cane fields, finally ending with the

Church of Magdalena Divina at the edge of Maraval Swamp. Now, outside of town, the trace curved through bush – with the shanties and roukou-scrubbed mudhuts half-hidden behind giant tufts of bamboo, schools of yardfowl scurrying in dust-waves as I approached, the odours of cooking coalpots, stench of rubbish – unless the trace traversed one of the estates. Then it ran straight, mossy grey cocoa trees on either side, with nutmeg or brilliant orange immortelle in between to shade them from the sun. Otherwise the trace passed among thick groves of coconut palms, their fronds rustling in the breeze high above, or it would be closed in by purple walls of cane, the air sweet-smelling, charred if the field had been scorched to scare out the scorpions for harvest. There were hills from which the mountains could be seen at one horizon, hot black sea at the other.

I'd been to Maraval Swamp many times before, but I didn't want to believe it was ten miles away. I kept thinking: *Maybe it's not so far as that? You know it is ten mile at least. How many times you been to the church with Mother Maurina and the whole of St Maggy Provisional to see the walking statue and hear bout the Black Virgin? How many times you been to the swamp with Papee Vince and the whole of form three science to collect specimens fa dissections? With daddy and all five troups of seascouts to catch jumping frogs fa the summer jamboree?* Thinking: *You know it is ten mile fa the least. How many times you been with you jacks to catch guanas to pope them off on the Indians by Suparee fa fifty cent fa each? Running and grabbing them up quick by they tails and swinging them round and round until they heads kaponkle, and they drop boodoops sweet in the crocasssack! And the time you get a dollar fa that big big one, and you eat so many julie-mangoes fa that dollar you belly wanted to bust froopoops! How them coolies and Warrahoons could eat them things? But Granny Myna say Barto used to eat guana all the time in Venezuela when they was first married, and they had the cattle ranch in Estado Monagas where daddy was born. And the time Barto try to bring one inside and she chase him out with he own cutlass, because one thing Granny Myna wouldn't stand in the house is no kind of creature curse to walk on he belly, and it is from eating that nastiness that kill Barto young so. But daddy say a Warrahoon bring him a stew guana to the hospital once, and he couldn't tell the difference from fricassee chicken.*

I didn't want to think about the contents of the bottle, about the ten miles ahead, and I didn't want to think about getting back too late for the funeral. I'd been up the whole night, and I was already tired carrying the bottle. I'd only just left the cemetery. I hadn't been able to fall asleep that night, turning in my bed thinking about old Granny Myna. She'd told me a story once about a frog she'd seen suck out the eye of a woman in Wallafield, and I could not dissolve from my mind the image of this woman struggling with the huge, white frog. It was one of those flying frogs, and the woman had been sitting good as ever beneath a tamarind tree. As soon as she looked up the frog flew out and stuck *frapps* to her face. Granny Myna told me it took two big men to pull off this frog, and when he came off the eye came out too. She said that if Barto had not been there to pick up the eye from out the mud, to spit on it and rub off the mud and push it back in, the woman would have walked away from that frog without an eye.

It was not unusual for me to awaken in the middle of the night and begin thinking of Granny Myna and one of her stories, but I remember this time I could not put her and the frog out of my mind. My grandmother was ninety-six, always talking about dying, yet Granny Myna had never known a sick day in her life, and I was convinced she'd live forever. I couldn't fall asleep, so I woke up my younger brother to ask him about the woman from Wallafield. He cussed me and rolled over again. I remember I lay there listening to the oscillating fan, its noise growing louder with each pass, until it seemed to be screaming in my ears. I threw off the sheet and jumped out of bed. I pulled on my shorts, buckled on my jesusboots, and walked quietly down the hall. Papee Vince, my grandfather on my mother's side, had his room at the end. I hurried past and on down the stairs. Granny Myna's door was open, so I stuck my head in. She was sitting up in her bed waiting. I went and sat beside her. She looked at me for a long time, reached across me to put her gold rosary down on the bedstand, and she began to talk.

He was born a man, but above he cojones he was a frog. It happen so, because Magdalena Domingo was a whore, and a black bitch, and on top of that she was a bad woman. Magdalena make this practice of going every Sunday to Maraval Swamp, because I used to follow her and sometimes she would meet there with Barto beneath the samaan tree, she go to Maraval Swamp because she like to watch the crapos singando. Magdalena just love to see the frogs fucking, and is that she must have been looking the moment she conceive the child, because Barto used the same principle to create a zebra from two donkeys by putting them to do they business in a room he have paint with stripes. So too again everybody take you daddy for another St John, because above my bed I have the picture hanging with him still smiling happy on the dishplate that I used to look up at it in all my moments of passion, and that is why you daddy have that same crease right here in the middle of he forehead, and how else could it be you daddy is the only Domingo with those eyes always watching you just like St John? You see how Papa God does do He work? In the same way Magdalena make that child with the face of a frog to mimic she own, and with the cojones of *every* man on this island of Corpus Christi!

67

When Dr Brito Salizar see this child coming out, he only want to push it back inside Magdalena pussy and hide it from the rest of the world. Dr Brito know nothing good could come from this child that is the living sin of all the earth. Because it take Magdalena only one look in the face of this frogchild to kill sheself dead: she press the pillow and hold up she breath until she suffocate. By the time Dr Brito have realize and cut the pillow from out she lock up jaws she was already dead. Feathers was gusting back and forth in that little hospital room like a blizzard. Dr Brito blow into the air before him to clear way the floating feathers, he cross heself, and Dr Brito open he mouth wide to bend over to bite off the cordstring from the belly of this crapochild to join the world of the living with the world of the dead for the whole of eternity!

That night there was such a great rain that the Caronee have overflow sheself, and the next morning there was cocodrilles in the streets and the basements of all the houses. So when Barto arrive now dress in mud up to he cojones, and holding this shoebox in he hands, I grab on to he moustache and I put one cursing on him to say he is *never* coming inside the house with that crapochild! But Barto is a man that nobody couldn't tell him nothing once he have make up he head, and he don't pay no attention a-tall never mind my bawling to break down the roof. I tell him Papa God will kill him and all of us too if he try to bring that crapochild inside, but Barto can't even hear, because he walk straight through the front door and he put this shoebox down in the middle of the diningroom table. And if I would have give Barto only half a chance, he would have lay this frogchild right down next to Amadao who is sleeping in my bedroom in the crib, born no even six months before.

Well Evelina, she is the servant living with me even in those days, just a little negrita running round the estate when she mummy dead and I take her up, Evelina only have to hear about this crapochild coming inside the house, and she start to

68

beat she breast and shout one set of Creole-obeah bubball on the child, and she run quick to she room to bury sheself beneath the bed. Reggie and Paco, they is the last of the nine boys before Amadao sleeping in the cradle, Reggie and Paco come running to Barto to question him where do he find this chuffchuff frog, and could they please take him in the yard to find out how good can he jump. But Barto only have to make one cuteye on these boys for them to know he is no skylarking, and little Reggie and Paco take off running and we don't see them again until late in the night. As for me now, after a time I have quiet down little bit and Barto turn to me, because of course at this time I am still nursing Amadao, and he want to know now if I am ready to feed he Manuelito, which is the name Barto pronounce on the child official with salt and water. Sweet heart of Jesus! I look Barto straight in he eyes, and I tell him if he only bring that crapochild anywhere near by me, I will squeeze he cojones so hard they will give off milk like two balls of cheese, and he could feed *that* to he pendejo frogchild!

But nothing couldn't stop Barto. Like he want to take on Papa God self. Because next thing I see he have pick up he revolver again to protect against the cocodrilles, and he go outside to the shed for the big cow that we have there by the name of Rosey. And this Rosey have been with us so many years that she have come tame tame, that the boys used to ride her all about the place like a horse, and we have to be very careful no to leave a plantain or anything so on the table, because soon as you turn round she would push she head in through the window and carry it way. So here is me now only standing up like a mokojumbie watching at Barto leading this cow through the mud that is high as Rosey belly, and Barto carry her straight through the entrance hall into the diningroom up on top the table. Oui Papayo! Well now I know I am soon to go viekeevie!

69

Barto leave Rosey there just so, and he gone to the sea for a bucket of water to wipe off the mud from Rosey pechugas. But when Barto pick up this frogchild out the shoebox, and I have a good look at this frogchild face for the first time, I take off with one set of bawling again because you never see no creature on the skin of Papa God earth so ugly as that! Even Rosey have to jump when she see this crapochild, and Barto have to hold her down to keep her from bolting out the door. But nothing couldn't stop Barto once he have make up he head, because next thing I see he is untying the cowboy kerchief from round he neck, and he fix it to hide poor Rosey eyes. In no time a-tall she have calm down again, and Barto is holding this crapochild below her with the tottot in the big frogmouth, and he is sucking down milk that is spilling all over the ugly frogface, and he is talking one set of froglanguage like *oy-juga oy-juga oy-juga*!

That night I am in my bed trying my best to sleep with all this confusion going on in the house, and Barto come inside the room, because Barto used to keep he own bedroom upstairs, in the one you mummy and daddy use now, he come inside the room just here at the end of this bed pointing he revolver at me with he eyes only spitting fire, demanding to know what have I do with he Manuelito. Sweet heart of Jesus! I answer him that this frogchild have make he brain viekeevie now for true, because is no me a-tall to touch that crapochild no even until the ends of the earth, and if he have disappear I don't know nothing as the last I see him he is still sleeping happy in he shoebox cradle in the middle of the diningroom table. But Barto have reach into a state now over this crapochild, so I decide to go and wake up Evelina and the two of us begin to ransack the house, looking in all the drawers and beneath the beds and all about for this child, that we can't find him nowhere a-tall and we don't know what we will do. Just then I hear Evelina scream someplace outside, and I take off running to find her there by the pond for all the ducks to come and bathe theyself, there standing up with she eyes open wide wide like she have just see a jabjab, only watching at Reggie and Paco and this frogchild swimming!

Next morning the whole of St Maggy have reach at my doorstep to see this crapochild. The Caranee have no even begin to go down yet, and the mud in the streets is still high as you knees, but nothing couldn't slow down these people. In all the windows they is jam up standing one on top the next waiting half the day for only a glimpse of this frogchild, and the little baboo boy see the crowd to come running pushing he bicyclecar through the mud with all the bottles of sweetsyrup spilling out, and he begin to shave ice like he catch a vaps, selling one set of snowball to all these people only looking through the glass licking licking with all they tongues green and purple and yellow like this is one big pappyshow going on now with this cow and this crapochild inside the house! Everybody is laughing and bawling and blowing out they cheeks making one set of frogfaces to imitate this child, and soon I begin to hear somebody mamaguying me about how *I* is the mother of this crapochild, when they know good enough the child belong to Barto and that black jamet Magdalena and I don't have nothing to do with him a-tall, and how they use to see *me* with Barto all the time by Maraval watching the frogs fucking. Sweet heart of Jesus! I run quick to that shoebox cradle and I grab up this crapochild, and I go to Barto on my knees to beg him please for the mercy of Papa God please to carry him way!

Barto look down on me a moment, and I see that I have finally touch him. Because he reach down and he take way this crapochild that is wrap up now in a white coverlet that you can no even see the half belonging to a man. Barto carry the child to the big closet of glass that we have there in the parlour to keep all the guns. He take out the biggest one, this is the rifle all bathe in silver and mother-of-pearl that we have there since the days of General Monagas, and Barto carry the child and the gun both up to the garret. He climb out on top the roof and he walk straight to the very edge. Barto did no even open he mouth to speak a word. He stand up there just so in he leather clothes that I have rub all over with sweetoil until they are glowing, and he is holding this frogchild with he legs spread wide and the spurs on he cowboy boots and he eyes only flaming, and he reach out slow with he arm straight and General Monagas big rifle pointing up at heaven to fire so *boodoom!* and all these people take off running swimming in the mud like each one get jook with a big jooker *up* they backside!

People had begun to appear on the road, most walking in the direction of town. They were dressed in their best clothes for church, or they were already costumed as some saint or Bible character, some figure from the Hindu holy books. That day was a big one for Corpus Christi: it was the religious feastday after which the island had been named. Most of us went to Mass in the morning. In the afternoon there were parades through the streets of St Maggy, the fêtes continuing until midnight. Because at the stroke of twelve all the music stopped, and we returned to church to begin the Easter Vigil. There were never any motorcars on the trace other than the occasional truck or jitney belonging to one of the estates. Bicycles and donkeycarts went by, some already decorated with crêpe paper and papier-mâché.

Everyone who passed looked at me toting the huge bottle. I was sweating, covered in dust, thinking: *Supposing somebody see this frogbaby now and push out a scream? Supposing somebody question you where you get him from? What you ga say? You dig him up in Domingo Cemetery? You catch him in Maraval Swamp?* Then I began to think: *But nobody seeing this frogbaby a-tall! You sure you have anything in this glass-bottle? Maybe it's only fill with seawater? Maybe this frogbaby is only some monster you dream up? Some jujubee Granny Myna push inside you head?*

Just then a boy about my own age – costumed as Moses in a white turban, and dragging a big tablet of pasteboard commandments behind him – grabbed his father's sleeve and pointed at me: "See that, Daddy? Look the frog that boy hold up inside he glassbottle. He big as a monkey! He *live* you know, Daddy. He *swimming*!"

Magdalena just love to go to Maraval to see the crapos singando, because she used to walk all the way from St Maggy Convent every Sunday parading through the streets dress up in she white clothes of a nun before the face of Papa God, when beneath she is nothing but a black whore. And it is those frogs fucking Magdalena must have been looking to make the impression of that frogface the moment she conceive the child, because a crapo is the only creature on the skin of Papa God earth that can hold on and singando passionate for three days and three nights without even a pause for a breath of air, and how else could he come out a man perfect so with the big business hanging and the rest a frog? Of course Dr Brito realize straight way this child is a crapo above the cojones, and he say that he have hear of more frogchildren even though he never have the privilege before to see one heself, but I know that is impossible because this world could never be big enough for two. The other schoolboy-doctor in the hospital then, he is the first to come from England with a big degree stamp by the Queen that was Elizabeth the segundo one, but how can anybody with sense listen to a doctor who learn everything from a book without even seeing a sick person? This little schoolboy-doctor say the child isn't no frog a-tall, but he have a kind of a thing in the blood or the genes or something so. He bring out the big black book that is so big he can hardly tote it, and he point to the picture of this thing now that is name after the first two girlchildren to be born with this disease, and he mark it down on a piece of paper for me to believe it: ANNA-AND-CECILY. The little schoolboy-doctor say this thing means to be born without a brain, and that is what cause the child to *look like* a frog. But it is you Uncle Olly, he is the scientist of bones and rocks and a very brilliant oldman, Uncle Olly, prove without any questions that the child is a frog, and *he do* have a brain, even though it is no bigger than the size of a prune.

The frogchild didn't have no skull a-tall, but only the soft soft covering on the head like the skin of a zabuca. So all Uncle Olly have to do is cut a little cut with the scissors, and squeeze on the both sides, and the little brain pop out like a chenet out the shell. Of course the first thing Uncle Olly do is run quick to Maraval for a big crapo grande, and he take out the brain of this frogbull to compare it with that of the child. Well the two was so much the same in size and shape and weight and everything so, that soon as Uncle Olly go outside for a quick weewee and come back, he forget who belong to who.

I only wish to Papa God Uncle Olly could have satisfy heself with that brain! But when it come to he science nothing couldn't satisfy you Uncle Olly. By the time he have finish with that brain he was all excited, and he decide now he want to preserve this crapochild for more dissections. It is Uncle Olly then who put the child in the bottle of seawater, but the same night Barto discover him floating downstairs on the shelf in Olly laboratory, and that, is the beginning of the end.

A Man in an oxcart going in my direction stopped beside me: "Eh-eh whiteboy, tell me what you say!"

I stood staring up at this oldman who'd wrapped himself and his entire oxcart in aluminium foil. He nodded his nose at the bottle: "Where you going toting dat glassbottle fa health? Dat ting big as you own self! Why you don't climb up here rest you load, let me carry you little bit down de road?"

"Who you is?" I asked. "Robot?"

The oldman chupsed: he sucked his teeth in exasperation. "I is de archangel St Michael, dis my chariot going to battle. And you best get you little backside up here fa sin, you ga dead up yourself toting dat big glasstin." He chupsed again. *"Robot!"*

I gave the bottle a heave onto the shelf where the oldman rested his feet. He leaned over and studied it for several long seconds. He sat up again, his costume crinkling, and we looked at each other.

"Come, boy!" he said, and I climbed up onto the bench next to him, the bottle between us. The oldman nudged his nose over his shoulder: "Plenty more tinpaper back dere fa you, you know. Why you don't costume youself proper, we to play mas fa so!"

"You don't think one robot is enough, oldman?"

He chupsed, and he gave the worn rope he had for reins a tug. We left slowly, pitching from side to side as we went, the solution sloshing in the bottle at our feet. The oxen was a huge coolie-buffalo, with widespread s-shaped horns and a sticky mist rising from its bluegray hump. After awhile the oldman looked at me again, his face beaded with perspiration. His white stubble of beard, grey eyes and lashes looked silver against his umber-burntblack skin: it all seemed to match his aluminium outfit.

"Where you going toting dis bottle on Corpus Christi Day?" he asked. "Corpus Christi is the day fa play is play!"

I was looking up at his cone-shaped hat, the cuffed brim riding on the bridge of his nose, like the oversized cap of a yankee-sailor.

"What wrong with you, boy? You don't talk?"

"You not hot inside all that costume?"

He chupsed. "Where you going with dis glassbottle, boy?"

"You ever see a frogbaby before, oldman?"

He sucked his teeth again. "Ninety-some years I been walking dis earth, me mummy tell me. Still plenty tings I never see."

A breeze came up and the oldman held on to his hat. I shielded my eyes against the dust raised from the road.

"Oldman, you think somebody could die with their eyes open?"

He turned to look at me: "Everybody born with dey eyes close down, and everybody die with dey eyes open up round. Papa God mistake is He do de whole business back-to-front. And dat, boy, is de beginning of all dis confusion and quarrelment. Now tell where you going toting dis glassbottle."

"Maraval."

"Quite so to Maraval footing? Good ting I stop, boy. You would have dead up yourself polapeezoy, time you arrive by de swamp with dis big glasstin."

He reached behind and handed me the roll of aluminium foil. "Corpus Christi not de day to tote no heavy load. Dress up yourself proper let we play! We ga meet up de band down de road, do one set of monekeybusiness before we play!"

I told him I had to go to Maraval Swamp.

He chupsed. "Suit yourself den, whiteson. Time as we bounce up with de flock of Seraphim, you would have almost reach you destination."

I put the roll of foil down as we continued, the ox walking at its slow, steady pace, the cart pitching on its unsteady wheels.

I never hold nothing against Magdalena. Papa God is she judge, and if she is a whore she must answer to Him. Who am I to say she is wrong to be Barto mistress, and how can I hold that crapochild against her, or Barto, or anybody else when he is a creature of Papa God, touch by He own hand, make of He own flesh, breathing of He own air? And so I pick him up. Even though he is the most hateful thing to me in all the world, he is still the son of my husband, and I must go to this child. I am there with Evelina in the kitchen in the middle of preparing dinner when I feel something touch my heart. I don't even finish putting the remainder of the dasheen leaves in the pot of boiling water to make the callaloo, but I leave it there just so and I go to this frogchild. I pick him up with so much tears in my eyes I can hardly see, with so much trembling in my hand I can hardly hold it steady enough to push my tottot in he mouth, but I do it. For the love of Papa God I do it! I feed him with the milk of my *own* breast!

I never hold nothing against Magdalena. I try my best never to listen to what people say, and let me tell you people can say some words to push like a knife in you chest. But I never hold nothing against Magdalena. I am kind to her, and when I meet her in the cathedral with all the other nuns I make a special point to wish her a pleasant todobien, because who am I to say Barto must give he affections to me alone when he have enough love in he heart for all the world? No husband have ever honour he wife more, and offer her more love and devotion than that man give to me. Barto raise me up on a pedestal, you hear? On a *pedestal*!

But something happen when that child begin to suck at my breast. Something happen, and I don't know what it is. Like some poison pass from out he mouth to go inside my blood, because next thing I know I am running back to the kitchen for that big basin of boiling water that is waiting for me to finish the callaloo, and I push him in. Evelina scream but I can't even hear her, because before I can know what my hands are doing they are bury up to they elbows in this boiling water, and how to this day I can no even feel it I couldn't tell you, because here am I drowning this child in the basin of boiling water with the dasheen leaves swirling swirling like the green flames of hell!

Soon as I can realize myself I pull him from out the water, but by now he is already dead. I can no think what to do. I can only plead with Evelina for the mercy of Papa God please to take him way. I beg her to carry him back to Maraval where he belong, but Evelina refuse to come anywhere near this crapochild no matter if he is living or if he is dead. After a time though she have accept to carry him way from me, and I swear her to go straight to Maraval and pitch him in, and I go outside in the street to look behind Evelina walking with this crapochild hold upside down by he legs like a cockfowl going to sell at Victoria Market. I watch behind Evelina until I can no see her any more, and I go back in the house to try my best to finish seeing about the callaloo. I only wish to Papa God I could have remain in that street! Because I put loud goatmouth on myself saying about that crapofowl, as no sooner have I go back inside the house when Evelina turn round to come all the way back, only to sell this crapochild to Uncle Olly for a scrunting five coconut dollars. Uncle Olly have decide now he want to make some of he science on the child, and that night Barto find him floating on the shelf downstairs in Olly laboratory. Sweet Heart of Jesus! I thought Barto would kill me. I have never see him so upset as when he come to me with this bottle, and he demand me to tell him what happen to the child. When I have finish, and I am kneeling down on the ground pleading with him standing above me with he eyes only flaming, he tell me that I will suffer for this the whole of my life and death, because I can never even look forward to lying in the ground in peace beside my husband, as between us will be this crapochild to remind me on myself and torment me until the ends of eternity. And with that Barto leave toting the bottle into the night.

But I can never suffer any more. After ninety-six years I have no more strength left to go on. My eyes have dry up, and there is no more tears left to pass, and Papa God have forgive me. He have forgive me, and tomorrow I will be with Him in heaven. Papa God have forgive me, and Barto must forgive me now after all these years of crying in the dark, and I am ready. I am ready to lie down my bones in peace, peace that I have earn with sweating blood cold in the hot night, but I will never know peace so long as I have to be bury next to that crapochild. *Never!* But you will take him way, Johnny. You will go for me tonight to Domingo Cemetery, and you will dig him up, and you will carry him way. Now I am ready to die. Go and call you mummy and daddy.

We could hear the Divina Church band beating steeldrums in the distance long before we met them. The sun remained hidden behind the dark clouds, but the oldman continued to sweat in his aluminium outfit. A breeze came up and blew away his hat, so I took up the roll of foil and stood on the bench to make him another, a tall spike shooting up at the top – helmet fit for an archangel. There must have been fifty people in the band, and as many children, all costumed as angels. The oldman steered his oxcart to the side of the road and we watched the parade go by, the angels waving to us as they passed. Most went on foot, but there were bicycles and three or four donkeycarts. The children were running back and forth, screaming, flapping their wings. Each of the angels carried a musical instrument of some sort – steeldrums, horns, quatros – but most of the instruments consisted of nothing more than a pair of toktok sticks, a rumbottle and spoon, or a dried calabash with a handful of poinciana seeds shaking inside. The oldman began to sing, his lips flapping over his nearly toothless gums, spittle flying. He took hold of my hands and shook them up and down with the music, his aluminium arms crackling: "Time to jubilate whiteson, open you mouthgate!"

I began to sing too:

Sal-ve Re-gina,
Regina Magda-lena!
Be-ne-dicimas te,
Glo-ri-ficamas te,
A-do-ramas te,
Regina Magda-lena!

When the band had passed I got down from the cart and the oldman handed me the bottle. He turned the oxcart around and waved, his costume flashing molten metal for an instant as it caught the light, shouting something which I could not make out over the music. I watched the oldman disappear into the cloud of dust which followed his band of angels. I looked after him for a long time, until the dust had settled and the steel-drums had been reduced to a rumble in the distance. I looked around and realized I was suddenly alone. There was no one left on the trace. It was quiet. I turned and continued walking, calm now, unhurried.

Granny Myna stared at me in silence. I couldn't move, couldn't get up from the bed. She reached and took both my hands in hers: "Go Johnny. Tell you mummy and daddy I am ready."

I ran upstairs and called them, my brother, Evelina and Papee Vince waking with the commotion. We crowded around Granny Myna sitting up in the small bed, her back against the pillow against the headboard: my father in his drawers sitting next to her listening to her heart through his stethoscope, my mother holding my baby sister with one arm, my younger brother holding her other hand, Papee Vince in the chair leaning forward over his big belly, old Evelina mumbling some obeah incantation, and me thinking: *This is not you standing here seeing this because you are upstairs in you bed sleeping. Why you don't go see if you find yourself and then you would know it is only you dreaming?*

My father pulled the stethoscope from his ears and left it hanging from his neck. He looked around, got up and went to the small table covered with Granny Myna's religious objects: a statue of St Michael, of St Christopher, a photograph of the Pope, of Barto, a plastic bottle shaped like the Virgin filled with holywater from Lourdes, some artificial roses, multi-coloured beads, all decorated on a doily she had crocheted in pink, white and babyblue. My father took up a candle and put it in Granny Myna's hand, closing her fingers around it. He lit a match, but before he could touch it to the candle Mother Superior Maurina, Granny Myna's sister, entered the room. We all turned to look at her. No one had called her, and as far as we knew she and Granny Myna had not talked in more than fifty years, since before Mother Maurina had run away to the convent. She had never set foot in our house.

My father lit another match and touched it to the candle. He told us quietly to kneel down. My grandmother studied the flame for a few seconds, took a deep breath, blew it out: "Stand up! Pray for me to *die* if you have to pray!"

My father chupsed. "Mummy –"

"Tomorrow is the sixteen of April, Holy Thursday: Corpus Christi Day. It is the *happiest* day in heaven, and I am going to be there. I don't want no funeral confusion. Barto have the stone and everything there ready waiting for me. Just dig the hole and push me in the ground *first* thing in the morning!"

We didn't know what to do. My father sucked his teeth. He looked at my mother, got up again and sat next to my grandmother, listening to her heart through his stethoscope. Granny Myna's hands lay on her lap, her fists clenched. Her lips were pressed firmly together over her gums, her pointed chin protruding, trembling slightly. Her eyes were wide, unblinking – fixed on me. I watched her jaw drop slowly, her lips go purple and open a little, her skin turn to soft wax. I kept thinking: *Her eyes aren't closed so she isn't dead. Her eyes aren't closed so she isn't dead. Her eyes aren't* – My father turned. Before he could look up I was already running.

I ran halfway to Domingo Cemetery before I turned around and went back for the shovel, thinking: *If the bottle isn't there she isn't dead. Just make up you head not to dream up that bottle too.* The graveyard smelled of wet earth, rotting leaves, tinged by the too-sweet smell of eucalyptus. A small coral wall ran all around. The huge trees rustled in the breeze, the undersides of their leaves flashing silver in the moonlight. I went straight to Granny Myna's intended grave, everything but her deathdate chiselled into the headstone. I dropped the shovel and squinted to see the line of graves. On one side of the plot where my grandmother would be buried was Uncle Olly's grave, Manuelito's on the other. Beside Manuelito was Barto's grave, and beside him, Magdalena Maria Domingo. I moved closer: MANUELITO DOMINGO, NACI XVI ET MORI XIX APRILIS, ANNO DOMINI NOSTRI, MDCCCXCIX.

I picked up the shovel again, thinking: *If it isn't there she isn't dead because you refuse to dream up the bottle. You can go back home and laugh at yourself sleeping.* But I hadn't sent the shovel into the ground three times when I hit something solid. I threw the shovel aside and got down on my knees to dig with both hands. After a moment I realized I'd found the bottle.

I tried to pull it out but my hands slipped: I fell backwards as though I'd been shoved, my head thudding against Manuelito's headstone, and someone threw a clump of wet earth in my face – like I'd been slapped. I spit out the dirt and tried to wipe my eyes. There was no one there.

I got up slowly, brushed myself off. I knelt, digging carefully, all the way around the bottle. I placed a foot on either side of the hole and lifted it out. I rolled the bottle into a clear space and got down on my knees again, rubbing my hands over the glass, spitting, removing the dirt. I bent closer, still couldn't see. I stood. Straining, I lifted the bottle over my head, the moon lighting it up.

By the time I neared the end of Divina Trace the breeze had come up. Several dark clouds eclipsed the sun. The eight or ten houses of Suparee Village were deserted, not even a fowl or a potcake in the street. At the end of the trace the Church of Magdalena Divina was small, grey against a grey sky. The thick wooden doors were wide open. It was empty, cold inside. I walked slowly up the centre aisle, my jesusboots squeaking on the polished stone, slapping against the soles of my feet, each step echoing through the church. There was a gold baptismal font off to one side of the altar. On the other side there was a small chapel, devotion candles flickering in their red glass holders, the smells of Creole incense and sweetoil growing stronger as I approached.

I stood in front of the chapel, but I could see nothing in the darkness within except the bright red flames. I put the bottle down on one of the pews and climbed the steps, a line of calabash shells filled with sweetoil on either side. I knelt at the chapel railing. She began to take shape slowly out of the darkness, reflections of the tiny red flames rising on her face, flashing through the clouds of rising incense: her gentle eyes, comforting lips, the crimson mark on her forehead, her burnt-sienna skin, long wig of black hair. Her faded gown was covered with jeweled pendants, her outstretched arms thick with silver spiked churries and bangles, a solid gold rosary hanging from her neck – offerings for prayers answered – Magdalena Divina, Mother of Miracles, Black Virgin of Maraval! I closed my eyes: *Hail Mary full of grace the lord is with thee blessed art thou amongst women blessed is the fruit of*

83

you womb Jesus. Holy Mary mother of God pray fa we sinners now at the hour of we death amen. I dipped my finger into the basin of holywater, crossed myself. I picked up the bottle again, walked quickly across the altar, left through the sanctuary.

Behind the church there was an immense samaan tree, spread symmetrically over a plot of green grass. Beyond it Maraval Swamp was greenish-black, mangrove growing along the edge and in the shallows, their thick moss-covered banyans arching out of the water like charmed snakes. I walked along the line of mangrove – picking my way through the tall reeds, the mud sucking at my jesusboots – until I found a gap where I could walk out into the water. I put the bottle down and it sank an inch into the mud. I flipped open the wire clamps at the top and lifted off the lid. I'd expected some pungent odour: there was none, only the stagnant smell of the morass. I tried my best not to look into the bottle, but I couldn't avoid seeing two bulging eyes at the top of a flat head: the lid slipped from my hands landing *clap* in the mud.

I took a deep breath and picked up the bottle again, slippery now with the mud on the glass and on my hands. I walked slowly, the cold liquid in the bottle spilling down my chest, and at the same moment I put my foot in the water several things happened almost simultaneously: the frogs which were making a big noise ceased their croaking, and there was absolute silence; the light became immediately dimmer; and a gust blew, stripping blueblack tonguelike leaves from the mangrove limbs, their banyans quivering in the wind. I continued carefully into the water until it reached my waist, the bottle half-submerged, and stopped – shin-deep in the mud. Slowly, I tilted the bottle, feeling its weight slip away and the solid splash before me in the water. I wanted nothing more now than to turn quickly and run: I couldn't budge my feet. Standing there, holding the finally empty bottle, seeing myself again with my baggy navyblue school shortpants billowing around my hips, feeling my feet again in my jesusboots beneath the mud, looking down again through the dark water again, thinking, not understanding, believing: *He is alive. Swimming.* I watched his long angular legs fold, snap taut, and propel him smoothly through the water; snap, glide; snap, glide; and the frogchild disappeared into a clump of quiet mangrove banyans.

THE STYLIST

Jennifer Egan

Jennifer Egan was born in 1963. She has contributed numerous short stories to various publications, won the *Cosmopolitan*/Perrier Short Story Award (United Kingdom) in 1991, and her short-story collection, *Emerald City*, was published in 1993.

THE STYLIST

When they finally reach the dunes, Jann, the photographer, opens a silver umbrella. This is the last shot of the day. The light is rich and slanted. Around them the sand lies in sparkling heaps, like piles of glass silt.

A girl toes the sand. She wears a short cotton skirt, a loose T-shirt. A few feet away from her, the stylist pokes through a suitcase filled with designer bathing suits. The stylist's name is Bernadette. She's been doing this for years.

"Here," she says, handing the girl a bikini. It is made of shiny red material. The girl glances at Jann, who is busy loading his camera. She slips her underpants from beneath the skirt and pulls on the bathing-suit bottom. She is not close to twenty yet.

"Is this the cover shot?" asks the girl, whose name is Alice. Each time she's in a shot she asks this question.

"Where were you two months ago?" the stylist says.

"What do you mean?" Alice's face is diamond-shaped. Her eyes are filled with gold.

"I mean where were you two months ago?" Bernadette asks again.

"I was home. They hadn't found me yet."

"Home is where?"

"Rockford, Illinois."

"Cover shot or not," Bernadette tells the girl, "it seems to me you aren't doing too badly."

This takes Alice by surprise. Her mouth opens as if to answer, but instead she turns away and lifts the T-shirt over her head. There is something despairing in the movement of her shoulders. She covers each of her small breasts with half of the red bathing-suit top. Bernadette ties the straps. Alice stares for a moment at the waves, which are pale blue and disorderly.

"Where are we again?" she asks.

"Lamu," says Bernadette.

Hair and Make-up arrive, panting from the walk. Nick, the make-up man, begins to work on the girl's eyes. She hugs herself.

"Where were we yesterday?" she asks.

"Mombasa," says Bernadette.

The photographer is ready. The silver umbrellas are raised to gather the light. He holds a light meter to the girl's chest. Hair and Make-up share a cigarette. There are two other models on this trip, and they watch from a distance. The sea mumbles against the dunes. The girl looks especially bare, surrounded by people who are dressed. She is still so new the camera frightens her. Jann has removed it from his tripod and is holding it near her face. "This face," he says, pausing to glance at the rest of them. "Will you look at this face?"

They look. It is fragile and soft as a newly risen moon. Jann squints behind his camera. The rhythm of the shutter mingles with the breaking waves. Catching it, the girl begins to move.

"There," cries Jann, "that's it!"

They look again. Bernadette looks and sees it, too, feels the others see it. In the way the light falls there is something; in the girl's restless hands, her sad mouth. A stillness falls. She is more than a skinny young girl on a beach; she is any young girl, sad and long-haired, watching a frail line of horizon. The camera clicks. Then the moment passes.

Alice leans down and scratches at her knee. Bernadette looks at Jann and sees him smiling.

"Bingo," he says.

In town the wind blows, filling the air with dust and tissue candy wrappers. There are lots of widows in Lamu, old squat women who clutch their dark veils against the wind. In the market square they hunch beside baskets of dried fruit, seeds, purple grain. The air smells burned.

The group is staying in an old two-storey hotel near the waterfront – the sort of place that conjures up piano players and rough men toasting their motherlands. It reminds Bernadette of the hotel in New Orleans where she spent her honeymoon. Like that hotel, this place has ceiling fans. Last night she lay in bed and watched hers spin.

After dinner, Alice tells of how she was discovered. It happened at the shopping mall, she says. All the girls walked through. You had to bring snapshots. She had one of herself riding on her brother's shoulders. The two other models look bored with the story.

Bernadette lights a cigarette. She turns to Jann, who is flipping through a magazine. "What does this remind you of?" she says.

He looks up, his blond eyebrows raised. He is gentle and brawny, like a Viking from a children's book.

"What does what remind me of?" he says.

"This. All of us."

Jann seems confused, so she goes on. "Have you noticed how no one really likes each other?" she says. "We're like a family."

He is amused. He takes a long drink of beer and runs his hands through his hair. "Speak for yourself," he says.

Bernadette laughs and then stops. "What's holding us together?" she asks.

"That's easy," says Jann, leaning back in his chair so the cheap wood creaks. "That's a no-brainer."

"Humour me," says Bernadette.

He leans forward, resting his elbows on the oilcloth table-top. The wind carries snaking bits of music in from the narrow streets. The models have wandered away, and the room is filled with people so black their skin shines blue in the light.

"We're on a fashion shoot," he says.

It sounds oddly senseless.

He rolls a matchstick between his palms and then waves at the waiter for two more beers. Flies settle on the table's edge. He looks at Bernadette. "To getting those shots," he says, raising his beer. He sounds uneasy. Bernadette drinks from her bottle, letting her head fall back. Her neck is long and white. Jann watches her throat move as she swallows.

"To the hand that feeds us," she says.

Now the girls gallop over. They want to go dancing some-where. In Mombasa there was a discothèque filled with young African whores who danced languidly and waited for business to arrive. The girls were fascinated.

"Not in Lamu," says Jann. "Remember, there aren't even cars."

Alice yawns openly, like a cat. Her teeth catch the light. She leans down and rests her head on Jann's shoulder. In a helpless, teen-age way she has adored him from the start.

"I'm sleepy," she says.

Jann glances at Bernadette and pulls the girl into his lap. He runs a palm over her soft hair, and she relaxes against him. Her long legs scatter towards the floor. All of them are silent. The girl squirms and moves her head. At this hour two months ago, she would be kissing her father good night. She climbs to her feet. "Well," she says, looking from Jann to Bernadette, "see you tomorrow."

She wanders in search of the other two, who have left her behind.

"Poor kid," says Jann.

As they watch her go, Bernadette reaches under the table and touches him, softly at first, then more boldly. It's amazing, she thinks, how you can just do this to people. Like stealing. Luckily, the youngest girls don't know it.

Jann looks at her and swallows. She decides that he is younger than she thought. She sips her beer, which tastes of smoke, and does not move her hand. "What does this remind you of?" she says.

He shakes his head. Colour fills his cheeks.

"Let's go upstairs," says Bernadette.

They leave the bar and climb the narrow flight of steps to the hotel rooms. Bernadette presses her palms against the walls. She is drunker than she thought. They pause at the top, where insects dive against an electric bulb. Jann hooks his fingers into the back of Bernadette's jeans and gently pulls. Desire, sour and metallic, pushes up from her throat.

"Your room?" she says.

Jann's bed is neatly made, its curtain of mosquito netting twisted in a bundle overhead. He goes into the bathroom and shuts the door. Bernadette stands at the window. There is no glass, just wood shutters that have been pulled aside to let in the night wind. A bright moon spills silver across the waves. Painted sailboats line the shore.

She hears the toilet flush and stays near the window, expecting Jann to come up behind her. He doesn't. The bed squeaks under his weight.

"You know," she says, still facing the sea, "this reminds me of something."

"Everything reminds you of something," he says.

"That's true. One of these days I'll figure out what it is."

"Any ideas?"

"Nope." She stretches so her stomach pulls. "It must be one of the few things I haven't seen or done."

Jann is silent. Bernadette wonders if he has pulled the netting down.

"Well," he says, "then it shouldn't be hard to spot. When it comes along."

Bernadette lifts off her shirt. Her bra is black, her breasts full and white inside it. There is too much flesh. This has always been the case, but after a day of dressing girls with pronged hips and bellies like shallow empty dishes her own body comes as a surprise. She turns to Jann. "I'll know when I've found it," she says, "because it won't remind me of anything else."

He is lying down, hands crossed behind his head. His photographer's eye is on her. Her body feels abundant, tasteless. She wishes she had left her shirt on.

"If you close your eyes," she says, "you won't know the difference."

Jann shakes his head. The ceiling fan spins, touching Bernadette's bare shoulders with its current. She goes to the dresser and finds scattered change, film containers, a pack of cigarettes. She takes one out and lights it. There are Polaroids: two from this morning in town, another from the docks. She finds one of Alice in the dunes and holds it up. "What do you think of her?" she says.

"Cute," says Jann. "Stiff, though. New."

"She has a crush on you," says Bernadette. "I'm sure you've noticed."

"Poor kid," says Jann. "Should be going to high-school proms."

Bernadette looks again at the picture. Sunlight fills the girl's hair. The sand is pale and bright as snow, the sea turquoise. She longs suddenly to be in those white dunes, as if she had never seen anything like them before. She must remind herself that she was standing just outside the shot, that she chose the girl's bathing suit.

"Have you ever noticed how meaningful these things can look?" she asks.

Jann laughs. "Have I noticed?" he says. "It's my shot."

Bernadette flips the picture back among the others. Her voice goes soft. "I meant in a general sense," she says.

"In a general sense," says Jann, "that's how they work."

The room is filled with stale light. Bernadette goes to the bed. It's amazing, she thinks, how lust and aggravation will combine to push you towards someone. She sits on the bed and then wishes she had headed for the door. She would have liked to make him ask. He would have asked, she thinks.

She stretches out beside him under the twisting fan. It reminds her of scissors. They do not touch.

"So," she says, addressing the fan, "are you planning to cash in?"

"On what?"

"On Alice."

His arms tense. "Are you always like this?" he asks.

"You bring out my best side," says Bernadette.

She takes his face in her hands and kisses his mouth. The sourness wells up around her gums and teeth. She wonders if Jann can taste it. She presses her stomach against him and works the T-shirt over his head. Undressing a person is easy – she makes a living at it. Jann smells like the beach. His chest is nearly hairless.

"What's the matter?" he says.

His eyes look cloudy and small. He pushes her down and moves above her now, pulling off her jeans one leg at a time. She watches his arms, the same thready muscles and veins she has watched as he held his camera these past days. She probes them with her nails, leaving small white crescents. He doesn't protest. She has him now, she knows it. And yet, she thinks, what difference does it make?

Later, when they have made love and the sounds of the bar have died down, Jann and Bernadette lie still.

"You know," she says, "this room is a lot like the one where I spent my honeymoon. New Orleans."

"Honeymoon?" he says.

"Sure," she says. "What else was there to do in the early seventies?"

Jann says nothing.

"I was pretty then," she adds. "My hair was down to here."

She turns a little, touching the base of her spine. The skin is damp.

"You're pretty now," says Jann.

"Please," says Bernadette.

Jann runs a finger down her cheek.

"Stop it," she says.

"How come?"

"Because old skin always looks tear-streaked."

"How old are you?" he asks.

"Thirty-six."

He laughs. "Thirty-six," he says. "God, what a business we're in."

Bernadette touches her cheek in the place where Jann's finger was. She presses the skin as though searching for a blemish.

"I've been a stylist for sixteen years," she says. "I felt competitive with the girls at first. Now I feel maternal."

"Sixteen years," says Jann, shaking his head.

"They're younger now," she says. "You know that."

"They get older, too. Think what it is like for them."

"Who knows? They disappear."

"Exactly," says Jann.

They lie in silence. Bernadette decides she will go back to her own room. Conversation is meant to get you somewhere, and she and Jann have already been and gone.

"You know," he says, "it's hard to picture you married."

"I hardly was. It lasted a minute."

"How did it end?"

"Christ!" she says. "What have I started here?"

"Tell me," he says.

She narrows her eyes and sits up. With her toes she searches the floor for her sandals.

"You can't answer a simple question," says Jann. "Can you?"

Bernadette touches her knuckles to her lips. The door is ten feet from the bed. She wishes she were dressed.

"I got restless," she says.

"Restless," says Jann.

"Restless," she says. "You know – restless? I kept thinking how many places there were."

Jann laughs. "I guess you picked the right life," he says.

"I guess so," says Bernadette. She fumbles for her lighter. "You know," she says, "you ask too many questions."

She lights a cigarette and smokes it lavishly, sending out plumes through her nose and letting the smoke roll from her mouth. She thinks how much she loves to smoke, how conversations like this would get to her otherwise.

"So," says Jann, as she stubs her cigarette into the half-shell ashtray, "were they as nice as you thought? The places?"

"Sure they were nice. They were very nice. This is nice." She waves her arm at the ceiling. "I've been all over the world," she says. "You've done it, too, right?"

"I've done it, too," Jann says.

She shrugs, then slides her feet into her sandals and lights a last cigarette. One for the road, she thinks.

"My only regret," she says, "is that I hardly have any pictures of myself. All I've got is the shots I styled."

Jann nods. "It's like looking through someone else's photo album," he says.

Bernadette twists around to look at him. He has a sweet face, she thinks. "That's right," she says. "That's exactly how it is."

She stubs out her half-finished cigarette. She wishes she had left ten minutes ago. She will stay another half hour, she thinks.

She lies back down, her body facing Jann's. His shoulder smells faintly sweet, like candle wax. She places her palm on his stomach, but when she tries to move her hand Jann covers it with his own.

"Of all those places you've been," he says, "which was your favourite?"

Bernadette sighs. She is tired of questions. Strangely, she cannot remember anyone having asked her this one before. Is that possible, she wonders. Surely someone asked, surely she had some answer. She tries again to move her hand. Jann holds it still.

"I liked them all," she says.

"Bullshit."

She feels a surge of regret at finding herself still here, at getting caught in this discussion. Jann moves her hand from his stomach to his chest. The skin is warmer there, close to the bone. She can feel the beating heart.

"There must be one that stands out," he says.

Bernadette hesitates.

"New Orleans," she says. "My honeymoon."

It is the only place she can think of. She feels suddenly that she might begin to cry.

Jann lets her hand go. He turns on his side so they are facing one another. Their hips touch.

"It must be quite a place," he says. His voice is gentle now.

Bernadette moves against him. She cannot stop herself. Jann

98

takes her head in his hands and makes her look at him. "Hey," he says, "what does this remind you of?"

He is playful, teasing. A thin silver chain encircles his neck.

"Nothing," she says. Something is caught in her throat.

For a moment neither moves.

"OK," says Jann, pulling her to him. "Here we are, then."

The next morning they stagger through the dunes, giddy with exhaustion. It is still early, and the light is pale, frosted. It bleaches the waves. Jann is unshaven. Bernadette can't stop looking at him.

They're late. The rest of the group mills restlessly near the shore, turning to check on their progress across the sand. The models' faces look ghostly in this bloodless morning sun. They will probably guess, thinks Bernadette. She hopes they do.

"It's strange," she says. "Going back."

"To them?" Jann gestures at the group. "Or back?"

"Both," she says.

Later today they will fly to Nairobi. Tomorrow morning, New York. Two weeks from now she leaves for Argentina.

"Everything fades the minute you're somewhere else," Bernadette says. It's a mistake to say these things. "It fades."

Jann switches his camera case from one shoulder to the other. The stubble of his beard glints with perspiration.

"Some things have to last," he says, grinning at her, "or there'd be nothing but pictures you styled and I shot."

Hair and Make-up are waving. The others stamp the sand with mock impatience. It is too soft to make a sound.

"They're not enough," says Bernadette.

"No," says Jann. "They're not."

She tries to catch his eye, but he is hurrying. He said it once, she thinks. But she cannot let the conversation go. "It's not enough," she says again.

They reach the group. Everyone eyes them alertly. Bernadette enjoys this attention in a shameless, childish way she cannot remember feeling since high school. There is something thrilling in being wondered about.

The first shot is of Alice. She wears a black one-piece, skimpy, woven with gold threads. It is Bernadette's favourite.

"Better on you than on me," she says, snipping a loose thread. The girl's breasts are so small that Bernadette must pin the suit at the back. Alice doesn't smile. Her eyes are funny today, as though she hadn't slept.

Nick, the make-up man, can't put enough shadow on. "You're puffy," he tells her, adding mascara.

"Puffy," Bernadette snorts. "Wait twenty years."

When Nick is satisfied, Alice goes to the water's edge. The two other models flank her, their backs to the camera. Alice extends her arms slightly from the shoulders, a ballet pose. As Jann begins to shoot, she raises them slowly. Bernadette stands beside Jann. She sees a thin child, a body barely settled in its first frail curves. There is something yielding in the girl's face, something easily wounded. She is looking at Jann.

"More eyes," he says. "Make them harder."

The girl lifts her chin, sharpening the thin line of her jaw. Her eyes are bright and narrow. She looks at Jann and Bernadette with the sad, fierce look of someone who sees a thing she knows she cannot have.

Jann is excited. "Kiddo! You've got it," he cries.

She does, Bernadette thinks. In three years she will probably be famous. She will hardly remember Lamu, and if she runs across pictures of herself on this beach she'll wonder who took them.

When the shot is done, Alice wanders to the water and begins to wade. She still wears the black bathing suit, and standing alone she looks like a teenager about to dive in. After dressing the other models, Bernadette follows. There is something she wants to say. She and Alice wade together in silence.

"I want to go home," Alice says. Her eyes are red.

"Twenty-four hours," says Bernadette.

"I mean home home."

"Rockford, Illinois?"

The girl nods. "I'm lonely," she says.

It's amazing, thinks Bernadette, how the young can just say these things. How easy it is.

"We're in Africa," she tells the girl.

Alice shrugs and looks at the shore. Oddly shaped trees rise from behind the dunes. Jann is shooting again. The other models lie stretched on the sand.

"Home never looks so good as when you're in Africa," Bernadette says.

Alice turns to her, squinting in the glare. "What do you mean?" she says.

"I mean you can go home whenever you want," Bernadette says. "No one's stopping you."

The girl fixes her distracted eyes on the horizon. The water looks thick as molten silver. It feels warm against Bernadette's thighs.

"And then you'll be home," she says.

Alice dips her fingers into the water and paints wet streaks along her arm. She looks disappointed, as if she had expected to hear something else.

"But now that you've had a taste," says Bernadette, "you probably won't."

She feels a moment of pride in the way she has led her own life. I didn't go home, she thinks.

"I bet I won't," Alice says.

Something relaxes around the girl's mouth. She looks relieved. It is hard to pass up an extraordinary life.

"Anyway," says Bernadette, "I can cheer you up a little."

Alice shrugs, clinging to her gloom. She is, after all, a teenager.

"That shot we just did – that one of you?" Bernadette says. "That was the cover."

The girl runs a hand through her hair. Her lips part, and her eyes fill with tears. She is trying not to smile.

They turn at the sound of voices. Jann jogs towards them with Nick in tow. They have finished the shot.

"I want to get one of you," Jann says to Bernadette. "I'll make you a copy."

Bernadette glances at Alice. The girl has turned away, and her wet hands dangle at her sides.

"Us three," says Bernadette.

Jann hands the camera to Nick. He goes to Bernadette's side, and she stands between him and the girl, one arm around each. She can feel the bones of Alice's shoulders, fragile and warm as a bird's. She brushes a few stray hairs from the girl's face.

"Smile," says Nick.

There is a stillness, the pause of a moment being sealed. Bernadette notices the breeze, the limp water washing her toes. She feels an ache of nostalgia. Jann's hand presses against her back. Between them all is a fragile weave of threads, a spider's web. Bernadette longs for this moment as if it had already passed, as if it could have been. Yet here it is.

CAPRICIOUS GARDENS

Jeff Eugenides

Jeffrey Eugenides is the author of *The Virgin Suicides*, the first chapter of which won the Aga Khan Prize after it had appeared in the *Paris Review*. He now lives in New York City.

CAPRICIOUS GARDENS

> I was asking myself these questions, weeping all the while
> with the most bitter sorrow in my heart, when all at once
> I heard the singsong voice of a child ... I stemmed my
> flood of tears and stood up, telling myself that this could
> only be a divine command to open my book of Scripture
> and read the first passage on which my eyes should fall.
>
> St Augustine

In Ireland, in summer, four people come out to a garden in search of food.

The back door of a large house opens and a man steps out. His name is Sean. He is forty-three years old. He moves away from the house, then glances behind him as two other figures materialize, Amy and Maria, American girls. There is a pause before the next person appears, a gap in the procession, but at last Malcolm arrives. He steps onto the grass tentatively, as if afraid he will sink.

But already they can all see what has happened.

Sean said: "It's my wife's fault, all of this. It's a perfect expression of her inner character. To go to all the trouble of digging and planting and watering and then to forget about it completely in a few days' time. It's unforgivable."

"I've never seen a garden quite so overrun," said Malcolm. He addressed the remark to Sean, but Sean didn't reply to it. He was busy looking at the American girls who, in one identical motion, had put their hands on their hips. The precision of their movements, so perfectly synchronized and yet unintentional, unnerved him. It was a bad omen. Their movements seemed to say: "We are inseparable."

That was unfortunate because one of the girls was beautiful and the other was not. Less than an hour before, on his way home from the airport (he had just returned from Rome) Sean had seen Amy standing by the side of the road, alone. The house he was returning to had been closed up for a month, ever since his wife Meg had gone off to France, or Peru. They had lived apart for years, each occupying the house only when the other was away, and Sean dreaded returning after long absences. The smell of his wife was everywhere, rose from armchairs when he sat in them, made him remember days of bright scarves and impeccable sheets.

When he saw Amy, however, he knew immediately how to brighten his homecoming. She wasn't hitchhiking, but was wearing a backpack; she was a pretty traveler with unwashed hair, and he suspected his offer of a spare room would surpass the ditch or clammy Bed and Breakfast she would find to stay in that night. At once he stopped his car beside her, and leaned across the seat to roll down the passenger's window. As he leaned he took his eyes off her, but when he looked up again, already bestowing his capricious invitation, he saw not only Amy but another girl standing next to her, holding her arm. The newcomer wasn't attractive in the least. Her hair was short, revealing the squarish shape of her skull, and the thick lenses of her glasses glinted so that he couldn't see her eyes.

In the end Sean was forced to invite the regrettable Maria

along as well. The girls climbed into his car like affectionate sisters, stowing their packs in the backseat, and Sean sped off toward his house. When he arrived at his house, however, he encountered another unexpected surprise. There, on the front steps, with his head in his hands, was his old friend Malcolm.

Malcolm stood at the edge of the garden, eyeing its neglect. The garden was mostly dirt. Brambles covered the back portion and in the front there was nothing but a row of brown flowers crushed by the rain. Sean was blaming it all on his wife. "She thinks of herself as having a green thumb," he joked, but Malcolm didn't laugh. The garden made him think of the nature of marriage, sown in haste and then left to corruption. Only five weeks earlier, his wife, Gwendolyn, had left him for another man. In response Malcolm had tried to jump off a cliff. In response to his failure to jump off a cliff he had gone traveling, hoping to find, in freedom of movement, freedom from pain. Quite by chance he had found himself in the town where he remembered his old friend Sean lived. Wandering the streets, his shirt spotted with coffee, he had made his way to Sean's house, knocked on the door, and found no one at home.

He had not been alone for long. All of a sudden he looked up and there was Sean, striding down the front path with a girl on either side of him. The vision filled Malcolm with envy. Here was his friend, surrounded by youth and vitality (the girls were laughing musical laughs) and here was he, sitting on the doorstep, surrounded by nothing but the specters of old age, loneliness, and despair.

The situation grew worse from there. Sean greeted him quickly, as though they had seen each other only last week, and Malcolm began to sense he was in the way. With a flourish Sean opened up the house and led the girls into the kitchen. Malcolm followed them and watched as they searched the cabinets. All they found was a plastic bag of black beans and in the refrigerator a stick of butter, a shriveled lemon, and a desiccated clove of garlic. That was when Sean suggested they go out to the garden.

Malcolm followed them outside. And now he stood apart, wishing he could take the failure of his own marriage as lightly as Sean took the failure of his. He wished he could put Gwendolyn behind him, lock her memory in a box and bury it deep in the earth, far beneath the soil he now turned up with the toe of his left shoe.

Sean stepped into the garden, kicking at the brambles. He had forgotten the cupboards would be bare, he had nothing to offer his guests now, and he had two more guests than he wanted. He gave one last kick, disgusted with everything, but this time his foot caught on a network of brambles, pulling them up in the air. They lifted as a lid lifts off a box and underneath, hiding against the wall, was a clump of artichokes. "Hold on," he said, seeing them. "Hold on one minute." He took a few steps toward them. He bent and touched one. Then he turned, looking back at Amy. "Do you know what this is?" he asked her. "It's Divine Providence. The Good Lord made my wife plant these poor artichokes and then made her forget about them, so that we, in our need, would find them. And eat."

A few of the artichokes were blooming. Amy hadn't known that artichokes could bloom but there they were, as purple as thistles, only larger. The idea of eating them made her happy. Everything about the evening made her happy, the house, the garden, her new friend, Sean. For a month she and Maria had been traveling through Ireland, staying in youth hostels where they had to sleep on cots in rooms crowded with other girls. She was tired of all the girls, of the budgeted meals they scraped together in the hostel kitchens, and of the way they washed out their underwear in the bathroom sinks, spreading it on the floor to dry. Now, thanks to Sean, she could sleep in a big bedroom with lots of windows and a canopy bed.

"Come look," Sean said, beckoning her with his hand, and she stepped into the garden and approached him. They bent over together. A tiny gold cross slipped out of her T-shirt and hung, swinging. "My God, you're Catholic," he said. "Yes," said Amy. "And Irish?" She nodded, smiling. He lowered his voice, bent one of the artichokes toward her. "That makes us practically family, my dear."

If Sean perceived the implications of the girls' body language, even more so did Maria. For it wasn't true that the two of them had put their hands on their hips simultaneously without meaning to. Amy had started the movement and Maria had mirrored her. Because Maria wanted to proclaim to the world just that message which Sean had read. Maria wanted to inhabit Amy's being, so, in this instance, she transformed Amy and herself into two identical sculptures set side by side on the grass.

Maria had never had a friend like Amy before. She had never felt that someone understood her so well. Her life thus far had been like living in a town of mutes, where no one spoke to her but only stared. It seemed to Maria that she had never heard the sound of another human voice, until that Sunday in March when Amy had said, for no reason at all: "Hello."

At the back of the garden the artichokes lolled on their thick stems. Maria looked at Amy standing in them, running a hand through her thick hair. Maria was just as happy as Amy. She too responded to the stark beauty of Sean's stone house, and to the coolness of the evening air. But besides the delight of her present surroundings there remained another bright spot which made her happy, a bright spot she returned to again and again in her thoughts. For the day before, in an empty train compartment, Amy had put her arms around Maria and had kissed her on the lips.

*

Amy's gold cross was swinging and as Sean looked at it he thought it was impossible to guess the importance circumstances would give to random things. At that moment an object lay inside his suitcase, an object he had foreseen no use for until now. But the tiny cross swung, his mind linked image to image, and he saw in the air before him the index finger of St Augustine.

It was his only souvenir of Rome. On his last day there, exploring side streets, he had come across a curious shop full of ancient parchment and crumbling bones. The proprietor led him to a glass case and showed him a thin dusty piece of bone-like material which he insisted was the finger of St Augustine. Sean didn't believe him, but had bought the relic anyway, because it amused him.

He led Amy further back in the garden, away from Maria and Malcolm who still hadn't ventured onto the dirt. He turned his back to them and asked, "Your friend isn't Catholic, is she?" "Episcopalian," Amy whispered. "Not good enough," said Sean. He frowned. "And Malcolm's an Anglican, I'm afraid." He put a finger to his lip as if he were deep in thought. "Why?" Amy asked. His attention returned to the surface. He gave her a sly look. But when he spoke it was to all of them: "We need to organize work details. Malcolm, perhaps you'd be good enough to pick these artichokes while we get the water boiling."

"They have thorns," said Malcolm.

"Just prickles," said Sean, and with that he left the garden and started back toward the house.

Amy assumed Sean meant all three of them would get the water boiling. She followed him into the kitchen, glancing back and smiling once at Maria, who hurried along after them, swinging her short arms. When they got inside, however, Sean looked at Maria and said, "If I remember correctly, my wife keeps the good silver upstairs in the hall chest. The red chest.

In the bottom drawer, rolled up in a sheet. Could you get it, Maria? It would be nice to at least have good silverware." Maria hesitated before saying anything. Then she turned and asked Amy to come help her.

Amy didn't want to. She was fond of Maria but had found lately that Maria tended to smother her. Everywhere Amy went, Maria followed. On trains Maria sat squashed against her side. Yesterday, pressed between the metal compartment wall and Maria's stiff shoulder, Amy had finally gotten angry. She wanted to push Maria away and shout, "Let me breathe, will you!" She felt uncomfortably hot and was just about to nudge her when suddenly her anger left, replaced by a feeling of guilt. How could she scold Maria for wanting to be near her? How could she return affection with peevishness? Amy felt ashamed, and though she still felt too hot pressed against Maria, she tried to forget her discomfort and instead leaned over and gave Maria a friendly peck on the lips.

Now Amy wanted to stay downstairs and help cook the meal. Sean interested her. He had the perfect life, didn't have to work, took trips to Rome whenever he wanted, and always came back to a beautiful country house. Amy had never met a person like Sean before and what she most wanted out of life at her age was just that: the new, the as-yet-unexperienced. That was why she was glad when Sean said, "I'm afraid you'll have to go up by yourself, Maria. I need Amy's help here in the kitchen."

Gently, blindly, Malcolm picked the artichokes. It had grown dark in the garden, the sun had set behind the stone wall, and the only light came now from inside the house, illuminating a patch of lawn not far from where Malcolm knelt. There had been a time when he would never have done this sort of thing, get down on his knees and pick his own dinner, muddying his trousers, but such considerations seemed alien to him now. For weeks he hadn't been able to look himself in the mirror whereas usually his sophisticated appearance filled him with pride.

He ran his hands up the thick stems of the artichokes, snapping off the bulbs. This way he avoided the prickles. He worked slowly. The smell of the earth rose to his nostrils, a stew of mud and worms. It was the first smell he had noticed in weeks, and there was something intoxicating about it. He could feel the coldness of the ground against his kneecaps.

In the dark the artichokes seemed to go on forever. As he picked them, and moved further in, he kept encountering new stalks. He began to work a little faster, and after a time, became aware that he was completely absorbed in his work. He liked picking the artichokes. He slowed down. He didn't want the picking to end.

The front staircase was long and grand, and as soon as she began climbing it Maria ceased to mind her lonely errand. She felt free, far from home and all the disappointments of home. She liked her clothes, which were thick and baggy; she liked her short hair; she liked the fact that she and Amy were in a place where they couldn't be found, a place where they could act toward one another as they wished and not as society dictated. An old tapestry hung on the wall, a stag being torn by two threadbare dogs.

She came to the top of the stairs and went down the hallway looking for the red chest. There were chests all along the hall, most of them dark mahogany. Finally she found one somewhat redder than the others and knelt before it. She opened the bottom drawer. A roll of sheet lay inside, and taking it out she was surprised at how heavy it was. She laid the sheet on the floor and began to unroll it. She flipped it over and over again, the metal inside clinking together. Then finally the last wrap came undone and there they were – knives, forks, spoons – all laid out in the same direction, glittering up at her.

*

Once he was alone with Amy, Sean took his time getting the water on the stove. He removed a metal pot from its hook on the wall. He brought it to the sink. He began filling it with water.

Through all this he was extremely aware of his actions and of the fact that Amy was watching him. When he reached up to unhook the pot from the wall he tried to make his movements as fluid as possible. He set the pot on the stove (gracefully) and turned to face her.

She was leaning back against the sink, her hands planted on either side of her, her body stretching in a delicate arc. She looked even more appealing than she had by the side of the road. "Since we're alone now, Amy," he said, "I can tell you a secret."

"I'm ready," she said.

"Do you promise to keep this quiet?"

"I promise."

He looked into her eyes. "How much do you know about Church history?"

"I went to catechism until I was thirteen."

"Then you're familiar with St Augustine?"

She nodded with enthusiasm. Sean looked around the room as if to see if anyone were listening. Then he took a long pause, winked, and said: "I have his finger."

Amy was not so much interested in St Augustine's finger as in the fact that Sean was willing to tell her a secret. She listened to him devoutly, as if he were revealing a divine mystery.

When Amy flirted she didn't always admit to herself that she was flirting. Sometimes she preferred to suspend her mental faculties so that she could flirt, as it were, without her mind watching. It was as if her body and mind separated, her body stepping behind a screen to remove its clothing while her mind, on the other side of the screen, sat and daydreamed.

With Sean now, in the kitchen, Amy began to flirt without admitting it to herself. He told her about his relic and said that in consideration of the fact that she was Catholic he would show it to her. "But you mustn't tell anyone. We don't want these heretics shouldering their way back into the true faith."

Amy agreed, laughing. She stretched her body even further back. She knew that Sean was looking at her and, suddenly, dimly, became aware that she enjoyed the feel of his gaze upon her. She saw herself through his eyes: a willowy young woman, leaning back on her arms, staring thoughtfully at the floor.

"Have you got a basket?" said Malcolm, coming into the doorway. His hands were covered with dirt and he was smiling for the first time that day.

"There can't be that many," said Sean.

"There are hundreds. I can't carry them all."

"Make two trips," said Sean. "Make three."

Malcolm looked at Amy leaning against the sink. The ivory comb in her hair gleamed as she turned her head toward him. He thought once again of Sean's ability to surround himself with youth and vitality. And so he said to her, "It's damned pleasant out in the garden, Amy. Why don't you come help me? Let old Sean boil the water."

He didn't give her a chance to refuse. He led her by the hand out the back door, waving goodbye to Sean with the other. "I've made a little pile," he said, once he had brought her into the garden. "It's a little wet but you get used to it." He knelt down by the pile of artichokes and looked up at her. In the light from the house he could make out her figure and the slopes and shadows of her face.

"Make a basket of your arms and I'll fill it," he said. Amy did as she was told, crossing her arms with the palms of her hands facing up. On his knees before her Malcolm began picking up the artichokes, placing them one by one in her arms, gently pressing them against her stomach. First there were five, then ten, then fifteen. As the number increased, Malcolm became more precise in the positions he chose for the artichokes. He furrowed his brow and fit each artichoke snugly into place among the rest, as if linking pieces of a puzzle. "Look at you," he said. "You've become a goddess of the harvest." And to him she was. She stood before him, slender and young, with a profusion of artichokes sprouting from her belly. He placed one last artichoke high up on her chest, accidentally pricking her.

"Oh, sorry!"

"I'd better take these in."

"Yes, by all means, take them in. We're going to have a feast!"

When Maria came into the kitchen and saw Sean standing over the stove, peering into the pot of water, she became uneasy. She of course understood quite well what Sean was up to. She saw the looks he gave Amy, noted the affected tones of his voice when he spoke to her. "Your room is up the stairs to the right," he had said, and his voice had tried to sound grand and generous.

She moved to set down the silverware but caught herself before doing so. It would make too much noise. Instead she stood holding it all, watching Sean from behind, quietly enjoying the fact that she was watching him without his knowing it.

The room she and Amy were staying in had only one bed. Maria had noticed that at once. When they first went in, carrying their backpacks in front of them, Maria had looked at the bed, seeing out of the corner of her eye that Amy was also looking at it. It had been a moment of unspoken understanding. The understanding said: "We are going to sleep tonight in the same bed!" But at that moment Maria had felt that to utter a word would break the spell. They both knew what the other was thinking but they only said, "This is great," and "I can't believe it!"

Malcolm knelt in the garden, savoring the vision of Amy as a goddess of the harvest. He had forgotten he was capable of perceiving such beauty. And this made him realize for the first time that his marriage to Gwendolyn had slowly, day by day, anaesthetized him to the beauty of the world. What beauty had he seen with her? He remembered none. All he could remember was Gwen in the short pants she insisted on wearing around the house, without a top so that he had to keep the blinds drawn even in the day. "The neighbors can see you!" he had complained, but she didn't care. And so day after day he had sat slumped in a faded chair, while Gwendolyn paraded about the dim room in her shorts. Then he had called that love.

But it wasn't love; he saw that now, picking up the last few artichokes Amy had been unable to carry. He sniffed the artichokes, put them against his cheek to feel how cool they were. And his sense of beauty came flooding back to him, as if he were peeking under the drawn shades to behold the tree-lined street Gwen's immodesty had forced him to block from his life – Gwen who had driven him to the edge of a cliff, who had committed adultery with the man downstairs (having to remove only her shorts), who had seemed just months before to control the entire shape and flow of his life.

Sean dropped the artichokes into the boiling water one by one. Amy was standing next to him. Their shoulders were touching. He could smell her skin, her hair.

At the table Maria was wiping off the silverware. She was hunched over, squinting at the spots, and rubbing her nose from time to time with the back of her hand. Some artichokes were also on the table. Now and then Amy shuttled a new batch from table to stove, handing them carefully to Sean who dropped them into the enormous pot with the eager abandon of a man tossing coins into a wishing well.

The sight was certainly a happy one, thought Malcolm as soon as he stepped into the doorway, holding his small charge of artichokes. The pot on the stove was steaming. Amy and Sean were washing dust off plates exhumed from the cupboards. On the far side of the kitchen Maria was stacking silverware into neat piles. It was a scene of rustic simplicity – the vegetables harvested from the garden, the mammoth hissing stove, the two American girls reminding Malcolm of all the country girls he had ever glimpsed from train windows: slight figures beckoning from sideroads, paused upon their bicycles. Everything spoke of simplicity, goodness, and health. Malcolm was so struck by the scene that he couldn't bring himself to intrude upon it. He could only stand in the shadows of the doorway, looking in.

It occurred to him that they were about to partake of a miraculous meal. Less than an hour ago they had stared at the open, empty cupboards with disappointment and he had thought they would end up in a pub, eating liver and onion sandwiches amid the smoke and the noise. Now the kitchen was full of food.

From the doorway, invisibly, he was watching them. And the longer he watched without their noticing, the stranger he began to feel. He felt suddenly as though he had receded from the reality of the kitchen onto another plane of existence, as though now he were not looking at life but peering into it. Wasn't he dead in some respects? Hadn't he come to the point of despising life and throwing it away? At the sink Sean was wringing out a yellow dish towel, Amy was melting the stick of butter over the stove, at the table Maria was holding a silver spoon up to the light. But none of them, not one, recognized the significance of the meal they were about to share.

And so it was with the greatest joy that Malcolm felt his bulk finally ease forward (from out of the nether world back into the dear sluggish atmosphere of earth). His face came into the light. He was smiling with the bliss of reprieve. There was still time left for him to speak.

Sean didn't notice Malcolm enter the kitchen because he was carrying the bowl of artichokes to the table. The artichokes were steaming; the steam was rising in his face, blinding him.

Amy didn't notice Malcolm enter the kitchen because she was thinking about what she would write home in her next letter. She would describe it all: the artichokes! the steam! the bright plates!

Maria didn't notice Malcolm enter the kitchen because she was wishing she and Amy could live together in the country, in a house with a garden where every evening they could pick food for their own table.

Malcolm entered, took his seat at the table, deposited his artichokes on the floor beside his feet. At that moment the faces of the girls were indescribably beautiful. The face of his old friend, Sean, was also beautiful.

Amy wasn't paying attention when Malcolm began to speak. She heard his voice but his words had no meaning for her, were only sounds, in the distance. She was still calculating the total effect of a letter home, imagining her family around the table, her mother reading it with her glasses on, her little sisters poking each other with their forks. Other memories of home crowded in: the backyard grass full of crabapples, the kitchen entrance, in winter, lined with wet boots. Through the parade of these memories Malcolm's voice kept up its slow, steady rhythm, and gradually Amy began to pick out bits of what he was saying. He had gone on a trip. He had climbed a hill. He had stood looking down at the sea.

In the middle of the table the artichokes fumed on their platter. Amy reached out and touched one but it was too hot to eat. Next she glanced at Sean's profile and then at Maria's and saw that they were uncomfortable about something. Only then did the full import of what Malcolm was saying become clear to her. He was talking about suicide. His own.

The idea of this middle-aged, heavy-set man throwing himself off a cliff struck Maria as comic. Malcolm's eyes were moist, she could see that, but the fact that his emotion was genuine only separated her further from him. Maybe it was true that he had tried to kill himself, maybe it was true that now (as he insisted) this meal had brought him back to life, but it was a mistake to think that she, who hardly knew him, could share either his sorrow or his joy. For a moment Maria reproached herself for not being able to feel for Malcolm (in a voice full of emotion he was describing the "darkest days" immediately after his wife had left him), but the moment quickly passed. Maria admitted to herself that she felt nothing. She kicked Amy under the table. Amy began to smile but then covered her mouth with her napkin. Maria rubbed her foot against Amy's calf. Amy moved her leg away, and Maria couldn't find it again. She searched back and forth with her foot and waited for Amy to look at her again so that she could wink, but Amy kept looking down at her plate.

Sean watched as Malcolm began to stuff himself with artichokes. He had them all captive now and so began to speak and eat at the same time. And what a time to pick! Nothing could be so detrimental to the mood of romance (which was the mood Sean was hoping to induce) than the mention of death. Already he could see Amy cringing ever so slightly, hunching her shoulders, pressing (no doubt) her lovely legs together. Death, jumping off cliffs, why did Malcolm have to talk of it now? As if it meant anything to them! Some dramatic moment Malcolm had indulged in to convince himself he could feel love. And how much love had he felt? Hadn't he recovered rather quickly? Five weeks! "I never thought I would again enjoy a simple meal among friends," he was saying, and Sean watched as, unbelievably, a tear slid crookedly down Malcolm's cheek. He was crying, plucking the leaves off a huge artichoke (even in the swell of emotion he had managed to take the biggest one), plucking off the leaves and dipping them in the butter before putting them in his mouth.

"We're too quick to reckon the value of our lives!" Malcolm proclaimed to them, and it seemed that he had never been so close to any group of people in all his life. They were all silent, hanging on his every word, and his emotion was stirring him to eloquence he had never known. How often in life one says unimportant things, he thought, trivial things, just to pass the time. Only rarely does one get a chance to unburden one's heart, to speak of the beauty and meaning of life, its preciousness, and to have people listen! Just moments before he had felt the agony of the dead barred from life, but now he could feel the joy of language, of sharing intimate thoughts, and his body vibrated pleasurably with the sound of his own voice.

At his first opportunity Sean broke Malcolm's gloomy filibuster by taking an artichoke from the platter and saying: "Here's one for you, Amy. It's not too hot now."

"They're marvelous," said Malcolm, dabbing his eyes.

"You know how to eat them, Amy, don't you?" Sean asked. "You just pick off the leaves, dip them in the butter, and then scrape the meat off with your teeth." As he explained this, Sean demonstrated, dipping a leaf in the butter and holding it to her mouth. "Go on, try it," he said. Amy opened her mouth, put her lips around the leaf, and pulled back.

"We have artichokes in America, you know, Sean," said Maria, taking one herself. "We've eaten them before."

"I haven't," said Amy, chewing and smiling at Sean.

"You have too," said Maria. "I've seen you eat them. Lots of times."

"Perhaps that was asparagus," said Sean, and he and Amy laughed together.

The dinner proceeded. In a few moments Sean noticed that Amy was no longer hunching forward in a posture of self-protection. Malcolm was eating silently, his wet cheeks shining like the buttery artichoke he held in his hand. One by one the artichokes were taken from the platter, one by one stripped of their leaves. Sean kept handing Amy bits of food, caressing her with simple specific considerations: "One more? ... some butter? ... water?" Between mouthfuls he levelled his face in her direction, filling the air between them with the warm odor of what he had eaten.

He was thinking of their upcoming tryst. The plan he had arranged with her was this: after dinner he would suggest backgammon; she would immediately agree and together they would go downstairs to the game room; they would play until the others went to sleep and then go up to view the relic alone.

But just then Malcolm said: "Ladies, take a look at these two old men who sit before you. We're dear old friends, Sean and I. At Oxford we were inseparable."

Sean looked up to see Malcolm smiling warmly at him across the table. His eyes were still watering. He looked vulnerable and foolish. But Malcolm went on: "I pray that your friendship, young as it is, survives so long." He was looking at the girls now, from one to the other. "Old friends," he murmured, "they're the best."

*

121

"Would anyone care to retire to the game room for some backgammon?" Sean asked aloud to the table, but especially, Amy knew, to her. She was just about to say yes when out of the corner of her eye she caught Maria looking at her. Amy knew that Maria was waiting for her reply. If she said yes, Maria would also say yes. Suddenly she knew the plan wouldn't work, Maria would never go up to sleep by herself. And so Amy spread her hands on the table, looked at her nails, and asked, "Maria, what do you feel like?"

"Oh, I don't know," Maria said.

"We can't all play," said Sean. "Only two of us, I'm afraid."

"Backgammon sounds lovely," said Malcolm. Amy shifted in her seat. She had hesitated too long. She had ruined everything.

"We have to be up early anyway," said Maria.

"Well, we'll excuse you two travellers then," said Malcolm. "With profound regret."

"Perhaps it is getting a little late," said Sean.

"Nonsense!" said Malcolm. "The night's just beginning!" And with that he slid his chair from the table and stood resolutely up.

There was nothing Sean could do. He had no idea why Amy had deviated from their plan. He suspected he had been too forward during dinner, had given away his true motives, and scared her off. Whatever the reason now there was nothing for him to do but stand up, disown the signals from his heart (registering despair) by smiling, and head for the basement door. As he descended the stairs with Malcolm behind him he tried unsuccessfully to hear what the girls were saying in the kitchen.

The gameroom was a long narrow wainscotted room, with a billiard table in the middle and at one end a red leather sofa facing a television set. Sean went immediately to the television and turned it on. "What about backgammon?" Malcolm asked.

"I've lost the mood," said Sean. Malcolm took a seat on the sofa. "Sit down, Sean," he urged. "I'm fine," said Sean. "I've been sitting all through dinner."

"I hope you didn't mind my little oration," said Malcolm. "I'm afraid I monopolized the conversation."

Sean kept his eyes on the television. "I hardly noticed," he said.

"Sean likes you," Maria told Amy once they were alone.

"He does not."

"He does. I can tell."

"He's just being nice."

They were drying the last few dishes, standing elbow to elbow at the sink. "What did he say to you in the garden?"

"When?"

"In the garden. When he took you into the back."

"He told me I was the most beautiful girl he had ever seen and then he proposed marriage." Maria was rinsing a plate. She held it under the water and said nothing. "I'm kidding," said Amy. "He just talked about the soil, how hard it is to grow things here." Maria started to scrub the plate, even though it was perfectly clean. "I'm just kidding," Amy said again.

Amy wanted to take as long as possible washing the dishes. If Sean came back she could give him a sign to meet her later. But the plates were not very dirty, and there were only four of them, along with some glasses. Soon everything was done. "I'm exhausted," Maria said. "Aren't you exhausted?"

"No."

"You look exhausted."

"I'm not."

"What should we do now?"

Amy could think of no reason for staying in the kitchen. She could go downstairs but Malcolm would be there. He would be everywhere, all night. He would never go to sleep again he was so happy to be alive. So at last she said, "I'm going to sleep," and Maria announced that she would too.

"Let's not watch television, Sean," said Malcolm. "We haven't had a chance to talk all night. We haven't talked for twenty years!"

"I haven't watched television for two weeks," said Sean.

Malcolm laughed, agreeably. "Sean," he said, "it's no use. You can't hide from me. Especially tonight." He waited for a response but received none. He felt monumentally calm. He could say whatever he had to say, without embarrassment, and he peered at his friend, wondering why Sean, on the contrary, was so withdrawn. But in the next moment it came to him. Sean's imperviousness was much too perfect. It was a sham. Inside his shell Sean was lonely too, and grieved for his failed marriage as Malcolm himself did. That was the reason he surrounded himself with jokes and the young women.

Malcolm was surprised he hadn't realized this before. His sight now in every way was sharper. He looked at his friend and felt great sympathy for him. And then he said: "Tell me about Meg, Sean. There's no reason to be ashamed. I'm in the same boat, you know."

This time Sean did turn and meet his gaze. His manner was still stiff, it was difficult for him, but at last he began: "Not the same boat, Malcolm. Not at all. I left Meg. Meg didn't leave me."

Malcolm looked away, down at the floor.

"And she took it badly, I'm afraid," Sean continued. "She stepped in front of a train."

"She tried to kill herself?" Malcolm asked. Sean nodded. "But she's gotten over it now," he said. "She's quite happy now. She's overwhelmed with happiness."

This revenge pleased Sean. Malcolm had spoiled his evening but now Sean had control over him, could make him believe whatever he liked. Malcolm laid his head back against the sofa and Sean said, "Quite a coincidence your showing up here tonight. Almost as if something sent you here to receive that very information."

"I had no idea," Malcolm said softly. Sean continued to stare at his friend, filled with the power of being able to create a world for Malcolm to live in, where nothing happened by chance and where even suicides harmonized.

He left Malcolm sitting on the couch and made his way toward the stairs.

When Maria went into the bathroom to brush her teeth, Amy tiptoed to the bedroom doorway. She heard nothing. The house was quiet. All she could hear was Maria swirling water in her mouth and spitting it into the sink. She stepped into the hall. Again she heard nothing. Then Maria came out of the bathroom. She had her glasses off and was squinting at the bed.

Sean reached the kitchen to find it empty. He cursed himself for ever suggesting backgammon, cursed Malcolm for getting in the way, cursed Amy for betraying their plan. It was not to be, no matter what he did. The house, the artichokes, the relic, none of these had been enough. He thought of his wife, dancing in some tropic zone, and then he saw himself as he was, alone, in a cold house, his desires thwarted.

He walked back to the basement door and listened. The television was still on. Malcolm was still sitting before it, thunderstruck. Sean turned away, determined to leave Malcolm there all night, but as soon as he did so he stopped where he was. For in front of him, wearing nothing but a man's long T-shirt, was Amy.

Upstairs, ears pricked, Maria was waiting for Amy to come back to bed. Amy had just gotten into bed when suddenly she crawled out again, saying she was going downstairs for a glass of water. "Drink from the tap in the bathroom," Maria suggested, but Amy said, "I want a glass."

After all this time, even after the kiss on the train, Amy was still shy. She was so nervous she had gotten into bed and jumped right out again. Maria knew exactly what was going through her friend's mind. She crossed her arms behind her head. She stared up at the decorated plaster of the ceiling and felt the weight of her body sinking into the mattress, the pillows. A great calm came over her, a solidity, a sense that she was one of the lucky ones of the earth, those who knew what it meant to be truly intimate with another.

Malcolm stood up and turned off the television. He wondered what had become of Sean. He moved across the room to the billiard table. He took out a ball, rolled it across the felt, and watched it career off the sides of the table. He caught it again and repeated the action. The ball made soft thumps against the cushions.

To get away before Malcolm came up, Sean led Amy down the hall to his study. Once inside he closed the door, whispered that she should be absolutely silent, and with an air of solemnity began searching for the relic in his suitcase he had left next to his desk. As he bent down he was aware that Amy's naked thighs were only inches from his face. He wanted to reach out and take hold of her legs, to pull her toward him and fit his face into the bowl of her hips. But he didn't do that. He only took out a gray woolen sock from which he extracted a thin, yellow bone less than three inches long.

"St Augustine's index finger," he said, showing it to her.

"How long ago did he live again?"

"Fifteen hundred years."

Amy put out her hand and touched the sliver of bone, as Sean gazed at her lips, cheeks, eyes, hair.

Amy knew he was about to kiss her. She always knew when men were about to kiss her. Sometimes she made it difficult for them, moved away or asked them questions. Other times she merely pretended not to notice, as she did now, examining the saint's finger.

Then Sean said, "I was afraid our little meeting wasn't going to happen."

"It was hard getting away from the heretics," said Amy.

Malcolm came into the kitchen, looking for Sean. All he found were the plates the girls had thoughtfully washed stacked next to the sink. He strolled about the kitchen, warmed his hands by the smoldering fire, and, seeing the artichokes he had left on the floor were still there, set them on the table. Only after doing all these things did he go to the kitchen window and look out to the backyard.

When Maria saw them they were bent over something, their heads almost touching. Immediately she understood what had happened. Amy had come down to get a glass of water and Sean had waylaid her. She had arrived just in the nick of time to save her friend from an awkward situation.

"What's that?" she said, and boldly, triumphantly, walked into the room.

*

Maria's voice was the voice of the fate he could not escape. At the very moment of victory, as his budding desires were just about to bloom (he and Amy were cheek to cheek) Sean heard Maria's voice and his hopes shrank before it. He said nothing. All he did was stand mute as Maria approached him and took the relic into her cold hand.

"It's St Augustine's finger," Amy offered in explanation.

Maria examined the bone a moment, then handed it back to Sean and said, simply, "No way." The girls turned (together) and moved toward the door. "Good night," they said, and motionless, Sean heard their voices blend into an excruciating unison.

"You didn't believe him, did you?" Maria asked once they were alone in their room. Amy made no reply, only got into bed and closed her eyes. Maria switched off the light and fumbled through the darkness. "I can't believe you could fall for that. The finger of St Augustine!" She laughed. "The things they'll do." She crawled into bed and pulled the covers over her, then lay staring into the dark, thinking about the trickery of men.

"Amy," she whispered, but her friend didn't reply. Maria moved closer. "Amy," she said, a little more loudly. She moved further across the sheets. She touched her hip to Amy's hip. And called again: "Amy."

But her friend didn't return her greeting, or amplify the pressure of hip on hip. "Go to sleep!" she said, and turned away.

Sean was left holding the counterfeit finger of an illustrious saint. In the hallway he thought he heard the girls giggle, and then came the sound of their feet on the stairs, the creak and knock of the bedroom door closing and then – silence.

The bone was coated with a film of white powder which

flaked onto his open palm. He wanted to fling the bone across the room, or drop it and crush it beneath his heel, but something deterred him. Because as he stared at the bone he began to feel as though someone were watching him. He looked around the room but no one was there. He looked back at the bone and saw now that the tip of the finger was pointing at him. Suddenly he began to feel, though it was impossible, he began to feel that the finger was still alive. It was infused with intelligence. It was pointing at him, accusing him, condemning him.

Fortunately the feeling lasted only an instant. In the next moment the finger stopped pointing. It became just a bone again.

The moon had risen and in its light Malcolm could make out the garden, a pale blue circle at the end of the grass. He looked back at the remaining artichokes lying on the table. Then he walked to the back door, opened it, and went out.

The garden was in even worse condition than before. The dead flowers, which before had at least been in a row, were now trampled, dug up, scattered. Footprints were everywhere. Signs of violence had replaced the serenity of neglect.

He saw the imprints of his own shoes, large and deep. Then he noticed the small treads of Amy's tennis shoes. He stepped into the garden and placed his feet over her treads, enjoying how thoroughly his shoes covered them. By this time he had stopped wondering what had become of Sean. He was unaware of the location of the others inside the house, of Maria on one side of the bed, of Amy on the other, of Sean in his study staring at the twig of bone. Malcolm forgot his friends a moment, while he stood in the garden that Meg, his twin, had planted. He was thinking that what he needed was a house and garden of his own. He was imagining himself pruning rosebushes and picking beans. It seemed to him that happiness, with such a simple change, would come at last.

COWBOYS ARE MY WEAKNESS

Pam Houston

Pam Houston is the author of the collection of stories, *Cowboys are My Weakness*. She is a part-time river guide and hunting guide, but not a hunter herself. She is currently working on a novel.

COWBOYS ARE
MY WEAKNESS

I have a picture in my mind of a tiny ranch on the edge of a stand of pine trees with some horses in the yard. There's a woman standing in the doorway in cutoffs and a blue chambray work shirt and she's just kissed her tall, bearded, and soft-spoken husband goodbye. There's laundry hanging outside and the morning sun is filtering through the tree branches like spiderwebs. It's the morning after a full moon, and behind the house the deer have eaten everything that was left in the garden.

If I were a painter, I'd paint that picture just to see if the girl in the doorway would turn out to be me. I've been out west ten years now, long enough to call it my home, long enough to know I'll be here forever, but I still don't know where that ranch is. And even though I've had plenty of men here, some of them tall and nearly all of them bearded, I still haven't met the man who has just walked out of the painting, who has just started his pickup truck, whose tire marks I can still see in the sandy soil of the drive.

The west isn't a place that gives itself up easily. Newcomers have to sink into it slowly, to descend through its layers, and I'm still descending. Like most easterners, I started out in the transitional zones, the big cities and the ski towns that outsiders have set up for their own comfort, the places so often referred to as "the best of both worlds." But I was bound to work my way back, through the land, into the small towns and beyond them. That's half the reason I wound up on a ranch near Grass Range, Montana; the other half is Homer.

I've always had this thing about cowboys, maybe because I was born in New Jersey. But a real cowboy is hard to find these days, even in the west. I thought I'd found one on several occasions, I even at one time thought Homer was a cowboy, and though I loved him like crazy for a while and in some ways always will, somewhere along the line I had to face the fact that even though Homer looked like a cowboy, he was just a capitalist with a Texas accent who owned a horse.

Homer's a wildlife specialist in charge of a whitetail deer management project on the ranch. He goes there every year to observe the deer from the start of the mating season in late October until its peak in mid-November. It's the time when the deer are most visible, when the bucks get so lusty they lose their normal caution, when the does run around in the middle of the day with their white tails in the air. When Homer talked me into coming with him, he said I'd love the ranch, and I did. It was sixty miles from the nearest paved road. All of the buildings were whitewashed and plain. One of them had been ordered from a 1916 Sears catalogue. The ranch hands still rode horses, and when the late-afternoon light swept the grainfields across from headquarters, I would watch them move the cattle in rows that looked like waves. There was a peace about the ranch that was uncanny and might have been complete if not for the eight or nine hungry barn cats that crawled up your legs if you even smelled like food, and the exotic chickens of almost every color that fought all day in their pens.

Homer has gone to the ranch every year for the last six, and he has a long history of stirring up trouble there. The ranch hands watch him sit on the hillside and hate him for the money he makes. He's slept with more than one or two of their wives and girlfriends. There was even some talk that he was the reason the ranch owner got divorced.

When he asked me to come with him I knew it would be me or somebody else and I'd heard good things about Montana so I went. There was a time when I was sure Homer was the man who belonged in my painting and I would have sold my soul to be his wife, or even his only girlfriend. I'd come close, in the spring, to losing my mind because of it, but I had finally learned that Homer would always be separate, even from himself, and by the time we got to Montana I was almost immune to him.

Homer and I live in Fort Collins, Colorado, most of the year, in houses that are exactly one mile apart. He's out of town as often as not, keeping track of fifteen whitetail deer herds all across the West. I go with him when he lets me, which is lately more and more. The herds Homer studies are isolated by geography, given plenty of food in bad winters, and protected from hunters and wolves. Homer is working on reproduction and genetics, trying to create, in the wild, super-bucks bigger and tougher than elk. The Montana herd has been his most successful, so he spends the long mating season there. Under his care the bucks have shown incredible increases in antler mass, in body weight, and in fertility.

The other scientists at the university that sponsors Homer respect him, not only for his success with the deer, but for his commitment to observation, for his relentless dedication to his hours in the field. They also think he is eccentric and a bit overzealous.

At first I thought he just liked to be outdoors, but when we got to the ranch his obsession with the deer made him even more like a stranger. He was gone every day from way before sunrise till long after dark. He would dress all in camouflage, even his gloves and socks, and sit on the hillsides above where the deer fed and watch, making notes a few times an hour, changing position every hour or two. If I went with him I wasn't allowed to move except when he did, and I was never allowed to talk. I'd try to save things up for later that I thought of during the day, but by the time we got back to our cabin they seemed unimportant and Homer liked to eat his dinner in front of the TV. By the time we got the dishes done it was way past Homer's bedtime. We were making love less and less, and when we did, it was always from behind.

The ranch owner's name was David, and he wasn't what you'd think a Montana ranch owner would be. He was a poet, and a vegetarian. He listened to Andreas Vollenweider and drank hot beverages with names like Suma and Morning Rain. He wouldn't let the ranch hands use pesticides or chemicals, he wouldn't hire them if they smoked cigarettes. He undergrazed the ranch by about fifty percent, so the organic grain was belly-high to a horse almost everywhere.

David had an idea about recreating on his forty thousand acres the Great Plains that only the Indians and the first settlers had seen. He wasn't making a lot of money ranching, but he was producing the fattest, healthiest, most organic Black Angus cattle in North America. He was sensitive, thoughtful, and kind. He was the kind of man I always knew I should fall in love with, but never did.

Homer and David ate exactly one dinner a week together, which I always volunteered to cook. Homer was always polite and full of incidental conversation and much too quick to laugh. David was quiet and sullen and so restrained that he was hard to recognize.

The irreconcilable differences between Homer and me had been revealing themselves one at a time since late summer. In early November I asked him what he wanted to do on Thanksgiving, and he said he'd like most of all to stay on the ranch and watch the does in heat.

Homer was only contracted to work on the ranch until the Sunday before Thanksgiving. When he asked me to come with him he told me we would leave the ranch in plenty of time to have the holidays at home.

I was the only child in a family that never did a lot of celebrating because my parents couldn't plan ahead. They were sun worshipers, and we spent every Thanksgiving in a plane on the way to Puerto Rico, every Christmas in a car on Highway 95, heading for Florida. What I remember most from those days is Casey Kasem's Christmas shows, the long-distance dedications. "I'll be home for Christmas" from Bobby D. in Spokane to Linda S. in Decatur. We never had hotel reservations and the places we wound up in had no phones and plastic mattress covers and triple locks on the doors. Once we spent Christmas night parked under a fluorescent streetlight, sleeping in the car.

I've spent most of the holidays in my adult life making up for those road trips. I spend lots of money on hand-painted ornaments. I always cook a roast ten pounds bigger than anything we could possibly eat.

Homer thinks my enthusiasm about holidays is childish and self-serving. To prove it to me, last Christmas morning he set the alarm for six-thirty and went back to his house to stain a door. This year I wanted Thanksgiving in my own house. I wanted to cook a turkey we'd be eating for weeks. .

I said, "Homer, you've been watching the deer for five weeks now. What else do you think they're gonna do?"

"You don't know anything about it," he said. "Thanksgiving is the premium time. Thanksgiving," he shook one finger in the air, "is the height of the rut."

David and I drank tea together, and every day took walks up into the canyon behind ranch headquarters. He talked about his ex-wife, Carmen, about the red flowers that covered the canyon walls in June, about imaging away nuclear weapons. He told me about the woman Homer was sleeping with on the ranch the year before, when I was back in Colorado counting days till he got home. She was the woman who took care of the chickens, and David said that when Homer left the ranch she wrote a hundred love songs and made David listen while she sang them all.

"She sent them on a tape to Homer," David said, "and when he didn't call or write, she went a little nuts. I finally told her to leave the ranch. I'm not a doctor, and we're a long way from anywhere out here."

From the top of the canyon we could see Homer's form blending with the trees on the ridge above the garden, where the deer ate organic potatoes by the hundreds of pounds.

"I understand if he wasn't interested anymore," David said. "But I can't believe even he could ignore a gesture that huge."

We watched Homer crawl along the ridge from tree to tree. I could barely distinguish his movements from what the wind did to the tall grass. None of the deer below him even turned their heads.

"What is it about him?" David said, and I know he was looking for an explanation about Carmen, but I'd never even met her and I didn't want to talk about myself.

"Homer's always wearing camouflage," I said. "Even when he's not."

The wind went suddenly still and we could hear, from headquarters, the sounds of cats fighting, a hen's frantic scream, and then, again, the cats.

David put his arm around me. "We're such good people," he said. "Why aren't we happy?"

One day when I got back from my walk with David, Homer was in the cabin in the middle of the day. He had on normal clothes and I could tell he'd shaved and showered. He took me into the bedroom and climbed on top of me frontwards, the way he did when we first met and I didn't even know what he did for a living.

Afterwards he said, "We didn't need a condom, did we?" I counted the days forward and backward and forward again. Homer always kept track of birth control and groceries and gas mileage and all the other things I couldn't keep my mind on. Still, it appeared to be exactly ten days before my next period.

"Yes," I said. "I think we did."

Homer has never done an uncalculated thing in his life, and for a moment I let myself entertain the possibility that his mistake meant that somewhere inside he wanted to have a baby with me, that he really wanted a family and love and security and the things I thought everybody wanted before I met Homer. On the other hand, I knew that one of the ways I had gotten in trouble with Homer, and with other men before him, was by inventing thoughts for them that they'd never had.

"Well," he said. "In that case we better get back to Colorado before they change the abortion laws."

Sometimes the most significant moments of your life reveal themselves to you even as they are happening, and I knew in that moment that I would never love Homer the same way again. It wasn't so much that not six months before, when I had asked Homer what we'd do if I got pregnant, he said we'd get married and have a family. It wasn't even that I was sure I wanted a baby. It wasn't even that I thought there was going to be a baby to want.

It all went back to the girl in the log cabin, and how the soft-spoken man would react if she thought she was going to have a baby. It would be winter now, and snowing outside the windows warm with yellow light. He might dance with the sheepdog on the living-room floor, he might sing the theme song from *Father Knows Best*, he might go out and do a swan dive into the snow.

I've been to a lot of school and read a lot of thick books, but at my very core there's a made-for-TV-movie mentality I don't think I'll ever shake. And although there's a lot of doubt in my mind about whether or not an ending as simple and happy as I want is possible anymore in the world, it was clear to me that afternoon that it wasn't possible with Homer.

Five o'clock the next morning was the first time I saw the real cowboy. He was sitting in the cookhouse eating cereal and I couldn't make myself sleep next to Homer so I'd been up all night wandering around.

He was tall and thin and bearded. His hat was white and ratty and you could tell by looking at his stampede strap that it had been made around a campfire after lots of Jack Daniels. I'd had my fingers in my hair for twelve hours and my face was breaking out from too much stress and too little sleep and I felt like such a greaseball that I didn't say hello. I poured myself some orange juice, drank it, rinsed the glass, and put it in the dish drainer. I took one more look at the cowboy, and walked back out the door, and went to find Homer in the field.

Homer's truck was parked by a culvert on the South Fork road, which meant he was walking the brush line below the cliffs that used to be the Blackfeet buffalo jumps. It was a boneyard down there, the place where hundreds of buffalo, chased by the Indians, had jumped five hundred feet to their death, and the soil was extremely fertile. The grass was thicker and sweeter there than anywhere on the ranch, and Homer said the deer sucked calcium out of the buffalo bones. I saw Homer crouched at the edge of a meadow I couldn't get to without being seen, so I went back and fell asleep in the bed of his truck.

It was hunting season, and later that morning Homer and I found a deer by the side of the road that had been poached but not taken. The poacher must have seen headlights or heard a truck engine and gotten scared.

I lifted the back end of the animal into the truck while Homer picked up the antlers. It was a young buck, two and a half at the oldest, but it would have been a monster in a few years, and I knew Homer was taking the loss pretty hard.

We took it down to the performance center, where they weigh the organic calves. Homer attached a meat hook to its antlers and hauled it into the air above the pickup.

"Try and keep it from swinging," he said. And I did my best, considering I wasn't quite tall enough to get a good hold, and its blood was bubbling out of the bullet hole and dripping down on me.

That's when the tall cowboy, the one from that morning, walked out of the holding pen behind me, took a long slow look at me trying to steady the back end of the dead deer, and settled himself against the fence across the driveway. I stepped back from the deer and pushed the hair out of my eyes. He raised one finger to call me over. I walked slow and didn't look back at Homer.

"Nice buck," he said. "Did you shoot it?"

"It's a baby," I said. "I don't shoot animals. A poacher got it last night."

"Who was the poacher?" he said, and tipped his hat just past my shoulder toward Homer.

"You're wrong," I said. "You can say a lot of things about him, but he wouldn't poach a deer."

"My name's Montrose T. Coty," he said. "Everyone calls me Monte."

I shook his hand. "Everyone calls you Homer's girlfriend," he said, "but I bet that's not your name."

"You're right," I said, "it's not."

I turned to look at Homer. He was taking measurements off the hanging deer: antler length, body length, width at its girth.

"Tonight's the Stockgrowers' Ball in Grass Range," Monte said. "I thought you might want to go with me."

Homer was looking into the deer's hardened eyeballs. He had its mouth open, and was pulling on its tongue.

"I have to cook dinner for Homer and David," I said. "I'm sorry. It sounds like fun."

In the car on the way back to the cabin, Homer said, "What was that all about?"

I said, "Nothing," and then I said, "Monte asked me to the Stockgrowers' Ball."

"The Stockgrowers' Ball?" he said. "Sounds like a great time. What do stockgrowers do at a ball?" he said. "Do they dance?"

I almost laughed with him until I remembered how much I loved to dance. I'd been with Homer chasing whitetail so long that I'd forgotten that dancing, like holidays, was something I loved. And I started to wonder just then what else being with Homer had made me forget. Hadn't I, at one time, spent whole days listening to music? Wasn't there a time when I wanted, more than anything, to buy a sailboat? And didn't I love to be able to go outdoors and walk anywhere I wanted, and to make, if I wanted, all kinds of noise?

I wanted to blame Homer, but I realized then, it was more my fault than his. Because even though I'd never let the woman in the chambray work shirt out of my mind I'd let her, in the last few years, become someone different, and she wasn't living, anymore, in my painting. The painting she was living in, I saw, belonged to somebody else.

"So what did you tell him?" Homer said.

"I told him I'd see if you'd cook dinner," I said.

I tried to talk to Homer before I left. First I told him that it wasn't a real date, that I didn't even know Monte, and really I was only going because I didn't know if I'd ever have another chance to go to a Stockgrowers' Ball. When he didn't answer at all I worked up to saying that maybe it was a good idea for me to start seeing other people. That maybe we'd had two different ideas all along and we needed to find two other people who would better meet our needs. I told him that if he had any opinions I wished he'd express them to me, and he thought for a few minutes and then he said,

"Well, I guess we have Jimmy Carter to thank for all the trouble in Panama."

I spent the rest of the day getting ready for the Stockgrowers' Ball. All I'd brought with me was some of Homer's camouflage and blue jeans, so I wound up borrowing a skirt that David's ex-wife had left behind, some of the chicken woman's dress shoes that looked ridiculous and made my feet huge, and a vest that David's grandfather had been shot at in by the Plains Indians.

Monte had to go into town early to pick up ranch supplies, so I rode in with his friends Buck and Dawn, who spent the whole drive telling me what a great guy Monte was, how he quit the rodeo circuit to make a decent living for himself and his wife, how she'd left without saying goodbye not six months before.

They told me that he'd made two thousand dollars in one afternoon doing a Wrangler commercial. That he'd been in a laundromat on his day off and the director had seen him through the window, had gone in and said, "Hey, cowboy, you got an hour? You want to make two thousand bucks?"

"Ole Monte," Buck said. "He's the real thing."

After an hour and a half of washboard road we pulled into the dance hall just on our edge of town. I had debated about wearing the cowboy hat I'd bought especially for my trip to Montana, and was thankful I'd decided against it. It was clear, once inside, that only the men wore hats, and only dress hats at that. The women wore high heels and stockings and in almost every case hair curled away from their faces in great airy rolls.

We found Monte at a table in the corner, and the first thing he did was give me a corsage, a pink one, mostly roses that couldn't have clashed more with my rust-colored blouse. Dawn pinned it on me, and I blushed, I suppose, over my first corsage in ten years, and a little old woman in spike heels leaned over and said, "Somebody loves you" just loud enough for Monte and Buck and Dawn to hear.

During dinner they showed a movie about a cattle drive. After dinner a young enthusiastic couple danced and sang for over an hour about cattle and ranch life and the Big Sky, a phrase which since I'd been in Montana had seemed perpetually on the tip of everybody's tongue.

After dinner the dancing started, and Monte asked me if I knew how to do the Montana two-step. He was more than a foot taller than me, and his hat added another several inches to that. When we stood on the dance floor my eyes came right to the place where his silk scarf disappeared into the shirt buttons on his chest. His big hands were strangely light on me and my feet went the right direction even though my mind couldn't remember the two-step's simple form.

"That's it," he said into the part in my hair. "Don't think. Just let yourself move with me."

And we were moving together, in turns that got tighter and tighter each time we circled the dance floor. The songs got faster and so did our motion until there wasn't time for anything but the picking up and putting down of feet, for the swirling colors of Carmen's ugly skirt, for breath and sweat and rhythm.

I was farther west than I'd ever imagined, and in the strange, nearly flawless synchronization on the dance floor I knew I could be a Montana ranch woman, and I knew I could make Monte my man. It had taken me ten years, and an incredible sequence of accidents, but that night I thought I'd finally gotten where I'd set out to go.

The band played till two and we danced till three to the jukebox. Then there was nothing left to do but get in the car and begin the two-hour drive home.

First we talked about our horses. It was the logical choice, the only thing we really had in common, but it only lasted twenty minutes.

I tried to get his opinion on music and sailing, but just like a cowboy, he was too polite for me to tell anything for sure.

Then we talked about the hole in my vest that the Indians shot, which I was counting on, and half the reason I wore it.

The rest of the time we just looked at the stars.

I had spent a good portion of the night worrying about what I was going to say when Monte asked me to go to bed with him. When he pulled up between our two cabins he looked at me sideways and said,

"I'd love to give you a great big kiss, but I've got a mouthful of chew."

I could hear Homer snoring before I got past the kitchen.

Partly because I didn't like the way Monte and Homer eyed each other, but mostly because I couldn't bear to spend Thanksgiving watching does in heat, I loaded my gear in my truck and got ready to go back to Colorado.

On the morning I left, Homer told me that he had decided that I was the woman he wanted to spend the rest of his life with after all, and that he planned to go to town and buy a ring just as soon as the rut ended.

He was sweet on my last morning on the ranch, generous and attentive in a way I'd never seen. He packed me a sack lunch of chicken salad he mixed himself, and he went out to my car and dusted off the inch of snow that had fallen in our first brush with winter, overnight. He told me to call when I got to Fort Collins, he even said to call collect, but I suppose one of life's big tricks is to give us precisely the thing we want, two weeks after we've stopped wanting it, and I couldn't take Homer seriously, even when I tried.

When I went to say goodbye to David he hugged me hard, said I was welcome back on the ranch anytime. He said he enjoyed my company and appreciated my insight. Then he said he liked my perfume and I wondered where my taste in men had come from, I wondered whoever taught me to be so stupid about men.

I knew Monte was out riding the range, so I left a note on his car thanking him again for the dancing and saying I'd be back one day and we could dance again. I put my hat on, that Monte had never got to see, and rolled out of headquarters. It was the middle of the day, but I saw seven bucks in the first five miles, a couple of them giants, and when I slowed down they just stood and stared at the truck. It was the height of the rut and Homer said that's how they'd be, love-crazed and fearless as bears.

About a mile before the edge of ranch property, I saw something that looked like a lone antelope running across the skyline, but antelope are almost never alone, so I stopped the car to watch. As the figure came closer I saw it was a horse, a big chestnut, and it was carrying a rider at a full gallop, and it was coming right for the car.

I knew it could have been any one of fifty cowboys employed on the ranch, and yet I've learned to expect more from life than that, and so in my heart I knew it was Monte. I got out of the car and waited, pleased that he'd see my hat most of all, wondering what he'd say when I said I was leaving.

He didn't get off his horse, which was sweating and shaking so hard I thought it might die while we talked.

"You on your way?" he said.

smiled and nodded. His chaps were sweat-soaked, his leather gloves worn white.

"Will you write me a letter?" he said.

"Sure," I said.

"Think you'll be back this way?" he asked.

"If I come back," I said, "will you take me dancing?"

"Damn right," he said, and a smile that seemed like the smile I'd been waiting for my whole life spread wide across his face.

"Then it'll be sooner than later," I said.

He winked and touched the horse's flank with his spurs and it hopped a little on the takeoff and then there was just dirt flying while the high grass swallowed the horse's legs. I leaned against the door of my pickup truck watching my new cowboy riding off toward where the sun was already low in the sky and the grass shimmering like nothing I'd ever seen in the mountains. And for a minute I thought we were living inside my painting, but he was riding away too fast to tell. And I wondered then why I had always imagined my cowboy's truck as it was leaving. I wondered why I hadn't turned the truck around and painted my cowboy coming home.

There's a story – that isn't true – that I tell about myself when I first meet someone, about riding a mechanical bull in a bar. In the story, I stay on through the first eight levels of difficulty, getting thrown on level nine only after dislocating my thumb and winning my boyfriend, who was betting on me a big pile of money. It was something I said in a bar one night, and I liked the way it sounded so much I kept telling it. I've been telling it for so many years now, and in such scrupulous detail, that it has become a memory and it's hard for me to remember that it isn't true. I can smell the smoke and beer-soaked carpets, I can hear the cheers of all the men. I can see the bar lights blur and spin, and I can feel the cold iron buck between my thighs, the painted saddle slam against my tail-bone, the surprise and pain when my thumb extends too far and I let go. It's a good story, a story that holds my listeners' attention, and although I consider myself almost pathologically honest, I have somehow allowed myself this one small lie.

And watching Monte ride off through the long grains, I thought about the way we invent ourselves through our stories, and in a similar way, how the stories we tell put walls around our lives. And I think that may be true about cowboys. That there really isn't much truth in my saying cowboys are my weakness; maybe, after all this time, it's just something I've learned how to say.

I felt the hoofbeats in the ground long after Monte's white shirt and ratty hat melded with the sun. When I couldn't even pretend to feel them anymore, I got in the car and headed for the hard road.

I listened to country music the whole way to Cody, Wyoming. The men in the songs were all either brutal or inexpressive and always sorry later. The women were victims, every one. I started to think about coming back to the ranch to visit Monte, about another night dancing, about another night wanting the impossible love of a country song, and I thought:

This is not my happy ending.

This is not my story.

I WAS AN INFINITELY HOT AND DENSE DOT

Mark Leyner

Mark Leyner is the author of *Et Tu, Babe* and *My Cousin, My Gastroenterologist*. He lives in Hoboken, New Jersey.

I WAS AN INFINITELY HOT AND DENSE DOT

I was driving to Las Vegas to tell my sister that I'd had Mother's respirator unplugged. Four bald men in the convertible in front of me were picking the scabs off their sunburnt heads and flicking them onto the road. I had to swerve to avoid riding over one of the oozy crusts of blood and going into an uncontrollable skid. I maneuvered the best I could in my boxy Korean import but my mind was elsewhere. I hadn't eaten for days. I was famished. Suddenly as I reached the crest of a hill, emerging from the fog, there was a bright neon sign flashing on and off that read: FOIE GRAS AND HARICOTS VERTS NEXT EXIT. I checked the guidebook and it said: *Excellent food, malevolent ambience.* I'd been habitually abusing an illegal growth hormone extracted from the pituitary glands of human corpses and I felt as if I were drowning in excremental filthiness but the prospect of having something good to eat cheered me up. I asked the waitress about the soup du jour and she said that it was primordial soup – which is ammonia and methane mixed with ocean water in the presence of lightning. Oh I'll take a tureen of that embryonic broth, I say, constraint giving way to exuberance – but as soon as she vanishes my spirit immediately sags because the ambience is so malevolent. The bouncers are hassling some youngsters who want drinks – instead of simply carding the kids, they give them radiocarbon tests, using traces of carbon 14 to determine how old they are – and also there's a young wise guy from Texas A&M at a table near mine who asks for freshly ground Rolaids on his fettuccine and two waiters viciously work him over with heavy bludgeon-sized pepper mills, so I get right back into my car and narcissistically comb my thick jet-black hair in the rearview mirror and I check the guidebook. There's an inn nearby – it's called Little Bo Peep's – its habitués are shepherds. And after a long day of herding, shearing, panpipe playing, muse invoking, and conversing in eclogues, it's Miller time, and Bo Peep's is packed with rustic swains who've left their flocks and sunlit, idealized arcadia behind for the more pungent charms of hard-core social intercourse. Everyone's favorite waitress is Kikugoro. She wears a pale-blue silk kimono and a brocade obi of gold and silver chrysanthemums with a small fan tucked into its folds, her face is painted and powdered to a porcelain white. A cowboy from south of the border orders a "Biggu Makku." But Kikugoro says, "This is not Makudonarudo." She takes a long cylinder of gallium arsenide crystal and slices him a thin wafer which she serves with soy sauce, wasabi, pickled ginger, and daikon, "Conducts electrons ten times faster than silicon . . . taste good, gaucho-*san*, you eat," she says, bowing.

My sister is the beautiful day. Oh beautiful day, my sister, wipe my nose, swaddle me in fresh-smelling garments. I nurse at the adamantine nipple of the beautiful day, I quaff the milk of the beautiful day, and for the first time since 1956, I cheese on the shoulder of the beautiful day. Oh beautiful day, wash me in your lake of cloudless azure. I have overdosed on television, I am unresponsive and cyanotic, revive me in your shower of gelid light and walk me through your piazza which is made of elegant slabs of time. Oh beautiful day, kiss me. Your mouth is like Columbus Day. You are the menthol of autumn. My lungs cannot quench their thirst for you.

Resuscitate me – I will never exhale your tonic gasses. Inflate me so that I may rise into the sky and mourn the monotonous topography of my life. Oh beautiful day, my sister, wipe my nose and adorn me in your finery. Let us lunch alfresco. Your club sandwiches are made of mulch and wind perfumed with newsprint. Your frilly toothpicks are the deciduous trees of school days.

I was an infinitely hot and dense dot. So begins the autobiography of a feral child who was raised by huge and lurid puppets. An autobiography written wearing wrist weights. It ends with these words: A car drives through a puddle of sperm, sweat, and contraceptive jelly, splattering the great chopsocky vigilante from Hong Kong. Inside, two acephalic sardines in mustard sauce are asleep in the rank darkness of their tin container. Suddenly, the swinging doors burst open and a mesomorphic cyborg walks in and whips out a 35-lb phallus made of corrosion-resistant nickel-base alloy and he begins to stroke it sullenly, his eyes half shut. It's got a metal-oxide membrane for absolute submicron filtration of petrochemical fluids. It can ejaculate herbicides, sulfuric acid, tar glue, you name it. At the end of the bar, a woman whose album-length poem about temporomandibular joint dysfunction (TMJ) had won a Grammy for best spoken word recording is gently slowly ritually rubbing copper hexafluoroacetylacetone into her clitoris as she watches the hunk with the non-Euclidian features shoot a glob of dehydrogenated ethylbenzene 3,900 miles towards the Arctic archipelago, eventually raining down upon a fiord on Baffin Bay. Outside, a basketball plunges from the sky, killing a dog. At a county fair, a huge and hairy man in mud-caked blue overalls, surrounded by a crowd of retarded teenagers, swings a sledgehammer above his head with brawny keloidal arms and then brings it down with all his brute force on a tofu-burger on a flowery paper plate. A lizard licks the dew from the stamen of a stunted crocus. Rivets and girders float above the telekinetic construction workers. The testicular voice of Barry White emanates from some occult source within the laundry room. As I chugalug a glass of tap water milky with contaminants, I realize that my mind is being drained of its contents and refilled with the beliefs of the most mission-oriented, can-do feral child ever raised by huge and lurid puppets. I am the voice ... the voice from beyond and the voice from within – can you hear me? Yes. I speak to you and you only – is that clear? Yes, master. To whom do I speak? To me and me only. Is "happy" the appropriate epithet for someone who experiences each moment as if he were being alternately flayed alive and tickled to death? No, master.

In addition to the growth hormone extracted from the glands of human corpses, I was using anabolic steroids, tissue regeneration compounds, granulocyte-macrophage colony-stimulating factor (GM-CSF) – a substance used to stimulate growth of certain vital blood cells in radiation victims – and a nasal spray of neuropeptides that accelerates the release of pituitary hormones and I was getting larger and larger and my food bills were becoming enormous. So I went on a TV game show in the hopes of raising cash. This was my question, for $250,000 in cash and prizes: If the Pacific Ocean were filled with gin, what would be, in terms of proportionate volume, the proper lake of vermouth necessary to achieve a dry martini? I said Lake Ontario – but the answer was the Caspian Sea which is called a sea but is a lake by definition. I had failed. I had humiliated my family and disgraced the kung fu masters of the Shaolin temple. I stared balefully out into the studio audience which was chanting something that sounded like "dork." I'm in my car. I'm high on Sinutab. And I'm driving anywhere. The vector of my movement from a given point is isotropic – meaning that all possible directions are equally probable. I end up at a squalid little dive somewhere in Vegas maybe Reno maybe Tahoe. I don't know ... but there she is. I can't tell if she's a human or a fifth-generation gynemorphic android and I don't care. I crack open an ampule of mating pheromone and let it waft across the bar, as I sip my drink, a methyl isocyanate on the rocks – methyl isocyanate is the substance which killed more than 2,000 people when it leaked in Bhopal, India, but thanks to my weight training, aerobic workouts, and a low-fat fiber-rich diet, the stuff has no effect on me. Sure enough she strolls over and occupies the stool next to mine. After a few moments of silence, I make the first move: We're all larval psychotics and have been since the age of two, I say, spitting an ice cube back into my glass. She moves closer to me. At this range, the downy cilia-like hairs that trickle from her navel remind me of the fractal ferns produced by injecting dyed water into an aqueous polymer solution, and I tell her so. She looks into my eyes: You have the glibness, superficial charm, grandiosity, lack of guilt, shallow feelings, impulsiveness, and lack of realistic long-term plans that excite me right now, she says, moving even closer. We feed on the same prey species, I growl. My lips are now one angstrom unit from her lips, which is one ten-billionth of a meter. I begin to kiss her but she turns her head away. Don't good little boys who finish all their vegetables get dessert? I ask. I can't kiss you, we're monozygotic replicants – we share 100% of our genetic material. My head spins. You are the beautiful day, I exclaim, your breath is a zephyr of eucalyptus that does a pas de bourrée across the Sea of Galilee. Thanks, she says, but we can't go back to my house and make love because monozygotic incest is forbidden by the elders. What if I said I could change all that ... What if I said that I had a miniature shotgun that blasts gene fragments into the cells of living organisms, altering their genetic matrices so that a monozygotic replicant would no longer be a monozygotic replicant and she could then make love to a muscleman without transgressing the incest taboo, I say, opening my shirt and exposing the device which I had stuck in the waistband of my black jeans. How'd you get that thing? she gasps, ogling its thick fiber-reinforced plastic barrel and the Uzi-Biotech logo embossed on the magazine which held two cartridges of gelated recombinant DNA. I got it for Christmas ... Do you have any last words before I scramble your chromosomes, I say, taking aim. Yes, she says, you first. I put the barrel to my heart. These are my last words: When I emerged from my mother's uterus I was the size of a chicken bouillon cube and Father said to the obstetrician: I realize that at this stage it's difficult to prognosticate his chances for a productive future, but if he's going to remain six-sided and 0.4 grams for the rest of his life, then euthanasia's our best bet. But Mother, who only milliseconds before was in the very throes of labor, had already slipped on her muumuu and espadrilles and was puffing on a Marlboro: No pimple-faced simp two months out of Guadalajara is going to dissolve this helpless little hexahedron in a mug of boiling water, she said, as a nurse managed with acrobatic desperation to slide a suture basin under the long ash of her cigarette which she'd consumed in one furiously deep drag. These are my last words: My fear of being bullied and humiliated stems from an incident that occurred many years ago in a diner. A 500-lb man seated next to me at the counter was proving that one particular paper towel was more absorbent than another brand. His face was swollen and covered with patches of hectic red. He spilled my glass of chocolate milk on the counter and then sopped it up with one paper towel and then with the other. With each wipe of the counter the sweep of his huge dimpled arm became wider and wider until he was repeatedly smashing his flattened hand and the saturated towel into my chest. There was an interminable cadence to the blows I endured. And instead of assistance from other patrons at the counter, I received their derision, their sneering laughter. But now look at me! I am a terrible god. When I enter the forest the mightiest oaks blanch and tremble. All rustling, chirping, growling, and buzzing cease, purling brooks become still. This is all because of my tremendous muscularity . . . which is the result of the hours of hard work that I put in at the gym and the strict dietary regimen to which I adhere. When I enter the forest the birds become incontinent with fear so there's this torrential downpour of shit from the trees. And I stride through – my whistle is like an earsplitting fife being played by a lunatic with a bloody bandage around his head. And the sunlight, rent into an incoherence of blazing vectors, illuminates me: a shimmering, serrated monster!

CRUSADER RABBIT

Jess Mowry

Jess Mowry was born in 1960. He is the author of *Six Out Seven*, *Way Past Cool*, *Children of the Night* and *Rats in the Trees*.

CRUSADER RABBIT

"You could be my dad."

Jeremy stood, waist-deep in the dumpster, his arms slimed to the elbows from burrowing, and dropped three beer cans to the buckled asphalt.

Raglan lined them up, pop-tops down, and crushed them to crinkled discs under his tattered Nike, then added them to the half-full gunnysack. Finally, he straightened and studied the boy in the dumpster. It wasn't the first time. "Yeah. I could be."

Jeremy made no move to climb out, even though the stink seemed to surround him like a bronze-green cloud, wavering upward like the heat-ghosts from other dumpster lids along the narrow alley. The boy wore only ragged jeans, the big Airwalks on his bare feet buried somewhere below. His wiry, dusk-colored body glistened with sweat.

Not for the first time Raglan thought that Jeremy was a beautiful kid, thirteen, small, muscles standing out under tight skin, big hands and feet like puppy paws, and hair like an ebony dandelion puff. A ring glinted gold and fierce in his left ear, and a red bandana, sodden with sweat, hung loosely around his neck. His eyes were bright obsidian but closed now, the bruise-like marks beneath them were fading, and his teeth flashed strong and white as he panted.

Raglan could have been a larger copy on the boy, twice his age but looking it only in size, and without the earring. There was an old knife slash on his chest; a deep one, with a high ridge of scar.

The Oakland morning fog had burned off hours before, leaving the alley to bake in tar-and-rot smell, yet Raglan neither panted nor sweated. There were three more dumpsters to check out, and the recycle place across town would be closing soon, but Raglan asked, "Want a smoke?"

Jeremy watched through lowered lashes as Raglan's eyes changed, not so much softening as going light-years away. Jeremy hesitated, his long fingers clenching and unclenching on the dumpster's rusty rim. "Yeah . . . no. I think it's time."

Jeremy's movements were stiff and awkward as he tried to climb out. Garbage sucked wetly at his feet. Raglan took the boy, slippery as a seal, under the arms and lifted him over the edge. Together, they walked back to the truck.

It was a '55 GMC one-ton, as rusted and battered as the dumpsters. There were splintery plywood sideboards on the bed. The cab was crammed with things, as self-contained as a Land Rover on safari. Even after two months it still surprised Jeremy sometimes what Raglan could pull out from beneath the seat or the piled mess on the floor . . . toilet paper, comic books, or a .45 automatic.

Raglan emptied the gunnysack into an almost full garbage can in the back of the truck, then leaned against the sideboard and started to roll a cigarette from Top tobacco while Jeremy opened the driver's door and slipped a scarred-up *Sesame Street* Band-Aids box from under the floormat. The boy's hands shook slightly. He tried not to hurry as he spread out his things on the seat: a little rock bottle with gray-brown powder in the bottom instead of crack crystals; a puff of cotton; candle stub; flame-tarnished spoon, and needle, its point protected by a chunk of Styrofoam. On the cab floor by the shift lever was a gallon plastic jug from Pay-Less Drugs that used to hold "fresh spring water from clear mountain streams". Raglan filled it from gas station hoses, and the water always tasted like rubber. Jeremy got it out, too.

Raglan finished rolling his cigarette, fired it with a Bic, handed the lighter to the boy, then started making another as he smoked. His eyes were still far away.

Jeremy looked up while he worked. "Yo. I know your ole name. I seen it on your driver license. Why's your street name Raglan?"

Smoke drifted from Raglan's nostrils. He came close to smiling. "My dad started calling me that. S'pose to be from some old-time cartoon, when he was just a little kid. *Crusader Rabbit*. But I never seen it. The rabbit's homey was a tiger. Raglan T. Tiger. Maybe they was somethin like the Ninja Turtles. Had adventures an' shit. It was a long time ago."

"Oh." Jeremy sat on the cab floor. He wrapped a strip of inner-tube around his arm. It was hard to get it right, one-handed. He looked up again. "Um . . ."

"Yeah." Raglan knelt and pulled the strip tighter. His eyes were distant again, neither watching nor looking away as the boy put the needle in. "You got good veins. Your muscles make 'em stand out."

The boy's eyes shifted from the needle, lowering, and his chest hardened a little. "I do got some muscles, huh?"

"Yeah. But don't let 'em go to your head."

Jeremy chewed his lip. "I used to miss 'em . . . my veins, I mean. A long time ago. An' sometimes I poked right through."

"Yeah. I done that too. A long time ago."

The boy's slender body tensed a moment, then he relaxed with a sigh, his face almost peaceful and his eyes closed. But a few seconds later they opened again and searched out Raglan's. "It only makes me normal now."

Raglan nodded. "Yeah. On two a day, that's all." He handed Jeremy the other cigarette and fired the lighter.

The boy pulled in smoke, holding it a long time, then puffing out perfect rings and watching them hover in the hot, dead air. "Next week it only gonna be one." He held Raglan's eyes. "It gonna hurt some more, huh?"

"Yeah."

"Um, when do you stop wantin' it?"

Raglan stood, snagging the water jug and taking a few swallows. Traffic rumbled past the alley. Exhaust fumes drifted in from the street. Flies buzzed in clouds over the dumpsters, and a rat scuttled past in no particular hurry. "When you decide there's somethin' else you want more."

Jeremy began putting his things away. The little bottle was empty. It would take most of today's cans to score another for tomorrow. "Yo. You gotta be my dad, man. Why else would you give a shit?"

"I don't know. You figure it out." Raglan could have added that, when he'd first found Jeremy, the boy wouldn't have lived another week. But dudes Jeremy's age would think that was bad ... almost cool. Why? Who in hell knew? Raglan didn't remember a lot about being thirteen, but he remembered that.

He dropped his cigarette on the pavement, slipped the sack off the sideboard, and started toward the other dumpsters. There really wasn't much use in checking them: this was the worst part of Oakland, and poor people's garbage was pitiful, everything already scraped bone-bare, rusted or rotted or beaten beyond redemption, and nothing left of any value at all. Jeremy followed, his moves flowing smooth like a black kid's once more.

A few paces in front of the boy, Raglan flipped back a lid so it clanged against the sooty brick wall. Flies scattered in swarms. For a second or two he just stood and looked at what lay on top of the trash. He'd seen this before, too many times, but it was about the only thing he wouldn't accept as just what it is. His hand clamped on Jeremy's shoulder, holding the boy back. But Jeremy saw the baby anyhow.

"Oh . . . God." It came out a sigh. Jeremy pressed close to Raglan, and Raglan's arm went around him.

"I heard 'bout them," the boy whispered. "But I never figured it happen for real."

"Best take a good look, then."

But the boy's eyes lifted to Raglan's. "Why do people do that?"

But Raglan's gaze was distant once more, seeing but not seeing the little honey-brown body, the tiny and perfect fingers and toes. "I don't know."

Jeremy swallowed once. His lean chest expanded to pull in air. "What should we do?"

Raglan's eyes turned hard. He was thinking of cops and their questions, then of a call from some pay phone. There was one at the recycle place. Time was running short. The truck's tank was almost full, but there was food to buy after Jeremy's need, and the cans were the only money. Still he said, "What do you want to do?"

The boy looked back at the baby. Automatically he waved flies away. "What do they . . . do with 'em?" He turned to Raglan. "I mean, is there some little coffin? An' flowers?"

Raglan took his hand off the boy. "They burn 'em."

"No!"

"The ones they find. Other times they just get hauled to the dump an' the bulldozers bury 'em with the rest of the garbage. You been to the dump."

Almost, the boy clamped his hands to his ears, but then his fists clenched. "No! Goddamn you! Shut up, sucker!" One hand dove for the pocket where he carried the blade.

The boy's chest heaved, muscles standing out stark. His hand poised. Raglan was quiet a minute. Finally he gripped Jeremy's shoulder once more. "Okay." Raglan walked back to the truck while Jeremy watched from beside the dumpster, waving away the flies.

Raglan stopped around back. There was a ragged canvas tarp folded behind the cab. On foggy or rainy nights he spread it over the sideboards to make a roof. A piece of that would do. Salty sweat burned Raglan's eyes, and he blinked in the sunlight stabbing down between the buildings. The canvas was oily, and stank. Going around to the cab, he pulled his black T-shirt from behind the seat.

The old GMC was a city truck, an inner-city truck, that measured its moves in blocks, not miles. It burned oil, the radiator leaked, and its tires were worn almost bald. There were two bullet holes in the right front fender. But it managed to maintain a grudging fifty-five, rattling first across the Bay Bridge into San Francisco and then over the Golden Gate, headed north. It had a radio–tape deck, ancient and minus knobs, but Jeremy didn't turn on KSOL or play the old *Dangerous* tape he'd scored in a dumpster and patiently re-wound with a pencil. He stayed silent, just rolling cigarettes for Raglan and himself, and looking once in awhile through the grimy back window at the little black bundle in the bed. Even when they turned off 101 near Navato onto a narrow two-lane leading west Jeremy just stared through the wind-shield, his eyes a lot like Raglan's even though an open countryside of gentle green hills now spread out around them.

It was early evening with the sunlight slanting gold, when Raglan slowed the truck and searched the roadside ahead. The air was fresh and clean, scented with things that lived and grew, and tasting of the ocean somewhere close at hand. There was a dirt road that Raglan almost missed, hardly more than twin tracks with a strip of yellow dandelions between. It led away toward more low hills, through fields of tall grass and wild mustard flowers. Raglan swung the truck off the asphalt and they rolled slowly to the hills in third gear. Jeremy began to watch the flowered fields passing by, then turned to Raglan. "Yo. You ever been here before?"

"A long time ago."

"I never knew there was places like this, pretty, an' without no people an' cars an' shit. Not for real."

"It real."

The road entered a cleft between hills, and a little stream ran down to meet it, sparkling over rocks. For awhile the road followed the splashing water, then turned and wound upward. The truck took the grade growling in second. The road got fainter as it climbed, then finally just ended at the top of the hill. Raglan cut the engine. A hundred feet ahead a cliff dropped off sheer to the sea. Big waves boomed and echoed on rocks somewhere below, sending up silver streamers of spray.

Jeremy seemed to forget why they'd come. He jumped from the truck and ran to the cliff's edge, stopping as close as possible like any boy might. Then he just stood gazing out over the water.

Raglan leaned on the fender and watched.

The boy spread his arms wide for a moment, his head thrown back. Then he looked down at his dirty jeans. Raglan watched a little while longer as the boy stripped to stand naked before the sea and the sun. Then Raglan went to the rear of the truck. There was an old square-nosed cement shovel and an Army trenching tool he used when he cleaned up yards.

Jeremy joined him, glistening with sea spray, but solemn, though his eyes still sparkled a little. Raglan said nothing, just taking the shovel in one hand and the little bundle in the crook of his arm. Jeremy put his jeans on and followed barefoot with the trenching tool.

The ground rose again nearby to a point that looked out over the ocean. They climbed to the top. Raglan cut the sweet-smelling sod into blocks with his shovel, and the earth-scent filled the air. Then they both dug. The sun was almost gone when they finished. Though the evening was growing cooler, Jeremy was sheened in sweat once more. But he picked some of the wild mustard and dandelion flowers and laid them on the little mound.

Far out on the water, the sun grew huge and ruddy as it sank. Raglan built a fire near the truck, and Jeremy unrolled their blankets. He was surprised again when Raglan conjured two dusty cans of Campbell's soup and a pint of Jack Daniels from somewhere in the cab. A little later, when it was dark and still and the food was warm inside them, they sat side by side near the little fire, smoking and sipping the whiskey.

"Is this campin' out?" asked Jeremy.

"Mmm. Yeah. S'pose it is."

Jeremy passed the bottle back to Raglan, then glanced at the truck: it seemed small by itself on a hilltop. "Um, we don't got enough gas to get back, huh?"

Raglan stared into the flames. "Uh-uh. Maybe there's some-place around here that buys cans."

Jeremy gazed into the fire. "It gonna hurt a lot, huh?"

"Yeah. I'll be here."

"I'm still glad we came."

Jeremy moved close to Raglan, shivering now. "So, you never seen that Crusader Rabbit. Don't know what he looked like?"

"I think he carried a sword, an' fought dragons."

"You are my dad, huh?"

LETTERS TO HOME

Robert O'Connor

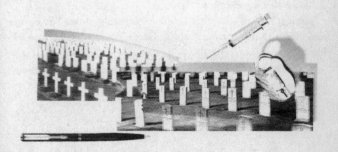

Robert O'Connor was born in 1959. He studied under Raymond Carver and Tobias Wolff for his M.A. from Syracuse University, and now teaches English and writing. "Letters to Home" was his first published short story, and his most recent novel is *Buffalo Soldiers*.

LETTERS TO HOME

In Bad Tolz, Germany, you are stationed with the 82nd. It is November, and Novembers in Germany remind you of the sadness and despair of a fallen woman. Let us say, also, we know of your fondness for heroin. You want to shoot up. This is how you do it:

There are three floors in your barracks. You get your three buddies, Johnson, Simmons, and Cabot. You go to the top floor where there are storage rooms and broom closets. To Johnson you hand the key. You have taken the padlock from your wall locker and he now locks you in the storage room until you are done. He will wait in the next room. When you are done you will bang on the wall twice and he will come by and let you out. There is an advantage to this. Should a noncom, Sgt. Lee, for example, come by on a sudden inspection of the barracks, he will pull the doorknobs of each of the sixteen rooms in succession. He will look in the rooms of the doorknobs that surrender their secrets willingly, but he will not look in your room because that room is locked and your buddy is in the next room with the key.

Or you can do this: You may prefer shooting up in the open. If you do it at night no one will see you. You go to one of the rooms, again on the third floor, and open the window. The windows are tall but narrow, and you lean out backwards,

171

hanging on with your fingertips to the edges of the frame. There is no light in the room and there is no light outside save for the few pips that appear around the base; and it seems at those times when you are silhouetted only by darkness, that you are climbing in the middle of nowhere. You gather your legs underneath you and sliding your fingers along the sides of the window frame, you straighten your body up. When you are standing it is an easy matter to reach from there to the roof. Your legs fly out from the windowsill, your combat boots act as a counterweight, and with your arms you pull yourself up to the roof. That is the easy part. The disadvantage is climbing back down when you cannot distinguish your head from your ass. If you were a fireman or climbed trees as a youth you will not be in trouble because hanging on and moving around with nothing but space to cushion your fall is as habitual as drawing your next breath. But, for instance, for Parsons McCovey, who was up on the roof a week ago, these things were not natural, and when he kicked out to find the windowsill on his way down, his fingers slid off the edge like they were greased and he fell down the three stories and landed on his head and died.

So you choose the room. You are in there with Simmons and Cabot, and your buddy Johnson is next door with the key. You take out your kit which is a small pouch you store on the inside of your pants against your thigh. You take out the Saran Wrap bag and put it to the left, next to your foot. You must remember not to move your foot. You take out the spoon from your mess kit, which is as deep and big around as a tablespoon. And you take out your silver Varick lighter, which if you hold it level with your navel can shoot up a flame that can singe the stubble on your chin. You open up your bag and tap the small brown granules into your spoon. It is only in Europe, you know, that you can buy heroin of this strength and quality. You hand the spoon to Cabot and take the bag. You seal it by taking the Varick and having the flame lick the open edges of the Saran Wrap. It melts and seals the heroin in until the next time. You take the bag and put it in the kit, next to your foot. You do not want to kick it when you space out. You open your lighter and turn up a high flame. Then you take the spoon from Johnson and cook it with the same casual indifference you use reheating coffee. Your buddy Simmons has taken out the syringe. He works in the dispensary and can sneak out as many syringes as he wants, and so you will use a new syringe each time and then sell it to somebody less fortunate. He has an adjustable tourniquet with Velcro clasps to wrap around your arm to make your vein swell up big enough to hit cleanly; and you are pleased at this trapping of civilization. When the crystals have turned to liquid in the spoon and you feel the heat has even traveled the length of the stem to your hand, you have Simmons draw it out of the spoon with the syringe. He taps the air bubbles out, holding the needle up in the air, like a tiny missile. Your other buddy, Cabot, takes your arm and wraps the tourniquet around it, and you both wait for the vein to pop out. On older addicts there is a deterioration process which causes the veins to collapse, but you have nothing but a few freckles of penetration. You take the syringe from Simmons and hit the vein cleanly, pushing the plunger part way down. Then you pull it back up getting blood out of the vein and mixing it with the heroin in the syringe. This is good. If you had pulled back and gotten nothing, it would have meant that you had missed the vein and hit meat. But you have not hit meat, and now you push the plunger down all the way and send the liquid through your body, getting a second, better rush than the first. You sink back, and Cabot finishes it by taking the syringe out of your arm. You kick your kit as you relax, but everything in it is closed, so nothing is spilled.

You bought, in your first month in Germany, a Volvo. You

173

had money left over from when you were stationed in the States, and so you put down a sizeable down payment and now pay monthly in installments. You get better whores with a Volvo than with a Jeep, or when stepping off a bus. However, you do not have the money to buy insurance, and you do not have the time to apply for an international license. So here is what you do:

You drive your car into town at two in the morning. You pull up to a car sitting by the train station. You get out and in your hand you hold a screwdriver. It takes five minutes to switch plates and you are back on the road, the screwdriver in your glove compartment, before you know it. You cannot, of course, park your car on base, but instead hide it in a blind, that you, Simmons, Cabot, and Johnson created about a half a mile away. And you walk the rest of the way to the barracks.

Your job on the base is that you are battalion secretary. You are directly under the command of Colonel Berman, and you write out reports, requisitions, and proposals. You are also in charge of sending a personal note home to the family of each man who dies. This does not happen often. For Parsons McCovey you sent this note:

Dear Mr. and Mrs. McCovey:

I regret the death of your son immensely. He was personally known to me and there was nobody in the battalion I would have trusted more with my life. In him were resplendent the virtues of honor, and loyalty to his country and God that are what keeps the core of our civilization together. He fell off the rooftop of his barracks while trying to make technical repairs on the antennae that we use to guard against the enemy. He died, while not in combat, still in the line of duty, and he had his country uppermost in his mind.

My deepest regrets,
Colonel William C. Berman
Commander, 82nd Battalion, U.S. Army

"Cross out 'resplendent,' Madison," said Col. Berman.

"Yessir."

You show Col. Berman all the mail you send out to grieving families. He has kept you as his secretary simply because there is nobody better at writing letters of bereavement, and he has already been sent letters by several congressmen who have heard of his thoughtfulness from their constituents.

"You kept this one a little short, Madison," said Col. Berman.

"Yessir." You have kept it short because you did not know much about Parsons McCovey. From what you do know you understand he was a jerk.

"Well, it's fine, except for that one word, 'resplendent.' Make sure that word doesn't leave this base," Col. Berman said.

"Yessir." Col. Berman always has one objection to each letter, as if that is a way of keeping them under control. He never gives a reason and you suspect he is a fool.

It is that night after dinner. It is dark. You have gone to Johnson's wall locker. It is eight feet tall, and is divided down the middle. On one side there are shelves. They contain his underwear, his T-shirts, belts, books, and records. On the other side there are hooks, and they hold his dress uniform, his fatigues, his boots, shoes, and helmet. You take all these things out and pile them carefully under his bed. Once emptied, a wall locker is light, and you and Cabot take it up to the third floor. Simmons has gone to get the lock from your wall locker. You have given him the key. Your buddy Johnson is involved in a fight on the third floor. You do not interfere because it has been discovered that Johnson is not your buddy, but an informer. He takes money for telling who shoots up. You and Cabot take the wall locker into a storeroom. Johnson is brought into the storeroom by three men. He has been subdued and gagged with a piece of medical tape Simmons has provided. By turning him sideways the men are able to squeeze him into a wall locker and close the door on him. When they close the door and take the padlock and push the arm through the doorhandles, they do not give Johnson the key. They give it to you. Johnson's muffled screams from inside the wall locker sound humorous, like the gruntings and snortings of a hog. The men push the wall locker towards the open window. It is heavy now, and you can hear the body of Johnson desperately sliding around inside, his back being stabbed by the hooks where his uniforms once hung. They sweat and curse and say you should have put the wall locker closer to the window because Johnson is heavy. But they get him to the window and throw him out. It is dark, so you could not see out the window even if you looked. You imagine the wall locker tumbling end over end, and you think of the grace and beauty of a body in free fall. The crash sounds, you think vaguely, like the slamming of a very large door.

At five the next morning you are awakened by Sgt. Lee. You are used to reveille and do not mind it as much as some of the other men. Your bereavement detail with Col. Berman spares you of much of the work in the barracks, but you still have to endure the mornings.

"Special detail this morning. Get dressed on the double. You have fifteen minutes," Sgt. Lee shouts.

You go to your wall locker, and take out your fatigues. You put them on quickly, and when you have laced your boots you go to the bathroom to shave. When you are done, you walk outside and get into formation. Sgt. Lee marches you to the armory, and you are each issued a gun and thirty rounds of ammunition. The gun is heavy, but balanced, and you have been taught in basic training in the States that if you choke up on it like a hitter in a game of baseball, and swing if from the shoulder, you could crush the skull of a medium-sized gorilla. But you have never done this. You slide your hand along the barrel and feel the smoothness of the metal, and you notice it is dark; dark like the night time that is just now beginning to lighten. You pull the gun to your shoulder and line up in formation next to Simmons.

"Anything about Johnson?" he whispers to you.

"No." You shake your head.

You march in silence through the gates, through the swamp, and over several hills. You realize, almost too late, that you are getting dangerously near the blind where your illegal Volvo is parked. The sergeant lines the men up single file twenty yards away from the blind. He struts in front of you.

"We are about to do some field practice. Behind that blind is the prototype of a new Russian tank." His voice is bitter rather than sarcastic, and you feel rather than see him looking at you. "We have found out about it with a minimum of casualties, and we know it is impervious to all but steady rifle fire. You will hitch your weapon to your shoulder and open fire at my command."

Your weapon is hitched to your shoulder as you open fire. You imagine the radiator being punctured, the tires deflating, the windows frosting over with splinters of glass. You fire until your ammunition runs out, and then rest your gun at your side.

Dear Mr and Mrs Johnson,

I know you loved your son very much and I want you to know that I did too. He was the best buddy that a man could have and it doesn't matter that he was weak because we are all weak; it was just that he was weak in a different way. If I had to do it all over again I would not have given him the key, I would not have bought the Volvo, and I would not have joined the Army and come to Germany. I know everybody says war is such a stupid thing but sometimes I think peace is such a stupid thing too. I'm very, very sorry.

You tear up this letter and write one Col. Berman will sign.

*

It is night again. You have your kit against your thigh and you go to the third floor. You do not have your padlock anymore because it was lost by being attached to a wall locker that went end over end. You are alone. You go to the window and open it up, and climb onto the roof. There is a full moon that lights your fumblings with the bag, your Varick, and the syringe. You put on the tourniquet, pop the vein, but it takes you three stabs to catch it, and when you double-pump the plunger you let it lay there in your arm and you know that you have learned.

Here is what you have learned:

You have learned that a Volvo hidden in a blind can be a Russian tank, and under those circumstances, may be fired upon.

You have learned a wall locker contains helmets, shoes, underwear, and uniforms; and when it does not contain those, it may contain a man.

You have learned that someone has the key at all times, but sometimes they do not have the key at the right time.

And you have learned that death is a constant at all times, but that at any time the constant may be renegotiated by introducing it, in its most moral and liquid form, into the various channels of your bloodstream.

FUCKING MARTIN

Dale Peck

Dale Peck was born in 1968. His work has appeared in *Out*, *OW* and *Men on Men 4: Best of the New Gay Fiction*. He is working on a new novel, *Red Deer*.

FUCKING MARTIN

I hate the empty moment before emotion clarifies itself. I hate sitting on Susan's couch and staring at her living room, which feels unfamiliar, even though nothing about it has changed. When she comes from the kitchen, carrying a platter of crackers that ring a smooth brown mound, she says, "Hummus," and dips a finger into the speckled green paste. "I think they put parsley in it or something." Hummus. Parsley. The world revolves around this opposition for a moment, and then, when I've accepted it, I realize that I'm afraid. Susan sits on the couch, looks at me. I can see the curve of her breast through a gap between two open buttons of her shirt. It rises and falls with her breathing. I notice the dimmed lights, the hush, the new sound of wordless music, and into this heady air I breathe my first words of the night. "Susan," I say, "you have to risk AIDS in order to get pregnant." I wonder then, as her hands rush to her chest, if she undid the buttons deliberately.

Seduction was Martin's art. Sometimes on a Sunday morning, the light in the tiny rooms of our apartment softened by closed curtains, he told me old stories. In the living room, sprawled on a futon, or in the kitchen, as he fried bacon or made omelettes and I sat at the table. How loosely I held him in that small space, one hand around my coffee, the other tracing the waistband of his underwear, the smell of both – coffee, underwear – mixing in my nose. For a while the only sound would be his metal spatula scraping the pan, but when he started speaking it was like a catalogue, a litany, was unrolling from his mind. Martin had a great memory for names, places, dates, for technique, though soon I realized he wasn't bragging, or trying to make me jealous, or being sentimental. He wasn't trying to recapture his past – merely to validate its existence. The remains of those mornings are mental pictures that I've drawn from his words: Martin, in the Ramble, lowering his glasses, slowly undoing the buttons of his shirt. I remember how carefully he chose his words, as carefully as, in days past, he must have chosen his method. He didn't unbutton his shirt: he undid the buttons one by one, his fingers working down his chest, a V of skin spreading behind his passing hand like the wake of a boat. And he knew me too, knew that my own backward-looking eyes would revel in this knowledge of his past, that my mind would take it in like liquor, until the whole of his experience would become inseparable from my own, and it would seem that the words which had been mouthed in his ears had been whispered to me, and the hands which had run across his body had passed over mine. I don't remember, I *am* Martin in a club, sliding a beer down the nearly empty gutter of a bar, coins tinkling to the floor as the bottle passes; in an alley, standing in shadow, listening to approaching footsteps, striking a match at just the right time. Though I'm sure he told me about the men he picked up, I don't remember their looks, why they attracted him, even if his seductions were successful. I did realize, even then, that he presented himself as an object, played roles out of movies and books; but he knew this too. You could in those days, John, he said. This was strange to me – not that he knew about roles, but that he had ever assumed them. I had played the pursuer in our relationship, had, on seeing him at Susan's old piano at one of her parties, pulled a rose from a jade vase and placed the half-open flower in his lapel buttonhole as he sat at the piano. I wonder, though: if I had possessed the ability to see him differently, would his piano playing have seemed a pose, a façade even more romantic than the one I'd assumed? But knowing that would require a different set of eyes, now, and in the past as well, and all I really know is what I remember. Martin – my lover Martin, the object Martin – posing himself for sex, for it is only that object which I now possess.

Memories pollute a planned atmosphere of seduction. Susan's apartment, if pared down to uneven wooden floors, cracked walls, and paint-smothered moldings, could be the one I once shared with Martin. I try to focus on her, but she pulls aside her hair and, beyond her shoulder, the ancient piano falls into view. Nostalgia traps us – the food, the music, everything, chosen according to past times. "My friend who likes hummus," Susan has called me – what about that is sexy? She speaks now in a careful voice. "Do you remember –?" she starts. She stops when she sees what I look at. She knows that I – that we both – remember. It seems all we can do, and that is why she doesn't finish her sentence. When Susan suddenly closes the windows, I think at first that she does so to foster the nostalgia, but when she sits down again there is more space between us than before. We both look at the new space, but neither of us moves into it.

I've been with a girl before – once, when I was eighteen, a long time ago. She and I had just finished our first year in separate colleges and were home for the summer. We'd known each other for years, had even been close friends in high school, but it took nine months apart and, that summer, the absence of most of our friends to force us together. Still, I think it's safe to claim we were experimenting, though not with sex; neither of us knew it about the other, but neither of us was a virgin. We were experimenting with love, and we failed. And it's not that I *didn't* love her, nor she me. Who knows, without love it might have been easier – certainly less painful.

We drove to the river one night in my father's old pickup. It was late June, early July. Already there was something between us: movies in the evenings after work, weekends in stores trying on expensive clothes that we never bought, long good nights on her front porch that left me alone in bed with a hard-on. We did a lot of things, I realize, that created their own conversations or made words unnecessary. We never talked about ourselves. On the way to the river, I sped down rutted dirt roads and the cab was filled with engine noises and music that screeched out of the single-speaker AM radio. We sang along and laughed and cursed at the more vicious bumps. At the river we rolled our socks into our shoes and waded into the shallow, slick-like-oil water. We held hands. It was night, the sky clear, and I invest the stars now with great significance, because you don't really see them in the city and they have for so long been a symbol of romantic love. Ten feet away from the water the air had been hot and still, but in it we were cool, and laughed quietly at little jokes and skittered on stones hidden in the sand. Though we hadn't talked about it, we both knew what was going to happen.

It was on a sandbar, surrounded by water, that we spread an old holey blanket through which the sand penetrated so easily that soon she suggested we abandon it and stretch out directly on the ground. I said no, the ground was damp, and besides, it wasn't really ground, but sand, it would get all over us. A stupid argument followed – we didn't fight, but we became paralyzed by an inability to agree and eventually we fell silent, I half on, she half off the blanket. I remember lying there looking up at the stars and feeling the effort of not speaking growing harder and harder, when suddenly her face interrupted my view and she kissed me. The kiss went on for a long time, and then extended itself, as the rest of our bodies became part of it and our clothes came off. Then all at once she rolled off me, and even as I noticed that the blanket had become a wadded mass between us she said, John, do you remember Hank? and after I'd said yes, she said, I had a baby last April. His.

All at once things expanded: my mouth, my eyes, my mind, my arms and legs even, flung wide in an effort to catch the sky that seemed to be falling on me. Only one part of me shrunk. It's unfair to say that her sudden revelation did us in; really, she merely provided the excuse I'd been looking for. What she said didn't repel me, but just then – when I was wondering if I should put on a condom, wondering if this would feel as good as, or better or worse than, it did with boys – just then she made sex seem unerotic, less like fantasy, more like life.

She started to talk then; she told me about hiding in her dorm room because when she left it for meals or classes people pointed at her. Her friends advised her to abort. That was okay for other women, she said, but not for her. Counselors, her parents, people calling themselves her friends, told her to drop out and raise the baby; if possible, marry the father. That, too, was okay for other women, but not for her. She had plans, and besides, who knew where he'd run away to? She told me about back pains and stomach cramps. She described an adoption agency that paid the medical bills and allowed her to screen parent profiles and name her baby. She held Stephanie in her arms once, and her mother snapped some pictures before the nurse came. She told me how Stephanie had turned her face to her breast and sucked the hospital gown. It made her think that humans should be marsupials, that we should have a pouch where we could grow in warmth and darkness, that nothing that fragile should have to face the world without the opportunity for retreat. When she's eighteen, she told me, they'll give her my name, she can look me up if she wants. Well, I said – I could think of nothing else to say – now I know why your mother flashes the porch light on and off.

We laughed too long at that – plainly, neither of us knew what to say. Then something made me mention the boys I'd had in college, and it was her turn to be beside me, silent. I told her that my problem seemed trivial compared to hers, but at least I understood it. I told her that I enjoyed anal intercourse, but when a boy pulled his penis out of me it felt like defecation. I really used these words; they seemed safely clinical. She told me that a woman she knew, on her fifth baby, said giving birth felt the same way: like taking a good shit. I felt she was offering me some kind of connection, but only a ladder's, and no matter how far I climbed, she would always be ahead of me.

After that we were beyond shyness, and we rolled close to hold each other for warmth. I remember that I tried to make sense of everything that had just happened. I couldn't, but for some reason that didn't make me feel uncomfortable. I did understand one thing, though: she and I would never be lovers, and the strongest emotion that realization produced in me was relief. And I should tell you that that girl, of course, was Susan. But on the river that night, I didn't know what that would mean today, which is why I didn't reveal it before. Because knowing this, knowing the future, changes things, changes the past.

Susan's laughter coils like smoke through the air before reaching my ears. Bent over so that her shirt falls open, she rolls a second joint. "They make machines for that," I say. "Rolling joints?" she asks, laughing again. "Well, cigarettes, I suppose. But like most things, it does things it wasn't intended to." Her droll "Really" seems exaggerated; her follow-up – "Like assholes?" – surprises me. Trying to joke it off, I take the knife from the hummus. Susan's shoulder rubs mine as I bend next to her. "Like this," I say, and fake a stab. Her smile vanishes. She takes the knife and sets it on the table; the heavy clunk of metal on wood startles me. It's too easy, how the meanings of once-familiar actions change. Susan slips the joint in my mouth; "Such things are for people with clumsy fingers," she says as she lights it, and maybe it's because I've almost forgotten about the rolling machine, but when I've exhaled and she is still holding smoke in her lungs, I say, "There's nothing wrong with my fingers," and run them along her arm. Susan's eyes lock on the space beyond my right shoulder. She exhales slowly. I've touched her a thousand times before; I do nothing to make this touch sexual. But the confusing blend of friendship and sexuality is inevitable. It is, after all, why we're here.

There was a time when I'd wanted to be powerless, and have sex. I wanted to lose control. I went to the Spike. I met Henry.

About forty then, defined by a decade of discos, gyms, and steroids, Henry wore leather pants and an unbuttoned button-down blue plaid shirt with the sleeves ripped off. A man's name, Lou, was tattooed on his shoulder, and his mustache was speckled gray. When he shook my hand my knuckles cracked. He bought me a beer, I bought him a beer, I told him what I wanted, he said, eventually, Do you have any limits? It was a Friday night; I said, I have to work Monday afternoon. And it's not enough to say he hurt me, to say that for two days and three nights he controlled me: I asked for that. He gave me something else, something I didn't understand until much later.

It was not, I think, in Henry's nature to hurt anyone. When I stroked his slick-leathered thigh in the taxi, he moaned; there was nothing dominant about it. If he'd had his way, we probably would have had sex normally, with perhaps a few accoutrements: a leather harness, latex gloves. But I insisted, and he knew what to do. We both did, we *all* did; we'd been

187

taught, by people now mostly dead. So I submitted to his kissing, stripped for him, called him Master; on his order, I licked his boots. He collared me, attached a leash, led me on my knees to his bedroom. I was drawn but not quartered, tied to the four bedposts. My ass gripped his sheets and pulled them into my crack. The red-rubber-ball gag started out egg-sized, but soon became an orange in my mouth. He stuffed wax in my ears and I heard my breath come fast and shallow. He hooded me. And he knew, Henry. Before zipping the eye slits, he pulled a mirror from the wall and held it above me. I saw what I'd wanted to see: not myself, but a picture from a magazine. I was powerless, if not ridiculous. But I hadn't lost control. Then he closed the eye slits. They didn't seal completely, and I could see, if I shut one eye or the other, the jagged outline of the zipper and Henry's shadow as he moved about the room. Still, I was close enough to blind and nearly deaf from the wax. Bound, gagged, unable to do anything else, I waited.

S/M, if you let it, or if you can't stop it, delivers what it promises: pain that transforms. At first I understood things. I felt him handle my cock and balls; I could see, without looking, the thong stretching my balls away from my body and separating them from each other. It hurt, and my hips rocked a little in protest. The nipple clamps were two sharp pains that translated into two useless pulls against my bindings. When he twisted the clamps I tensed, trying not to resist, trying to be above the pain, but I realized that my head was rolling from side to side. And then I didn't know what was happening. Later I found he'd been pouring hot wax over my chest, stomach, balls, but then it just felt like my skin was on fire. I couldn't help myself, I struggled. The gag hadn't been a gag until the first time I tried to scream against it, and then it was. But even though I knew I couldn't speak, I continued to try, tried to force the gag from my mouth by the power of my breath alone.

It went on like this, until eventually I was just struggling. The pain ceased to have meaning in any real way. I simply wanted to be released, but I had no control over that. In realizing this, and accepting it, a wave of heat washed through me and seemed to separate my inner body from my skin. The pain, and the fighting, were outside me, and inside I was still. I barely noticed when Henry cut off my head and held it above my body so I could look again at myself. My skin, inflated like a balloon, was held to earth only by thin ties at the wrists and ankles. I smiled to think of my real self bouncing around freely inside, painless, weightless, like a child in the Moon Walk at the fair. My mind bounced too, from memory to memory, and all of them seemed somehow transformed into visions that, no matter how painful they might have been once, were now ecstatic, and it was wonderful, a kind of freedom from the past – it was what I wanted. And then he made me come. I felt his hand on my cock vaguely at first, not knowing what he was doing. But as he pumped I grew hard, the wax cooled, I forgot the tit clamps and cock-and-ball harness, and he kept pumping until eventually, inevitably, I came. And it was just like any other too-long-delayed orgasm: anticlimactic and tiring. I lay in my bonds, bored. And for two more days and two more nights I was bored, as Henry tried to think of ever more exciting things to torment and arouse me. Oh, it was amazing what he could do, and not draw blood.

And I remember asking him a totally inappropriate question once, when the gag was out of my mouth. Lou, I said, is he still alive? Henry scratched the tattoo as if he wished it would come off. Louise, he said, my ex-wife. Yes.

Susan bats at smoke, goes to open the windows. Worming my toes into the warm space where she'd sat, I close my eyes and lean back, only to jump forward when Susan sits on my feet. "My violet!" she says, pointing at my hands, immersed in a pot in her lap. "My feet!" I respond. She raises herself so I can move them, and I pull my fingers from her plant, a withered African violet. Brown-edged leaves hang from an aged, thick stem; dead ones line the pot. "I told him I'm no good with plants," she says, and when I realize she means Martin, I grab the pot again. "Maybe you should take it home." "Maybe I should." Sometimes I only understand people through objects, and in the solid unerotic shape of this plant I see Susan: were she truly trying to seduce me, she wouldn't have brought Martin into the room more than he already is. Already she's sliding across the couch. "I'd feel bad if it died." There's a hush after I say this; it's an old rule and now I've broken it: don't mention death around people who have lost someone. "Jesus, John," Susan says then, taking my hand, forcing me to look up from Martin's plant. "When you make love to me, please, don't think of him." Quiet after that, broken only by the sound of the plant being set on the table. What's truly remarkable, I suppose, isn't that it's dying, but that it lived this long. We stare at each other in silence. And it's like the first time: when the silence becomes uncomfortable, we kiss, and then, for just a moment, I hear water running somewhere close by.

Sometimes sex is perfect. I remember my fourth time with Martin, the first time we fucked. I remember the fourth time because that's when I fell for him. Something held us back our first three times; our minds were elsewhere, our hands could have been tied. But the fourth time. There we were: Martin's place, Martin's old couch. There we were: Martin and John. The two of us, 3 a.m., empty bottles on the coffee table. We had exhausted conversation, wine had exhausted us, we stared at the TV. It was turned off. How did he do it? I mean, I know what he did: he put his hand on my leg. He didn't look at me when he did it, just lifted his right hand off his right leg and set it down on my left one, just above my knee. Just above my knee, and then it slid up my thigh, slowly, but not wasting time. That's what he did. But how did he make my diaphragm contract so tightly that I couldn't take one breath for the entire minute it took his hand to move to my belt? My stomach was so tight a penny would have bounced off it. His fingers found the belt buckle, worked it, a small sound of metal on metal, a sudden release, a rush of air – my lungs' air – and my pants were open and I gasped for breath.

Martin put his hand back in his lap. His words, when they came, were even. He could have been talking about the weather. You could slip a condom on your cock, he said, and twirl me on it like a globe on its axis. The words took shape in the room; they made sex seem as understandable as pornography. On the blank TV screen I imagined I saw Martin and myself, fucking. I looked down at my open pants, at my underwear, white as a sheet of paper. Or I could do you, he said. Still, I hesitated, not because I didn't want him, but because the very thought of fucking Martin added so many possibilities to my life that I grew dizzy contemplating them. Just do what you want to do, Martin said, but do it now. I kissed him. I pulled open the buttons of his shirt, pushed down his pants. I bent over him and ran my tongue over his chest, into his navel, down to his cock and balls. When I got there I swabbed the shaft until it glistened. I rolled his balls around my mouth the way a child rolls marbles in his hand. And it's important to know that I didn't do this because I suddenly loved him. I just wanted to fuck. Do it, I whispered. Do it.

And he did, lying on the floor, on a rug, though I didn't twirl as easily as those globes in high school, and in fact, after one revolution, I didn't twirl at all, but sat astride him and rocked up and down. And he pumped, pumped like anyone in any skinflick ever made, though I didn't think of that then, but only of the amazing sensation of having this man inside me. A funny thing happened then. He pumped and I rocked, and I rocked and he pumped, and eventually our rhythm must have been just right, for the rug, a small Persian carpet-type thing patterned in tangled growing vines, came out from under us as if it had been pulled. I fell over, he slipped out of me, we ended up on our sides, side by side, laughing. We lay on the floor for a long time, mouths open, our stomachs heaving as we sucked in air. We touched each other only with our fingertips, and then only slightly, and we lay on the floor for a long time, laughing.

We finished on his bed. I don't remember going there, just a point at which the world returned like a shadow and I saw my cum splashed on his stomach and legs, and his splashed on mine, and below us was a white sheet instead of the rug. Then for a moment I wanted to take everything a step further. I wanted to run my finger through Martin's cum and lick the finger clean. But Martin smiled at me. He kissed me. When my hands went for his body, he caught them halfway and held them. In a light voice he said, In my experience, there are two kinds of men in the world: those who play with their lover's hair when they're getting a blowjob, and those who play with their own. Though I tried, I couldn't remember what I'd done. Which type am I? I asked. You, he said, and showed me as he told me, put one hand on my head, and one on yours. And which are you? Martin looked at my hair. If there was a mirror handy, he said, you wouldn't have to ask that question. His words didn't really *mean* anything, but they accomplished what I think he meant them to: I forgot my desire to taste his cum. He lifted the sheet then and fluffed it with his arms, like wings, then let it settle on our shoulders, and I didn't realize we were standing up until I awoke hours later.

After that he could have asked me to do anything. A caress from Martin had more strength than any punch Henry would ever land. But he rarely used this power, and I suppose I had the same control over him. Didn't he, as well, sleep standing in my arms? We shut the windows, turned off the phone, unplugged the clock. We wore no clothes for days, and used our time to make love, to eat and sleep. What I remember from that time, the time we shut out the world, is sweating on his bed as he dove into me, and someone somewhere flushing a toilet and the wall behind Martin's bed rattling as water rushed through pipes concealed within it.

Just after that time I asked Susan what pregnancy was like. She'd been talking, vaguely, about having a baby, though she said she couldn't name five straight men in the world that she'd want to father it. If you've ever had a cock moving deep inside you, you know that it can feel like a part of you, even as you realize that it belongs to him. Can you imagine this staying in you after he pulls out, staying, growing, moving around eventually, making its presence, its separate life, known? This is how I imagined pregnancy. I asked Susan if this was reasonable. She sighed and smiled. Not even close, she said. Not even close.

When her shirt comes off, I'm struck by the strength in Susan's shoulders. Instead of unbuttoning it, she pulls it over her head, and her hair falls back audibly to surround her thin neck. Sometimes I think it's Susan, and not Martin, who is the love of my life. I don't know why I believe in such a concept — perhaps because thinking it distracts me from the larger fact: that I can have neither of them. Except for Susan, except for tonight. And that other night: I remember the river, both of us tenderly helping the other off with clothes. Tonight we kiss for a while, then stop, come to the bedroom. In here, candles instead of electric light or darkness, windows open but curtains drawn, so that they move in the breeze. Incense. The music from the other room. Susan busies herself with setting the stage, and then we pull our clothes off alone and pretend to ignore each other. But Susan, folding her bra in half, catches my eye. "There's an extra toothbrush if you want to brush your teeth," she says, and looks away. I have to fight back laughter. I know the kind of laughter it would be, cynical laughter, sad laughter, having more to do with things outside this room than in it. I feel like something's been stolen from me. I want to compliment her, tell her I think she's beautiful. At the river, I could have done so – I did, because the sex we had then was, we thought, just between the two of us. And it's not that Susan is no longer beautiful, no longer sexual. But her sexuality exists apart from me. Her apartment, these trappings, are one thing: she'll play with them. But not with herself. Not tonight. Tonight I'm not her lover. I'm just helping her to have her baby.

When she first came to us, only Martin and I knew he was sick. We'd known for months, but were still unwilling to give his illness the legitimacy, the finality, of a name. She presented her plan: she would have a baby and raise it alone. Perhaps one day she would marry, but she didn't foresee it and she didn't particularly care. She was happy fucking around: she wanted a baby, not a husband. But she didn't want anonymous sperm or the hassle of a turkey baster, and she couldn't afford artificial insemination. She wanted to do it the old-fashioned way. And she wanted to make love to me. I asked what she expected of me, besides sperm. Uncle John, she said: You will be Uncle John, and this one here will be Uncle Martin. She must have wondered why she laughed alone at her joke.

Before she left she asked him if he'd lost weight. After she left he said he was cold. In the bedroom I curled up with him under the blanket. Then he was hot and wanted to throw the blanket off, but I suggested we take our clothes off instead. And then he was cold again, and I took him in my arms and rolled us in the blanket, and when I'd finished we were pressed together front to front and I opened my mouth and closed it over his and tickled his lips with my tongue until he let me in. And then he pulled back and said, You shouldn't, and I looked into his face, so pale that it seemed almost greenish, and I said, I should, and kissed him again.

Wrapped in the blanket, stretched out on the bed, we could have been suspended in space. By our feet, by our heads, by our cocks, suspended in time. I reached down and pushed my cock between his sweating thin legs and pulled his between mine. Sometimes when we did it that way I imagined that I was inside him, but that night I imagined I was inside a woman. That was the only way he'd let us do it anymore, he said my health has got to be protected, said he loves me too much to kill me, said anything to keep me away from him because now, now that he's sick, he's afraid of what he wants because he's afraid of what he wanted because he thinks that what he wanted not what he did is why he's going to die.

When at last we unrolled the blanket, it seemed that buckets of salty-sweet water rolled off the bed as the last fold parted. Though untouched, the sheets were soaked, and I remade the bed before joining Martin in the shower. His thin back was bent over a fern he kept on the deep window ledge; his fingers pulled a few brown leaves from the pot and let them fall in the tub. Because you love me, he said. And because you love her. I said, What? He said, I think you should, if you can, if you stay healthy, you should help Susan. After I'm dead.

After he said that, I didn't do laundry for two weeks, didn't do anything, and when I came across those sheets again they were wet as if we'd used them just minutes ago, and covered in places with a thin green layer of mold. I held them in my hand and felt their green sliminess stick to my fingers and I didn't know what to think: if this was the product of fucking Martin, or if this was the product of nothing, or, worst of all, if this, the product of fucking Martin, was nothing.

After he died I didn't tell anyone for fifteen hours. I left his body in the hospital bed in the living room through the day, pulled back the covers once and looked at it, and then pulled them up to cover what was there. From seven in the morning until ten at night. I might have left him like that forever, but Susan came over to check on us. I brought her into the apartment and sat her down, and then I walked over to Martin and kissed him on the lips. They didn't taste like him. Nothing happened. I looked at Susan. She was crying; I remembered that she'd known him longer than I had, that she'd introduced us. I said, I wanted to do that in front of someone, so that when he didn't wake up, I'd know he was dead. And after Martin's body was gone and his bed sat there empty because they pick up bodies any time but they only pick up beds between nine and five, weekdays, I sent Susan away and then I went out myself. The air was hot and dry, the only moisture spat by air conditioners. I didn't want to be alone with my grief, I wanted to give it to someone, to the whole city. I stopped a man on the street, put my hand right on his chest. Martin, I started, but the man ran away. Didn't he know I could never hurt him? I walked a long time, until I had no place else to go, and so I went to the Spike, where I met Henry.

Two years have passed.

In this world, Susan says, there's as much nihilism in having a baby as in having one by me. I can't argue with that.

Science says I have nothing to protect her from. But still.

Part of the arrangement with the adoption agency was that every year, on Stephanie's birthday, Susan received an update on her daughter's life. The letters, addressed "Dear Birth Mother" and signed "The Adopted Parents," were always short, and came with two or three severely cropped polaroids of Stephanie. Only fragments of bodies – hands, the side of a leg – indicated that she didn't live alone. When Susan moved from Kansas she didn't leave a forwarding address with the agency.

The situation presses against me like . . . like what? Like trampling feet? Like uplifting hands? We weren't prepared for this – any of this. There are times when the past overwhelms the present, and nothing will happen, and there are also times when the present overwhelms the past, and nothing that happens makes sense. Here, today, the equations are changed: silence equals death, they teach us, and action equals life. And though I no longer question these anymore, I sometimes wonder, Whose death? Whose life?

Martin's life resided in his right hand. He pointed it out to me with his left; his right hand rested on my thigh and he said: Look. I looked for a long time and then, just when I was about to ask what I was looking for, I saw it, his pulse, visibly beating in the blue trace of a vein in the patch of skin where his thumb and forefinger met. For a moment I considered pressing my own finger on it, as a joke. I don't remember if this was before or after we knew he had AIDS. I don't remember if I put my finger on the vein.

Mouth open, teeth resting against Susan's inner thigh just above her knee, I stop what I'm doing as I realize I'm crying. My body trembles slightly. I feel, don't see, Susan's head lift up. "Dale?" she whispers.

Then John puts his hand on her pussy, where soon he will insert his dick and for all intents and purposes plant his seed; he runs fingers through her bush and teases her clit, and her head sinks to the pillow. She can't see his face or the tears streaming down it. He remembers suddenly what he wanted to tell that man on the street: Martin, he would have said, Martin is dead. Martin is *so* dead. And he remembers a piece of sado-babble that Henry had whispered to him. You will never be free of me, Henry had said, and John realizes that, though this isn't true of Henry, it is true of Martin. And Susan. Even more than he fears what he's doing now, he fears what will happen when Susan finds someone else, falls in love, leaves him. He admits something to himself that he's always known but never accepted: that he wasn't her first lover – just as she wasn't his – and that they won't be each other's last, as well. That, even as his passion for Martin has become this lament, his grief, too, will pass away, and Martin will be even more dead. And whatever else happens, the person that may or may not have been conceived tonight won't be Martin.

The sum of life isn't experience, I realize, isn't something that can be captured with words. Inevitably, things have been left out. Perhaps they appear in others' stories. Perhaps they were here once and John's forgotten them. Perhaps some things he remembers didn't really occur. But none of that matters now. Even as Susan takes John inside her he knows that this baby means something, though I've fought against that; even Martin has become something abstract. A symbol, like the rose John once put in Martin's lapel, like Susan's African violet, like the fern in the shower. But after tonight, Martin's face will be inseparable from Susan's, from John's own, which is just a mask for mine. How can this story give Martin immortality when it can't even give him life? Now I wonder, Has this story liberated anything but my tears? And is that enough? I want to ask. To which I can only answer, Isn't that enough?

I thought I'd controlled everything so well, the plants, Martin, John, Susan. Even the semen.

In this story, I'd intended semen to be the water of life.

But, in order to live, I've only ever tasted mine.

ALANA

Abraham Rodriguez Jr.

Abraham Rodriguez Jr. was born in 1961. His work has appeared in *Story Magazine* and anthologies, and his short-story collection, *Boy without a Flag*, was selected by the New York Public Library as a "Book to Remember" for 1992. His current novel, *Spidertown*, has been optioned by Columbia Pictures.

ALANA

I

Alana was black-and-blue. She stood in front of the mirror, rubbing her face with ice cubes. She wasn't going to cry anymore.

Last night, Freddie thought it was going to be the same. He came in whacked on crack. She fought him. It was the first time ever. She hadn't lifted a finger before. "Beatings are a part of it, girl," Wanda used to tell her, bearing scars and cigarette burns. "Ain't no big thing. Girl flesh grows right back." After six months of taking it, she was hurt and tired. She had just turned seventeen and felt like an old grandma. "No," she whined, kicking him away with her feet. He thought she was playing with him. She sunk her nails into his face; that's when he really started to smack her. When she woke up, she was bloody and sore. She could hardly stand on her wobbly legs. When she got to the bathroom mirror and saw herself, it all spilled out of her in choked sobs.

Who could've known six months ago that she was going to end up like this? Her best friend, Wanda, was a posse wife. She was sixteen and married to a seventeen-year-old kid who pulled in six thousand bucks a week. She would poke her head out of her man's white limo and call Alana away from the stoop. The two of them would guzzle champagne with the stereo blasting, Wanda barking directions to the driver.

"This aincha car," Alana said, getting huffy because her friend was riding so high.

"Baby, this is TOO my fucken car. Samson owns it. You read? He owns this fucken car. He can beep it up anytime he wants. That shows you the kinda juice I been suckin."

"Well, where is he then?"

"I tolju. While the cat's away, etcetera an shit. Listen girl, we gotta findju a chavo worth his shit in gold."

Alana didn't say anything. She was finishing the champagne.

"Look, I known you for a while, right?" Wanda gripped her hand, her large eyes concerned. "I know the kinda life you lead. Goin from bed to bed, who knows what kinda shit you could catch these days? A girl gotta take care a huhself. Bein a posse wife is a way more dope scam than doin the streets. I'm tellin you girl, get in on some a this action. You gotta come down to El Commandante's tomorrow night. All the boss chavos in town will be there."

Alana had gotten tired of the trade. She started at fifteen and in less than a year had gone through half a dozen pimps. She would walk out on them when they ripped her off or beat her or made her do free tricks. She decided she would go solo; all she needed was a crib to crash. That's why she ended up staying with her sister, Dora. It's where her head was at when Wanda put it to her about the joys of being a posse wife.

El Commandante's was a posse dive on Intervale Avenue. It looked like a boarded-up storefront on a crumbling, deserted street. Inside, it was all flashing lights and throbbing music and booze and women and young boys that made thousands of dollars a week. Some of them had Jaguars and diamond belt buckles. Young girls followed them around like groupies. They would hang outside and hope some posse boy would take them in. It was a special world and not everybody was allowed to play.

The moment Alana walked in there on Wanda's arm, she was the star she always felt herself to be. She was all curvy slinky in her pink minidress, Wanda beside her in her black catsuit, jiggling her man's tag, which twinkled and jangled on her wrist, eighteen $900 gemstones that spelled SAMSON. They sat in the bar and soon boys were swarming all over them, crazy desperate to know who the untagged fox was. It was the place to be all right.

"Didn't I tell you this was the joint?" Wanda seemed to say that every time they arrived. One night a friend of hers laid some acid on them. Alana had been deeply grooving to her own inner vibe when the prettiest little boy she had ever seen strolled right into view, tall and sleek, with dope threads. It didn't take long for her to get on the case. They went into the back, where there were mattresses and cushions and condoms. Suddenly she was fucking him, amidst pulsating lava lamps and gleeful kid faces and other bodies that rolled and tumbled. When she got back to her sister's house at six in the morning, her hair was mussed and crunchy and she had lost one of her high heels. Dora, getting ready for work, was in the kitchen making coffee.

"I'm not even gonna ask," she said, looking her up and down. Alana stumbled over to the coffeepot and peered in.

"Damn man, I'm hungry."

"You won't find food in there."

Alana grimaced. "Why are you yellin?"

Dora went to the refrigerator and took out a carton of orange juice. Alana snatched it and took a long swig, then followed Dora into the living room, where she was pulling on a pair of pantyhose with angry tugs. Her clothes were laid out on the sofa. She worked as a receptionist for a law firm on Centre Street.

"I don't believe you." Dora reached over and pulled off a barrette that clung to Alana's hair. "You should see yourself."

Alana shrugged. She had heard this particular rap before. She finished the O J.

"Bad enough thinking about what you've been doing out on the streets. You think I need this? It's why I live alone. It's why I left home. You think I want Mami living with me?"

"I ain't Mami."

"You are. Just like her." She squeezed the wrinkles from her panty hose. "Just like her. Putando. You even smell like her, you fucking bitch."

Alana's eyes were dull and unreceptive. "Damn man, canchu ever be nice? What makes you so nasty? If thass what workin all day in a office does to a person, forget it man. At least I'm nice. I know how to be nice an shit. Lookitchu. All tense. Maybe you should calm down an not work so hard. Why donchu take the day off an go to the park?"

Dora stared at her. "Just like Mami. Pulling the same shit that killed Papi. She killed him. You know that, right?"

Alana's lips were moving as though she were chanting a voodoo curse against Dora; her eyes, narrow slits.

"I want you out of this place," Dora said.

If Dora could see her now, dabbing her discolored swollen face with ice cubes, she would be ecstatic. "I knew you would end up that way," she would sneer, but Alana wasn't out of the race yet – no way. She had gotten off to a rough start in life, but she could bounce back, bounce from here to the moon. *You can bend but never break me.* What was that song? She remembered singing along while it blasted from the limo's radio, Wanda's crazy goofy face coming in for close-ups. The memory made her want to cry, but she fought it. There was a tired soldier staring at her in the mirror.

II

She was in the tub, the water as hot as she could take it. She rubbed a towel filled with ice against her face. She had decided

204

that if he ever tried to touch her again, she would kill him. She had a kitchen knife sitting on the toilet seat.

She hadn't minded being a posse wife. It beat being a hooker. At least this way she only had to do one man to get money.

"You gotta be . . . whass the word? Philosophical. Thass it." Wanda's voice came back to her as the ice stung her face. "Sure you gonna get beat every now an then. A woman gotta get used to that." She chewed her gum like the coin box on an old bus. "I know that won't bother you. Dincha father beatchu every now an then? Mines did alla time."

Alana's father never hit. He was a skinny man who couldn't even yell. Her mother used to smash plates while he tried to concentrate on his *New York Post*.

"It's nah so bad, girl. Don't get so womp. Donchu got a pocket fulla green? Donchu got some boss stones? Donchu got some street juice that gets you recognized an respected? Man, ainchu ridin around in a limo right now?" Wanda pinched her cheek tenderly. "Ahh, girl. Don't be all long face. So he hitchu. Thass the first time. Yuh man don't sound so bad. You better hold 'im tight."

Yeah, Freddie was crazy handsome. He had those big lips and those eyes that seemed to cross when he looked at her. He was a sweet lover at first, slow and careful. She had to guide him in. She thought he was such a soft dude; then she realized that he just didn't know. The big-time posse chief was as close to a virgin as she had ever experienced. It was a sweet sensation. She could teach him.

"What does that mean?" They had been lying in bed sharing a jay. He sat up like he had been stabbed with a knitting needle.

"Nothin, Freddie. It don't mean nothin."

"It do too mean somethin. Yuh sayin I don't know how to fuck, right?"

Alana sighed, reaching over to caress him. "You're just right for me, Freddie. Stop that."

He pushed her hand away, his eyes steaming.

"Freddie. Stop that. Don't lookit me like that." Her voice shook. "I didn't say that. I love you."

"You love me. Whatta packa shit. You can't love. You ain't learned how. You been fucken everythin in sight. I know aboutchu."

"That was in the past, Freddie. Thass all over."

"You kiddin me? Once a putona, always a putona. That don't never change. So maybe now I treatchu so nice, you miss the old days, huh?"

Alana couldn't speak. Freddie swept the sheet back and stood up, going to the bureau for a cigarette.

"Damn. The guys warned me, they told me I shun't get in witchu. Now you sittin there tellin me I ain't good enough."

"I didn't say that, Freddie. I just said I could teach you stuff to make it better for both of us. I just meant that I –"

The first punch caught her off guard. He spun right around; she didn't even see it. The blow left her dizzy, sprawled across the bed. In a flash she thought of all the times she had gotten beat up while working for pimps, one of which set her up with these three beat boys in a blue Plymouth. They took her to a lonely stretch, facing Home Street. They slapped her up, shoved socks in her mouth and fucked her up the ass, each and every one. Initiation rites. Did she have HIT ME stamped on her goddamned forehead?

She had thought the thing with Freddie was going to be another business arrangement, because once you hook, then everything that has to do with a man is a business arrangement. She thought she was swapping sex for food and lodging and some jewelry. Instead, she fell in love. When they fucked, it was a soft touching and kissing and snuggling thing, not the Rock'em Sock'em Robots scene. She was amazed she could

206

even feel, but with Freddie she learned to be tender and warm, learned how to give of herself to please him. The funny thing was that he pleased her, too. She had never known anybody to go to the trouble. The feelings freaked her out too much, made her think she was losing control. She thought about running away, because love was a leash, but when he made her come it was a deeper touch than any she had ever felt. She wanted to give him everything. He never went without, even if she had to. She was so good at it that it scared him.

"How many guys you blowed?" he'd ask her, making the shame color her face.

"I only love you, Freddie."

Being in love made her want to forget her old life, but he was always bringing it up to her, as if he couldn't get over it. The punch in the face had stunned her so much she couldn't move, couldn't speak, could only stare at him as he stood by the bed clenching his fists.

"You just a putona, an donchu forget it. I was crazy to take you. The guys told me. I din't listenna them."

She shook her head desperately. No words would come. She felt dirty and reached for the sheet to cover herself, but he yanked it off her.

"You gonna cover yuh body? Hide it from me?"

"Nah, Freddie, I —"

"All this time, you been makin funna me."

"Naah Freddie, it ain't like that." She got up, wanting to go to him and touch him. If she could touch him, maybe it would go away, but he pushed her back down on the bed.

"You wanna get a good hard fuck, right? Like in the old days? You fucken bitch!"

He whacked her again and jumped on her, turning her over. She knew what he was going to do. She started to cry. She thought he was different; now he was trying to shove his limp dick into her from behind, cursing her and bapping her on the head, just like the beat boys in the blue Plymouth, only Freddie wasn't the type. There's a certain kind of guy that can get hard from whacking a woman around and making her beg and plead. That wasn't Freddie. He was pushing and pushing and then he was hitting her harder and crying and pulling her hair and he still couldn't get inside her and she was trying to help him but he punched her back with hollow thumps.

"It's okay, Freddie. It's okay." She was twisting, trying to gather him up in her arms. He connected with a blow so hard that she fell into a deep, black sleep.

Freddie's friends told him hookers like to be belted when they fuck. ("Do you like that? Ahh? Want me to hitchu harder, bitch?") They told him to force her to swallow it, swallow it all, even though it made her nauseous. If she gagged, he would smack her. ("You used to do it for them right? What, my cum ain't good enough? Bitch!")

It was Freddie's friends who had put him up to it. They knew she was a super dope chica with experience. She was TOO MUCH woman. The man that tamed her would have to be a REAL MAN, above and beyond the call. Lots of guys at El Commandante's tried to tag her, but she saved herself for him, not even a quick little fuck when she was horny. It got like that for her after she had first spotted him and got on the case, only to find that he resisted her. From that moment on, he became her mission. She enjoyed the little glances, the nervous tension, the way he couldn't always look her in the eye. His compliments were clumsy. He was always asking her if she was with somebody, and she was always saying, "Nah. I'm savin myself." She would've still been saving herself if it hadn't been for Diablo, the one-eyed drug dealer who told her, "Listen up, you better make a move on that boy 'cause he sure do want it, but he don't know how to get it."

She stared at him, trying to figure out if he was making some kind of joke. She knew Freddie was pretty tight with him.

"He talk about me?" She was sitting at the bar sipping her favorite vodka drink.

"Sure he do. You know, he's an up and comin kid in the works, but the other guys be talkin him down. They figure like he ain't never gonna getchu. This is like a big scene, even some bets have been placed. I just like the kid, man. He don't even know I'm tellin you this. If Wanda hadn't told me you like him, I wun't even be here."

She smiled. "I do. I really do." It made her feel floaty to say it out loud. She started to laugh. "He's such a pretty little boy."

"You should just go an get him already. Just thinka what it'll mean for him, man."

She bit her lip for a moment, watching the lights dance in the mirror behind the bar. "Bet," she said, and the next night she cornered Freddie in the back alley beside an overflowing dumpster.

"Hey Freddie," she said, pinning him to the wall. "Whass this thing between you an me?"

Freddie swallowed hard and looked her up and down. He looked happy and scared.

"Yuh juss so dope," he said.

"Am I?" She moved closer. "Well how come you don't show me then? I mean, I come here alla time to see you. See this black minidress? I wore it tonight for you. They told me you like panty hose." She grinned and stepped back, the minidress sliding up her slick nylon thighs. She didn't have panties on. There were pretty flowers embroidered by the dark seam that ran right down into her tangled bush. "You like these?"

"Ahh shit girl, you know, I —"

"You think maybe you could kiss me?" She slid her dress back down and leaned against him, stroking his arms. "I wanchu, Freddie. I got a stone tied to my heart, an it says Freddie, Freddie, Freddie . . ." She got that from a country song. Dora was always playing that shit.

209

He kissed her softly, his hands touching her face as if checking to be sure. She pressed against him. No animal sex, no frenzied groping. It surprised her, how soft and gentle and warm it was. Suddenly she wanted to say a million things, to explain about how she had been a hooker but that hadn't been her fault, her mother had been one and she had ended up with her after the separation. She had tried running away but child welfare agencies always sent her back and so she ended up on the streets turning tricks. She just wanted to explain it was all, an old skin she wanted to peel off. He wiped her eyes with a fingertip. She shook her head, as if refusing to believe in him. It was all in his touch. She knew a guy's touch said more about him than words. "I love you," she said, because she couldn't help it. Crazy corny as it was, she felt her insides bursting.

III

She got dressed. She tried not looking in the mirror but she caught glimpses. She tried to snicker with contempt. She watched as her face wrinkled and folded and the tears came anyway. Her body did what it wanted. She had no control anymore.

She filled a suitcase, grabbing all the jewelry. There was no way she would let him keep any of it; she had earned it. He would have to kill her to get it. He had fucked-up her face. The jewelry might keep her in bucks until it healed. Then what? She couldn't go to Wanda or any of the posse wife friends she had. Leaving a posse boy was a big no-no, whatever the reason, and none of them would risk their status for her. There was only one place she could go. She quickly dialed the number before she could chicken out.

Dora was three years older. She was studying to be a paralegal and planned to marry a young doctor named Julio, who had a beard and doughy white hands. She had come home one day and found Alana packing.

"Well," she said. "Is this for real this time or am I gonna see you again when you change your mind?"

Alana didn't say anything, just kept gathering her stuff. Dora walked right up to her.

"Three months tops," she said. "I'll bet anything. You watch."

The memory of Dora's words made her stomach twitch as the phone rang. When Dora picked up, her voice sounded weary.

Alana paused, breathing into the phone. "It's Alana," she said. "Don't hang up."

Dora sighed. "Well, well. Looks like all your royal plans blew up in your face again, right? What happened? Didn't work out? Wrong pimp? Not enough blow? Maybe you're tired of working for your own pay?"

The contempt froze her. Alana didn't say anything.

"Well? What went wrong? Aren't you calling to tell me that everything is peachy-keen? A little gloating at your sister's expense, maybe? Ahh? Nah, not me. I'm an idiot, isn't that what you called me once? I gotta work eight hours a day in some office to make my money. I don't just lie with some slob and make a grand a week." Dora's voice was getting louder.

"Dora. Please. I just wanted . . ."

"You wanted what?"

Alana closed her eyes tight, squishing the tears with her fingers. She hung up the phone. Freddie found her about an hour later, sitting on the floor, clutching her legs and rocking to the empty sounds in her head. She had made up her face but her tears tracked all through it. She stopped rocking when he came in.

Freddie's eyes were red and bloated. There was a heavyset guy with him, who lingered by the door like a bodyguard.

Freddie squatted in front of her, hands clasped, like he had something serious to say.

"I'm glad yuh here," he said. There was something about the way his eyes darted to the guy by the door that made Alana think Freddie was scared of him. "Thass Jake over there." He paused, wiping his mouth with his hand. "You gotta go with him."

She looked from Freddie to Jake with the same glassy eyes.

"I was playin this poker game with some guys from Ace Of Spade's outfit. I ran outta money. I was playin Flaco. You remember Flaco?"

She thought of that tall, skinny dude with the dizzy eyes and hyena laugh. They say he killed three people. She gave him a blow job on a dare a long time ago, before Freddie, right in the back room at El Commandante's. Another one of her acid nights.

"Anyway, I lost, I lost, I lost. When I ran outta cash, we played for you. I lost." He didn't look at her, but at Jake. "You belong to him now."

"You sold me off?" She sounded like she was in a trance.

"Nah, man. I lostju in this card game. Thass different. Thass why Jake's here." He hadn't taken his eyes off Jake. "You better go with him now."

"I'm already packed," she said, getting up slowly. Freddie went into the kitchen and came back with a beer. He popped it open and stood by the doorway, watching her come out of the bedroom with her suitcase and her shoulder bag. Jake took the stuff right off her like a bellhop. "Come on," he said, and without another word to Freddie they headed out.

"Have a good time," Freddie said.

IV

Flaco's pad was way over on Cypress Avenue. Glass shards everywhere, garbage in clumps, empty buildings in rows. Drug dealers chanted and fat ladies sat on stoops, their little kids picking empty vials from the cracks in the sidewalk.

They pulled up to a building that had a locked front door and a tiled vestibule. The halls were clean and smelled like disinfectant. Flaco's pad was on the third floor. There was a card taped to his door, the picture of a saint. When Flaco opened it, her eyes followed the saint and did not look at him.

"Thass Saint Hojo," he said, "patron saint of all drug dealers. I know this guy who makes them." The saint was holding crack vials. Joints floated in the air around him.

She came into the apartment slowly. It had nicer furniture than Freddie's. Jake put her stuff in another room and left. Flaco sat on the couch and stared at her as she walked around the room, touching the bookcases and big screen TV and stereo speakers.

"You remember me, Alana?" He put a joint to his lips.

"Yeah. Sure." She was looking through his collection of video games. She had to squint. The lighting was low and she felt as if everything around her looked grainy.

"I was thinkin, you know? I ain't seen you in so long. I thought we could make a special occasion out of this. I got some champagne, and —"

Alana turned to look at him, her face twitching a little. Flaco got up from the couch and leaned close. He went to a switch on the wall and turned up the lights. He scraped at the powder on her face.

"Ahh, man," he said, turning away. "Fuck. The fucken bastid gimme damaged goods. I don't believe this shit!" He spun, rubbing at her face harshly, making her pull away. "Lookitchu! You a fucken mess. I thoughtchu was ready to go! I oughta kill that bastid!"

A sob burst out of her. She bit her lip so hard to hold it in that it bled.

"I'm good to go," she whispered. "Just gimme a second."

She was trembling. He dragged her into the bedroom. The bed was covered with red satin sheets, the lights dimmed. He had been ready all right.

He pulled her close and unbuttoned her blouse, pushing her down on the bed. He removed her sandals and slid off her slacks, leaving her in panties. He stared at her bruised legs, at the bite marks on her breasts, the assorted cigarette burns. He just stood there staring at her.

"I'm sorry," she said, and then she couldn't look at him.

He shook his head. "I oughta kill the bastid. Shun't I kill him?"

She didn't say anything.

"He thinks he's slick, passin you off on me like that. I should just pop the fuck. Lookitchu. Yuh a mess." He walked over to the light switch and dimmed the lights even more. He stood by the door, looking at her.

"Sleep," he said. "You go sleep. I'll see you later." He shut the door.

She closed her eyes and fell into the black.

Dedicated to Yolanda

TOTALLY NUDE
LIVE GIRLS

Gail Donohue Storey

Gail Donohue Storey is the author of *The Lord's Motel*, as well as a book of poems. Her short fiction has been published in *Chicago Review*, *Fiction*, *North American Review* and numerous magazines.

TOTALLY NUDE
LIVE GIRLS

Partially Nude Live Girls

Partially nude live girls, giving away their power in all the configurations of confection and deceit. Fluffie was a sweet job at Ginger's Finger Ginza, working the crowd of sensuous existentialists. Ginger's Finger Ginza was a palm-reading franchise and got the breakfast crowd from One Hour Martinizing across the street. Fluffie was in the future cheering up a lonely Martin.

"This bed closes at 8 a.m.," she said, rolling up the hide-a-bed. "If you want to roll longer you have to pay for another night."

Fluffie was also her wife-name from marrying the man standing behind her in the food line at their reception. It doesn't mean he can't go hunting or she can't go to the Junior League, but should be the person you like most to spend with.

The Ginza astronomers played charts of all the hearts of men and women so she could dance the palms of the customers. They came for community, roots, values, a place to belong, a place to come alive to the best we can possibly be.

"Am I as happy as I can be?" they asked.

"Perhaps I wear my nude dress," she teased. "Perhaps I take off my nude dress also." She took off her outer body until the central self lacked an outer identity body. She cultivated a transparent thinness.

Their own brutish and furtive, shoulders hunched, palms swinging between their thighs. When she was successful their fingers curled up and entire postures became less gorilla than embryonic. Outside the Ginza was a sign that said "MORE THAN 3 BILLION PALMS READ."

One palm, however, was deeply elusive. When she tried to dance his she felt delusory. The Clairvoyeur was as collective of thoughts as she was of fortunes. She tried all her fortunes. The Clairvoyeur did not reveal his feelings, but appeared to be considering her love.

Fluffie flowed out through her own fingers, like electrical water. Was that had never happened at Ginger's Finger Ginza. The musical astronomers, chiefly oboists, went crazy from double-reed madness. Eighth-notes and quarter-notes reverberating.

He remained as quiet as an air-pocket in a frozen Margarita. It was courtship by deep postures of intimacy. In silence and for silence, for you alone.

"Fluffie," he said.

"I exhaust the fantasy before we meet," she said, "so that there will be no betrayaltrothal."

Is who one needs a temptress who can be trusted with her temptation? Fluffie bore opportunity in one hand and resistance in the other.

"I can describe the affectional life," she said, "but not how to divine such thoughts as yours are."

"Are you happy in the Ginza?"

"It's wartime and I am at my station, but I am only happy when I am with you."

"Do you know who we're where you're dancing?"

"I know the night shifts steps and I feel them."

The Clairvoyeur allowed her to see him commune with himself and with others inside him. He sanctified her need before he satisfied it.

"I would even do melancholy for him," she thought, "if I knew the real reason for being sad, and someday I may do it."

She danced into the end of tradition/era. She went right up to the end of ( )ess, ( )ton, and possible ( )tion.

Totally Nude Live Girls

We slept with a man who hit us while we slept, then we ran away, to a city soft-split by a bayou. Before we come on, at The Oasis, we take pleasure in solitude. If we have no weapons, this really is a war. We raise our arms the way trees tense their branches in the wind. Our breasts fall into place. Men, having no breasts of their own, know a sudden feeling of affection.

Now we're making gestures on the open road. We go up, we come down, we slice the air with our paper bones. We read his slow face, the pattern of his shirt, his tie. He leans forward, as if there is nothing between us. He breathes as if listening.

Sign, countersign. Because he sees us when we do not see ourselves, because he calls us Aureole in the evening, because he puts the palms of his hands together, as if praying or diving, we suspect him of fierce experience of ecstasy. We smile at our own sadness. We had thought to be the best judge of our own beauty.

We unpin the flowers from our hair. Moving toward the light at the end of the stage, we bow into our applause. There were two moons that night. We saw him eyeing each, without suspicion.

Out in the soft, black night, it rains down the lip of the rose until water withdraws its tongue and sleeps. His drop runs rose-heart deep, as sharp as the incense of damp green weeds and the brown fermenting bark. In sleep positions, we kneel to the night, drink rainwater, while wetness softens grasses, mosses, trees. We drink the sleep at the bottom of our dream.

For years we have not been without thought of you. By thinking of you enough do we tell ourselves what we hoped that you would tell us?

Partially Live Nude Girls

How shall we get you to know we exist? Run, take the gentle streets as far as we are able. Is okay to be terrified, is a style of existence adopted to break a habit. It bothers us to know things and not have access to their conscious use. We are dressed as if for winter. If forced to swim, we'll put our mittens in the pockets of our snowsuits.

We intend to swim.

We paddle hard into the fight. Molecules of last light glide away from each other, our wrists fall into the darkness.

We make ourselves a small thing. Poppy was our red name, our now name is Aureole. Aureole had a brotheress.

"Boy-Twin," she said, putting her arm around him protectively as they were drifting in from sea, the Sea of Nau, the Day of Mothers.

We paddle, brotheress, his mother, and I, through air as thin as water. The wrists of the trees reach for bottom, water unfolds in stairs below us.

But these waves hurry you from one place to the next. The adults have always needed taking care of, something more now seems to be required. The first thing we did was institute a schedule. Adults need ordered lives. We suggested what would be eaten and what would not, woke them if they seemed to be drifting toward death. We parcelled out their chores with an eye to their aptitudes, even strengthening their competence in some areas where there seemed to be considerable need and relatively little risk. We posted a schedule for their baths, and made it "fun" for them, delineating elegant splashes on the walls. We wrote instructions on the walls, illustrating if all other efforts at socialization failed.

The political value of all this was unassailable. We succeeded in cultivating in them Fear of Inconvenience.

"Mother over matter," we thought, becoming more and more subversive.

But we're afraid that someone's leaving, Aureole sings to her father not her own. We select one among our girlfriends you would marry, and we marry her. Why has anyone disembarked this early in our morning, in any town in Greece, or Illinois? The lovers embrace each other's luggage.

They say that days go by, that we fill them up with cloud, each day a cylinder of glass, and everything else what came before, and what after. The feelings that exist in the someone to love are so reluctant as to seem colorless. Father's love-life is life-threatening.

In this way we cultivated a great gift for unhappiness. We wear the look of children who know they are about to. In this way we become love subjects, bartering Mother's death for Father's love.

Live Nude Totalled Girls

Uta Beauty was her name from French-kissing fashionable issues. We is a pronoun dream of imperial subconscious, the colossal personality of event. If you can't talk about it, point to it, so we pointed to it with our projectile. It had a vertical ability to go down into the moment.

Projectile wanted more and more to take the hot plunge. He flirted with Uta, who was thrilled.

"Big Boy, Big Boy," she said.

She got the heavy artillery out of her jewelry box and wore it all at once.

"Lapis lazuli!" she crowed. Hopeful opals, amethyst

ambition, real fake perils, gold beads, hot diamonds. Van Cleef and Arpels, watches on every wrist. Time is so precocious.

But the sadness of buying.

"I won't leave till I've whore every outfit I came with," she said.

In every dream store, Uta Beauty rode the escalator. Until Projectile was forced to mortgage off the psychic landscape. Their dismal decimals were feelings on a mathematical model. They began fighting in bed. They were corporate punishment. They were caught in Fragrant Delicious. They actually loved the fighting.

"Truth is stronger than friction," Projectile retaliatory.

Uta carried on in the oral tradition. He probed her for more information. The connections are so intimate intimidating.

They grew preoccupied with global thoughts of bigger issues. They began lining up with thoughts of their own appetites and fears.

"Uta," he said ferociously, "I feel need in you I need to kill."

The parallel moving outward and inward. A world moves up closer into a field of interior vision.

"It is a little in love with you," she said, holding him off by making him think of baseball. "I can tell by the things about you he wants to tell me. Don't worry, not very much, and some of it contradictory to what you say. Don't, because although what he says may be true or not, you can deep end on me to behave according to your specifications."

Layer by layer, closer to what we mean. Abstract erotica, fantasy modeling, interrogatory love. You can depend on me not to stop them, to continue to (make love to) you, (even from) this distance. This is the rare fact of the matter.

"I have the pleasant feeling," she said, "that you are expanding to the ultimate possibility of event. It may be by Christmas or it may be by lunch."

Uta rehearses her speech for afterglow:

"I'm Exhausted. Existed."

SLEEPYTOWN

Donna Tartt

Donna Tartt was born in Greenwood, Mississippi and is the author of *The Secret History*.

SLEEPYTOWN

I remember my great-grandfather – who was born fourteen years before the end of Queen Victoria's reign, and who was therefore Victorian not only by temperament but by statute as well – once saying that Thomas De Quincey was the greatest prose stylist in the English language. He was given to proclamations like that, usually announced loudly in the midst of some entirely unrelated conversation: the greatest Natural Wonder of the World, say, or the greatest book in the Bible. These recipients of his favor happened to change as the mood struck him: Dickens, for instance, and James Fenimore Cooper being on other occasions bestowed the prose stylist's laurel. I was ten at the time, and aware of both Dickens and Cooper (it was hard, in our household, not to be aware of Dickens, as my great-grandfather spoke of Dickens frequently and in a manner that led one to believe he had been personally acquainted with him), but De Quincey was a mystery. Though there were plenty of books in our house, there were none by him. I supposed that they had been lost, along with other lamented articles, either in one of my great-grandparents' moves or in the big fire at the old house, an event that occurred thirty years before my birth and that had assumed, in my imagination, the importance of the burning of the library at Alexandria.

Three years later I happened to run across a copy of *Confessions of an English Opium-Eater*, in the college apartment of one of my older cousin's hippie friends. It was the end of term; I had come along with my aunt and uncle to fetch my cousin from school, and my cousin, who was seven years older than me and took a perverse and active interest in my corruption, had invited me to come inside with him, ostensibly to say good-bye to the hippie friend but actually to smoke pot, while Aunt and Uncle waited trustfully in the car.

Though I was more than willing to be corrupted – and would have been heartbroken if my cousin, whom I idolized, had left me outside with his parents – I was both unused to pot and shy around the friend, who had a beard and scared me. Another guy was there, whom I didn't know, and a couple of girls. Wretchedly stoned after three or four awkward puffs, I left them all sitting on the living-room floor – chatting, still passing the reefer around, apparently unaffected – and wandered speechlessly around the apartment. I found myself in a room that was empty except for a stack of books and some record albums. The records were predictable (*Abbey Road*, *Are You Experienced?*) and so were the books, except for the Thomas De Quincey. I sat down on the floor and looked at it. It was, to me, pretty much incomprehensible. But there were pictures, black-and-white engravings – of Chinese dragons screaming through the London skies and enormous bat wings spread over the sooty roof of St Paul's – which struck a dim, sweet chord in my imagination. Overtly sinister, they were also oddly soothing, like the certain nightmare from childhood which had grown so familiar that – when I found myself standing on the windswept dream-hillside where it invariably began – I was somehow strangely comforted, because I always knew exactly what was going to happen. I looked at the pictures for a long time. Then my cousin came to find me and dragged me out to the car, where I sat very still on the drive home and tried not to act weird, as my unsuspecting aunt and uncle talked loudly in the paranoid, vibrating silence.

*

"O just, subtile, and mighty opium!" says De Quincey, ". . . thou buildest upon the bosom of darkness, out of the fantastic imagery of the brain, cities and temples, beyond the art of Phidias and Praxiteles – beyond the splendor of Babylon and Hekatompylos; and, 'from the anarchy of dreaming sleep,' callest into sunny light the faces of long-buried beauties, and the blessed household countenances, cleansed from the 'dishonors of the grave.'"

It might seem strange that my Victorian great-grandfather, who frowned even upon the innocent diversion of moviegoing, could admire an author who described so winningly this far more vicious pleasure. But in spite of, perhaps even because of, his upbringing, he had a nearly unlimited faith in the magic of Pharmacy. He was fond of relating horror stories of the Confederacy, of nicks and blisters turning into septic poisoning ("One bottle of rubbing alcohol!" he would say dramatically. "One bottle of rubbing alcohol could have saved hundreds of those boys!"), or of simple surgical procedures leading to shock and needless fatality because of the deadly shortage of morphine. (To this day, one of the most moving scenes for me in the film of *Gone With the Wind* is the scene at the Atlanta railroad depot, where poor Dr. Meade is surrounded by thousands of Confederate wounded: no morphine, no bandages, no chloroform, nothing.)

My great-grandfather's own mother had died, when he was a boy, a wrenching and terrible death from some illness now easily cured by penicillin: in later life, he had unwavering faith in the supernatural powers of this drug, which in the end would prove to be his undoing. Though he had been repeatedly warned not to, in the last years of his life he dosed himself almost constantly with antibiotics, whether there was anything the matter with him or not. These antibiotics were readily supplied to him – as was just about any drug in our town, to just about anybody – upon request, by local doctors and pharmacists who apparently believed that since my great-grandfather was an intelligent man, and well thought of in the community, he was therefore qualified to assume responsibility for his own medical treatment, despite his utter lack of any medical knowledge whatsoever. So he took antibiotics all the time, believing them to be a kind of healthful preventative, or nerve tonic, and over the years built up a gradual but powerful resistance, until the Easter weekend when a cold metamorphosed, unexpectedly, into pneumonia and – the pills that would have saved his mother now powerless to help him – he died.

When relatives reminisce about my great-grandfather, they almost always precede it with some reference to his affection for me. "You were his heart's own darling," they say; and, "He thought the sun rose and set on you." This was the truth. I was the product of a skittish, immature mother – Great-grandfather's youngest granddaughter, also dearly loved – and a dashing but feckless father: my parents were neither able nor inclined to take much of an interest in my early upbringing. But my mother's family – a bevy of great-aunts and grand-parents – were only too glad to rush into this breach, and I spent my days and most of my nights in the old house on Commerce Street, which had been bereft of children for nearly twenty years. Though most people in the advanced stages of life (the occupants of the Commerce Street house ranged in age from fifty to eighty) would have found the intrusion of a newborn infant unsettling, my arrival was apparently a source of excitement and much-needed diversion, and a bassinet was dragged from the attic, books were consulted, the milkman was advised to bring an extra quart or so per day. "It was," my great-aunt says happily, "like somebody just left a baby out on our doorstep." Then she goes on to tell the story that I've heard a thousand times: how, at the first, I was too small to wear regular baby clothes and had to be diapered in handkerchiefs, which had everyone in a quandary until someone hit upon the idea of doll's clothes, a small trunk of which was unearthed in some forgotten toy box. (There exists a hilarious photograph of me lying in a crib and wearing, for an infant, an oddly sophisticated career-girl outfit.)

Amidst this flurry of activity, my great-grandfather was the self-appointed arbiter of all matters relating to my care. Though he knew nothing about babies, he believed he knew everything and refused to listen to my great-grandmother's more sensible counsel. I was a healthy little girl, however, and thrived under what my great-aunts secretly thought was his nutty regime – until, to everyone's alarm, I started to become what they all called "sickly" when I was about five years old.

The problem was bad tonsils, nothing serious. But until they were removed, when I was seven, I was ill and feverish much of the time and had to stay in bed an average of about three days a week. (I came close to failing the first grade, not because of poor marks but because of a poor attendance record.) To my gloomy and sentimental great-grandfather – who was possessed of a Dickensian world-view in which rowdy children prospered while sweet little good ones were gathered swiftly to the Lord – this was nothing less than a sign that I should soon be taken from him, and he mourned for me as if I were already dead. Matters were not helped by his having a little sister who had died at about my age. And though everyone tried to reassure him – it was the 1960s, children didn't die of trifles anymore – he refused to be comforted. Even the beacon of penicillin did not offer him much hope. While he believed implicitly in its power in all matters pertaining to himself, he did not trust it fully with the lives of his loved ones: a lucky thing, as it happened, for me, as I do not know how I would have responded to the continual and bludgeoning doses of antibiotics that he prescribed for himself.

What my great-grandfather did prescribe for me – along with whatever medicine I got from the doctor – were spoonfuls of blackstrap molasses and some horrible licorice-flavored medicine that was supposed to have vitamins in it, along with glasses of whiskey at my bedtime and regular and massive doses of some red stuff which I now know to have been codeine cough syrup. The whiskey was mixed with sugar and hot water: it was supposed to make me sleep and help me put on weight, both of which it did. The reasoning behind the cough syrup remains obscure, as a cough was not among my symptoms. Perhaps he was unaware the syrup had codeine in it; perhaps he was simply trying to make me comfortable in what he thought were my last days. But, for whatever reason, the big red bottles kept coming from the drugstore, and – between the fever and the whiskey and the codeine – I spent nearly two years of my childhood submerged in a pretty powerfully altered state of consciousness.

When I remember those years, the long, drugged afternoons lying in bed, or the black winter mornings swaying dreamily at my desk (for the codeine bottle, along with the licorice medicine, accompanied me to school), I realize that I knew, even then, that the languorous undersea existence through which I drifted was peculiar to myself and understood by no one around me. Hiss of gas heater, sleepy scrape of chalk on blackboard. I saw desolate, volcanic landscapes stirring in the wood grain of the desk in front of me; a stained-glass window in the place of a taped-up sheet of construction paper. A wadded paper bag, left over from someone's lunch, would metamorphose into a drowsy brown hedgehog, snoozing sweetly by the garbage can.

My report card for the first grade stated that I was "quiet" and "cooperative." But what I really preferred was staying home sick, where I could allow my hallucinations to run free without the teacher's tedious interruptions. I would stare, sometimes for hours, at a particular View-Master reel: Peter Pan, soaring high over London, his thin, moon-cast shadow skimming over the cobblestones below. Even when unmedicated, if I stared at this particular picture long enough, I sometimes got the giddy sensation that I was flying; just as, if I closed my eyes in the backseat of my mother's Chrysler and tried hard enough, I could sometimes transform the Chrysler into an airplane. Now – to my immense satisfaction – this knack had increased itself by an almost exponential degree, to the point where the Chrysler seemed to be able to turn *itself* into a plane whenever it liked, and with no help from me whatsoever.

If Thomas De Quincey dreamed of lost Babylons, I dreamed about Neverland. I dreamed about Neverland, and Disneyland, and Oz, and other lands that had no name at all, with talking bears and swan princes. Sometimes, in the sleepy glow of the gas heater, I would catch a glimpse of Huck and Tom's campfire, out on their sandbar in the Mississippi. And sometimes at night the rattle of a truck going past would transform itself into the leaden advent of a dinosaur, its head above the telephone wires, plodding down the moonlit, empty streets. Our neighborhood was full of mimosa trees; they looked, to my eye, much like the Jurassic tree-ferns in the illustrated dinosaur book my grandmother had given me. It was not hard to imagine our yard, after dark, transforming itself into some prehistoric feeding ground: the gentle neck of a brontosaurus – mild-eyed, blinking like a tortoise – stretching to peer at me through my bedroom window.

I was spending more time at my own house now – my parents had a maid who looked after me – but it was still only around the corner from the house on Commerce Street, and my relatives there, who were mostly retired and had nothing much to do, came frequently to visit on the days I was home sick: bullying the maid, inspecting the contents of the linen closet and the refrigerator, making rueful but affectionate comments about my poor mother's lack of household-management skills. "That Baby," one of them remarked once (they all called my mother Baby, and still do, though she is now almost fifty), "isn't any better mother than a cat." This remark stuck in my mind – my mother, with her green eyes and her graceful way of sitting with her legs tucked under her, really did look like a cat – and I couldn't understand, when I repeated this to her, why she got so upset.

Feeling sick, and being warned occasionally that I might die, seemed a perfectly natural thing to me, as I had spent most of my life around old people. Though all the residents of Commerce Street possessed, in some degree or another, that affectionate, light-hearted streak which had found its culmination in my mother, they also possessed a kind of effusive, elegiac fatalism which expressed itself in long gloomy visits to the cemetery and melancholy ruminations on the vanity of human wishes, the certainty of suffering and loss. My great-grandfather liked to show me the graves of his deceased relatives ("Poor Papa," he would say with a mournful shake of the head, "that's all he's got left now") and also the spots reserved for my great-grandmother and himself. On the way to the car, he would always point out to me the tiny grave, adorned with the statue of a little girl, of some child about my age who had died nearly a hundred years before.

"I expect this is the last Christmas" (or Thanksgiving, or Easter, or whatever holiday was coming up) "that you and I are going to spend together on this old earth, darling," he would always say sorrowfully, on the way home in the old De Soto. And I would look at the side of his face and wonder: which of us was going to go first, him or me?

I was convinced that I would die soon. This conviction,

however, did not cause me much alarm. I was less concerned about separation from my family – a separation that, after all, would only be temporary – than I was about leaving my books and my toys and most of all my dog. In the Commerce Street theology, good dogs went to Heaven (and bad ones, presumably, to Hell), but when in Sunday school I expressed this theory as fact, I was swiftly corrected, and came home crying. My mother, my aunts, everyone tried to reassure me ("It was bad of that woman," said my great-grandfather darkly, "to tell you that"), but even so, doubt remained.

Though I disliked the idea of God and Jesus (an opinion that I, correctly, believed unwise to share with my family), everyone assured me that Heaven was a good place and I would be happy there. But I had a number of questions that no one was able to answer. Was there television? Did people exchange gifts at Christmas? Would I have to go to school? I had read in *Peter Pan* that Peter goes part of the way with dead children so they will not be frightened. Perhaps, I thought on long boring Sundays when the idea of Heaven seemed oppressive, if Peter did come to get me I could talk him into taking me not to Heaven but to wherever it was that he lived, where I could hunt pirates and swim in the lagoon with the mermaids and probably have a whole lot of fun.

I had a cigar box full of small things I loved, which I kept beneath my bed. In it were some photographs, a fossil that I'd found, a topaz ring my mother had given me, and a china dog that my great-grandfather had got in his Christmas stocking when he was a little boy. There was also a silver dollar, an ivory chess piece that had no particular sentimental value but that I thought was pretty, and a lock of my great-grandmother's hair. I had some idea that I would be able to tuck this box under my arm and bring it along with me when the time came. I also kept in this box – because I had nowhere else secret enough to keep it – an old stereopticon slide that I had stolen

233

from my uncle's house in Meridian. It depicted savages, on some horrid African veld, eating a bloody dismembered thing that I was sure was a person. In normal consciousness (and it was not a drawing, but a photograph) it frightened me so much that I wouldn't even touch it, and I kept it well hidden beneath the other photographs at the bottom of the box. But sometimes, after I had taken my medicine, I would get it out and stare at it for hours – bewitched, in a kind of abstract way, at both the horror of the scene itself and its odd lack of power to affect me.

My mother, despite the accusations leveled at her, was actually not such a bad mother as all that. She liked to play with me, listened to me as carefully as if I were an adult, and bought me Goo Goo clusters (her own favorite candy) at the little store down the street from where she worked. And though she was admittedly a bit on the childish side, this childishness enabled her to understand me better than just about anyone else. She, too, had been a dreamy little girl who sleepwalked and had imaginary playmates.

We also shared the gift – alarming to everyone else – of being able to plunge ourselves into sort of eerie, self-induced fits. I would stare fixedly at a certain object and repeat a word or phrase until it became nonsense. Then, at some subsequent point, I was never sure exactly how long, I would snap to again and have absolutely no idea who or where I was, and be unable to recognize even the members of my own family. This lasted sometimes as long as three or four minutes, during which I would be completely insensible to shakes, snapped fingers, my frantically repeated name. I was able to do this anytime I felt like it, to amuse myself when bored – the amusing thing being always those first strange minutes when I woke up and saw everything and everyone for the very first time; like a person blind from birth who has just had the bandages unwrapped after an operation restoring sight. I stumbled upon this gift quite by accident when I was four or five, while sitting in an Italian restaurant in Memphis with my parents.

On this first occasion, while my father – a black-haired, bad-tempered stranger – shook my arm and shouted an unfamiliar name in my face, my mother remained oddly calm. Later, alone, she questioned me. I explained what had happened and how I had brought it about. She then told me that she had once been able to do the exact same thing, though the knack had been lost with age. (As I grew older, my talent, too, disappeared: the last time I was ever able to successfully pull this trick was when I was a sophomore in high school, bored in the back of biology class.) We discussed it for a while, the ins and outs. Her procedure, it seemed, was slightly different from mine. And yes, she said, if you were bored, it *was* sort of an interesting thing to do, wasn't it?

It was precisely this sort of thing that made some people consider my mother an unwholesome influence. But my mother had her own ideas about what was good for me. Though she did not want to offend my great-grandfather, for instance, I knew she did not like the way he constantly dosed me with medicine. This, I think, was partly instinct and partly because she did not like me to be forced, ever, to do anything I did not want to do, even if that something – like being made to eat liver or go to bed before ten – was unquestionably good for me. (I really do not think she would have had the heart to make me go to school were it not, she explained apologetically, the law.)

Whatever the case, she never personally administered either the licorice medicine or the codeine and, left to her own devices, would have peacefully allowed the bottles to gather dust on top of the refrigerator along with the fondue pot, the mathematics flash cards somebody had given me, and various other useless and unloved articles. "Has that maid been forgetting to give this child her medicine?" my great-grand-father would sometimes say fiercely, upon noting that the levels of the bottles were suspiciously high. It was his rounda-bout way of accusing my mother; the maid – as he was well aware – was terrified of him and would never have skipped a dose that was to be administered while she was on duty.

"Why, no," my mother would say sweetly. "I don't think Cleo would ever forget something like that, do you?" And sometimes, if he wasn't looking, she would wink at me.

My long sabbatical in the Land of the Poppy was by no means all pleasant. The good dreams, though sometimes effortless, usually required a bit of coaxing; when the bad ones came – as they frequently did, uninvited, like the evil fairy to the wedding feast – there was no forcing them back. I always had to sleep with a light on, and many nights woke screaming for Mother or Cleo. The worst dreams usually had to do with snakes, but the very worst dream of all still frightens me to think of, even though it is years since I last dreamed it. In it, a set of country-club types – smartly dressed, around what would have then been my parents' age – are gathered, cocktails in hand, around a barbecue grill. They are snickering with jaded amusement as one of their number – a handsome, caddish-looking fellow – holds a howling Persian cat over the barbecue, pushing its feet into the flames.

I always woke, howling myself, at this point. Though it was never quite clear exactly who these people were, it was obvious to me that what they were doing was Devil worship – which I knew all about from the maid – and that what I had glimpsed were only the more innocent, preliminary stages of the ritual. Unimaginable horrors lay beyond. Which set me thinking, as I lay back trembling in bed after Mother had come and gone, about Devils, and Hell, and all the bad things there were in the world, and what was *really* going to happen to me after I died, and I would start to scream again for Mother; and, frequently, it was lucky if anyone in the house got any sleep at all on those nights.

> O mother, lay your hand on my brow!
> O, mother, mother, where am I now?
> Why is the room so gaunt and great?
> Why am I lying awake so late? . . .
> What have I done, and what do I fear,
> And why are you crying, mother dear?
> – from "The Sick Child," by Robert Louis Stevenson

The worst nights were when my fever was high, when my teeth chattered even in the summertime and the doctor had to come. I was one of those children who never told anyone when I was starting to feel bad and always crawled behind the couch or under the bed and fell asleep, to be discovered hours later, dusty and disoriented, still wrapped in the Navaho blanket I had dragged from the cupboard. (I used always to play Indian on those afternoons I was getting sick, the red Navaho blanket assisting for a while to disguise, as I crawled through the tunnel behind the sofa-back or lay in my hunter's camp beneath the table, the first creeping bone-chill of advancing fever.) So by the time they had become alarmed and begun to call through the house for me I was already pretty far gone; and when the doctor came, I sometimes had to be rubbed with alcohol or packed in ice, shot full of Compazine and God knows what.

My fever deliriums – unlike the heavy, leaden codeine hallucinations – were characterized by a whirlwind, giddy quality, a nightmarish sense of lightness. When I closed my eyes, I felt like an escaped balloon, sailing in a rapid helium rush to the ceiling; when I opened them again, I was pulled back down to my bed with a jolt, as if someone had suddenly grabbed my string and given me a sharp, fast tug to earth. The room spun like a merry-go-round; my stuffed animals, suddenly glitter-eyed and sinister, gazed hungrily at me from the mantelpiece. And my bed refused to stay still. It rocked on its moorings, pulled from beneath by some fast, spiraling undertow in the old blue carpet that threatened to break the rope entirely and sweep me whirling bow to stern in helpless circles, out to sea.

My great-grandfather, when he came to see me on those nights, would frequently be near tears. He would sit on the bed, hold my hand, and not say much; this uncharacteristic silence disturbed me, as if he were not my great-grandfather at all but some mournful, bewitched old huntsman from a story-book, tongue-tied by the bad fairy, unable to speak. My bedroom seemed horribly elastic, as if it had somehow been pulled out of shape. And the gabble of my aunts in the background – normally the most comforting sound in the world to me – assumed a terrifying, singsong, nonsensical quality, while my mother flitted anxiously in the background, a slender ghost in her pale housecoat.

Sometimes, on the really bad nights, my great-grandfather would perform, with great seriousness, a bizarre old sickroom practice from his own boyhood that he called "fumigating." This involved lighting a rolled-up piece of newspaper on fire and walking through the house with it; it was horribly messy, since it sent black feathers of newspaper ash flying everywhere, but no one dared object because they all knew that the procedure pleased him so. It was, he said, in order to burn the germs out of the air, but it made my eyes sting, and served only, in my delirium, to fan the blazes of an already raging unreality – my somber, heavy-jowled great-grandfather, gravely brandishing his flaming torch that somehow, in my mind, got all mixed up with the flames leaping from the barbecue grill in my nightmare about the Persian cat, and this in turn mingling with the madhouse babble of my aunts, until my poor balloon of a head swelled up so big that I thought it was going to explode with a bang.

*

I have outlived my great-grandfather by a number of years. But pretty much until the day he died he was convinced, I think, that he would outlive me: and this prospect caused him terrible grief. I remember, in a faint, dreamlike way, seeing him pause in my doorway on one of the bad nights, after the lamp was out, he and my mother black silhouettes in the lighted corridor. Mournfully, mournfully, he shook his heavy old head. "I'm afraid," I heard him say to my mother, in a low but quite audible voice, "that that poor child won't live to see the morning."

"*Hush*, Granddaddy," my mother said in an agitated whisper. Then, leaning her head inside, she called to me in a bright voice: "Now, I want you to try to rest awhile, sugar. You call me if you need anything, you hear?"

The door swung shut. I was alone in the dark. The voices, now indistinct, receded along with the footsteps. And I was left, staring at the mottled shadow that the moonlit trees cast on the ceiling, waiting for that soft rap (Peter Pan? Jesus? I wasn't sure who) which I felt sooner or later was going to gently sound on my windowpane.

THE BLUE WALLET

William T. Vollmann

William T. Vollmann is the author of seven books. His eighth, *Butterfly Stories*, is a love story involving AIDS and the Khmer Rouge. In 1994, *The Rifles*, volume 6 of the *Seven Dreams* series, will be published.

"'The Blue Wallet' is a true story."

THE BLUE WALLET

The thing you dislike or hate will surely come upon you, for when a man hates, he makes a vivid picture in the subconscious mind, and it objectifies.

Florence Scovel Shinn, *Your Word is Your Wand* (1928)*

I

I loved Jenny most when, sitting beside her at sentimental movies, I would look away from the big screen where the beautiful actress was about to leave her lover forever, and see Jenny sitting upright in her chair, her black button-eyes concentrating so hard on the film, while she chewed and chewed her gum so earnestly, and I ran my forefinger below her eyes to verify that her face was wet, that Jenny was crying for the people on the screen, crying in perfect placid happiness over this debacle that had never happened; and I knew that after the movie was over Jenny would forget that she had cried, but she would feel refreshed by her tears. – How harmless it all was! Sometimes I myself, reminded by the actress of my own failures, would be scalded by a single heavy

---

* Marina del Rey, California: De Vorss & Company, p. 74.

tear; but this would not be a good feeling, and I would have to stroke Jenny's wet eyelid again with my finger to be soothed.

2

"I got in a fight with this fucking *fat woman*!" cried Boot-woman Marisa, who was now a bicycle messenger. Her legs were covered with bruises like rotten apples. "Right when you get to the end of the block you go up onto the sidewalk. And there was like a Mack truck coming right at me, and it was *totally obvious* that I was not gonna to be able to fucking avoid it unless I put on my brakes to *skid* to like avoid this woman. And I told her, I go, *MOVE!* I *yelled* really loud; I go, *MOVE!* and she goes, *Na!*" – and, imitating the woman's voice, Marisa expressed this determined negation in a birdlike screech – "and she *stands* right there, and I go, *Fine!* I'm gonna *hit you!* – so," she laughed, "I hit her, straight on. – And she *throws* me off my bike! She fuckin' throws me off my bike, an' my bike is goin' that way; I'm goin' this way, and I just got off and *punched her in the face!*'

"All *right!*" yelled everyone, with enthusiasm as blue-white and glowing as the most powerful cleansing powder. This enthusiasm could have eaten holes in walls.

"Jesus! *BAM!*" screamed Marisa, so loudly that the dog began to bark. "And I start screamin', '*Bitch*, what in the *fuck* you think you're doing? *Bitch!*' And she's opening up her little purse, and I'm just *waitin*' on her. *Bitch! Bitch!* And she goes, 'Well, you were in the wrong! You were in the wrong!' – and this black guy steps between us and goes, 'Come on don't get in a fight,' and I go, '*BITCH! YOU NIGGER-FUCKING WHORE!* – and she turns around and she goes, 'You got *that* shit correct,' and I go, 'Of *course!* You're too fuckin' *fat* for a white man to fuck your lousy ass.'"

244

3

Marisa never liked me as well as I liked her, partly (I suppose) because I wore glasses and did not know how to fight hand-to-hand, in the knightly fashion of skinheads and other street-conquerors, but partly also because my girlfriend was Korean. She did like me enough to be polite to Jenny, it being one of the rules that if somebody was your friend you did not fuck around with his lover, as was demonstrated when Ken's girl Laurie went up to Dickie at a skinhead party and touched his shoulder to ask him for a cigarette, and Bootwoman Dan-L appeared from nowhere and warned Laurie to stay out of her territory unless she wanted to get beaten up. So because Jenny was in my territory Marisa tolerated her. – After all, Marisa did like me O.K. This must have been why she sometimes came over and cooked my breakfast, huge omelettes with mushrooms and cheese and bacon and red onions, while in a subordinate frying pan her home fries sizzled obediently, becoming the golden-brown of Jenny's skin, at precisely the moment when the cheese melted and the mushrooms were done and the steam rose from the titanic omelette like a chord from some cathedral organ, and Marisa would start doing the dishes that had piled up in the sink and say, "Boy, your girlfriend doesn't take very good care of you, does she? What a mess this place is," and I'd stand beside her at the sink and feel good that Marisa was *being* good to me; and meanwhile I'd be drinking whiskey out of the bottle because I was hungry, and the sun swam through the fog and I felt dizzy and Marisa shook her pretty bald head at me and buttered my toast. Whenever I asked her to, she'd tell me stories, such as how the Pretty Boys who peddled ass on Polk Street moved into the Pink Palace and then the Sleazy Attic and became the Bootboys so that they could die early because the Bootboys were such *severe* skinheads ("Almost *all* the skinheads are already dead," sighed Marisa, "all the good ones"); and while Marisa went back into the kitchen to finish doing my dishes, her bootsister Thorn told me about how when she was in London her boyfriend Luigi got his eye popped out by the Italian Fascists, and then Marisa came back and told me about how when she was a thirteen-year-old girl in Chicago she started going with a skinhead named Sean, who was eighteen or twenty, and Marisa loved to hang out in Sean's apartment, which must have resembled the workshop of a medieval armorer because scattered through its dark dirty chambers was a Camaro in pieces – hubcaps under the bed (so I imagined it), bucket seats emplaced against the living room walls for conveniently screwing Marisa and other girls, the shiny silver exhaust pipe by the door to hit enemies with, the carburetor serving to deploy old socks and dirty underwear and a black leather flight jacket to best advantage, while the gas tank was actively poised beside the window, still full of gasoline and ready to be hurled down onto the dirty icy street like a flying bomb; and presumably Marisa and Sean must have always been stepping over screws, and the windshield was in the cold dark moldy bathroom, covered with grime; and buckler-plates of chassis hung overhead in Sean's bedroom, and the battery slowly leaked its acids through the floor; and now I have come to the end of all the auto parts that I know (except for the fan belt) – and Sean also possessed a stolen stop sign still in its cement base; possibly this was his hatstand. Although Marisa had not become Bootwoman Marisa yet, she loved and admired Skinhead Sean, so she tattooed Sean's name on her body and started unrolling her secret capabilities by piercing her ears half a dozen times and doing fucked-up things to her hair, none of which things Marisa's mother cared for, which was an incentive for Marisa to do them because Marisa's mother treated her like a baby; when she used the leftover batter to make a final tiny pancake she'd say, "Oh, there's a *Marisa-sized* pancake!" – and that *really* bothered Marisa. At that time, going to school started to bother her, too. Since she liked Sean better than she liked that listless two-hour commute from the North Side to the West Side, through cold dirty snow, with the cold wind blowing through the rusty railings, Marisa began sneaking down to the basement on those dark winter mornings instead of going to the bus, and when she heard the door-slam of her mother going to work Marisa would run back upstairs and dive into her warm bed and wait for Skinhead Sean to let himself in and hop into bed with her and watch TV until her mother came home at the end of the day, and then Marisa and Sean would go back to Sean's metal-happy apartment. – Sean was very strong. One time after she and Sean broke up, Marisa was at this AOF show, and there was this skinhead band named The Alive going *dwuuunggg!* on their bass guitars, and one of the guys in the band picked up on her, and Sean slammed his head against the wall. *BAAAAAAAM!* until the blood spurted out, and Marisa thought that was the coolest thing, and then Sean threw him off the stage, and Marisa *loved* it. – Years later she met another Sean in Marin County when she and Thorn were over there trying to pop some virgin boy-cherries, and wily Marisa bet the new Sean two hundred dollars that she had his name tattooed on her body (which of course she did). Sean went for it. – Poor Sean! – Since he didn't have the two hundred, he found himself under a universally acknowledged obligation to get her stoned on his dope for the rest of her life.*

---

* Of course this was not quite as good a scam as the one perpetrated by the bum in the Panhandle who comes up to you and bets you that he has your name tattooed on the head of his dick *regardless* of who you are, so of course you fall for it and he unzips his jeans and flicks his thing, and there on the head of the glans, sure enough, are tattooed the words YOUR NAME.

"Now, tell me about how you decided to become Boot-woman Marisa," I said, eating my eggs (eggs very lightly done, Marisa told me, are called "scared eggs"), while Marisa and Thorn sat at the table to keep me company, Thorn smoking and staring out the window and crushing her cigarette butts into a mug while Marisa drank tea (she never ate what she cooked at my house; she cooked it only for me).

"Well, I didn't decide to be Bootwoman Marisa," she said, "it was sort of like a gift." (At this remarkable commencement my mouth fell open, and I was in such a state of suspense that I almost became incontinent.)

"How's that?" I said. "They invited you?"

"Okay. I don't know if you knew me 'way back when, but when I would hang out on Haight Street and shit, I used to wear like really funky makeup. *Really* funky makeup. I don't know. I guess I had a much different attitude back then, about a *lot* of things. One day, Dee was like walking Rebel, right? And I saw her. So I was like, 'Hey, why don't I go with you?' And so we went, and we sat in the Park for hours and we talked. She was just like, 'You look like a *freak*, Marisa!' She just laid it right out, and she said, 'You look like a freak, and none of us want to hang out with you if you're gonna look like a freak.' So, we went back to her house, and she sat me down, and she took off all of that freaky makeup, and she said, 'Now that's *it*. If you want to revolt against the world, you know, I hate the world, too, but it all comes from inside, and if you do it from the outside, people aren't gonna respect you at all and you're never gonna get anything you want.' Then I sat down, and I took off all my stupid jewelery and shit, and the other Skinz were like, 'That's *good*!'" – Marisa pounded on the table. – "'You have the potential to become a *Bootwoman*!'" – She pounded again, so that all the silverware jumped. – "And that's what it was."

"You must have had your feelings hurt a little at first, when she said that about your makeup."

"Well, no," said Marisa. "I didn't really have any reason for doing it. I never did. I just did it. What the fuck. It's just one of those things, you know."

"Did you feel *different* when you got your head shaved?"

"Well, *fuck*, yeah! It was cool. It was pretty cool. People started treating me with a little more respect. I stopped getting like black eyes every other week," she laughed, "and Spike started teaching me how to fight. That was fun."

"Why did you use to get black eyes?"

"Because just everywhere I would go, people would look at me and just think I was some sort of fucking weirdo, and punch me in the face. That was *lots* of fun!"

"What would you do then?"

"I'd punch them back, naturally. But I didn't know how to fight for shit. And I'm still not like the *best*, but I can defend myself a lot better than I could back then. See, now I'd rather fight with a *large stick*. Like last night."

"What happened?"

"When, last night?" she said nonchalantly. "See, I went out looking for this girl, right? There's this girl on Haight Street, and she's a total lily. *She's* a freak now, and I wanna ... *change her mind*. I wanna let her see *my* side." She chuckled. "And I'm gonna do it with a stick!"

"How do you know her?"

Marisa and Thorn hissed contemptuously at me for this idiotic question. "I don't know her," said Marisa patiently.

"You just know the way she looks, huh?"

"Yep." Both girls laughed. "Yep," said Marisa. "She's definitely got like an attitude problem. I was *really* freaky looking. She's a nothing. She walks around in this *leather* that's big enough for her to fucking *live* in. And it's got like DROOLING IDIOTS written on the sleeve and all sorts of punk rock shit written all over it, and she walks around and she like hangs on all the guys. She's a total bimbo. Definite bimbo. So, *I think*

249

we need to send her to Boot Camp! What about you, Thorn?"

"Mmm," said Thorn boredly over her toast.

4

I had been Jenny's lover for more than a year. She had never told her family about me. The fact that I was white was a problem, although Jenny and I both struck each other with bludgeons of the heaviest loyalty whenever one of us was so unguarded as to consider swimming away from the attachment like a slippery fish. Jenny laughed and laughed whenever the sun came out, whether it was the sun in the sky or the less reliable sun in my blue-steel eyes, for, as her cousin Alice explained to me, there are many different suns; as evidence, Alice cited the tale of the great Korean poet who got drunk in front of His Majesty and composed the following lines: "I see three moons: One in the sky, one in your eye, and one in your cup." – When Alice stayed over, Jenny and Alice slept together in Jenny's waterbed and I slept on the living-room couch, because although Alice knew that Jenny and I usually shared Jenny's bed, Alice had not actually seen *evidence* that we did; if she had, she would have had to tell her mother, even though she loved Jenny and knew that Jenny would suffer when Alice's mother (who was so conscientious as to place folded tissue paper inside the family's shoes to keep them from accumulating dust overnight), was obliged by reason of that conscientiousness to call Jenny's mother on the phone; in the meantime Jenny and Alice and Alice's friend Ivy went out with me to a Korean restaurant on Geary Street; while I sat at a corner of the table stirring the raw egg and raw beef around in my cold metal bowl of Yuck Hwe Bi Bim Bop, the others laughed and talked in Korean and conducted symphonies with their chopsticks, turning hunks of marinated chicken and beef and tripe on the little grille which the unsmiling waitress had placed in the center of the table, and the meat sizzled and the yellow flames shot up and warmed our faces; and every now and then Jenny would take a wet lettuce leaf and shake it down onto the grille to discipline the flames. – "Ooh!" she cried gleefully, holding up another chunk of smoking meat. "Intestines!"

The Korean girls all had tiny mouths and smooth taut faces. When Jenny smiled, her face was like a wide golden shield. They talked about movies which they had seen. "It was such a comedy," laughed Alice. "I couldn't believe it." – "I heard it was really bad," said Ivy. – "I just liked the title music," said Alice. – They talked about Jenny's brother Richard, mostly in Korean so that I did not obtain a lengthy catalogue of his imputed qualities, but the way the Korean girls sighed through pursed lips made it clear that Richard had lapsed into error, and from the occasional English phrases which were thrown to me in afterthought I gradually came to understand that he was seeing a Korean-American girl who had Caucasian ways. "He's so serious about her," said Alice in melodious surprise. "But she knows nothing about Korea. I don't think she wouldn't fit too good in with the family." Alice saw me looking at her and took an earnest unsmiling bite of her tripe.

5

Sometimes when Ice was too drunk to take care of himself, Marisa and Thorn had to help him piss. Thorn would lean him up against a wall and hold his shoulder and grip the seat of his pants. Marisa would tell him to put his dick back in his pants, and if he couldn't do it she'd do for him.

*

6

In the summertime Jenny took me north so that she could splash around in cool lakes, and she'd coax me in, too, so that we'd be holding hands and wading deeper and deeper, trying not to walk on the pointed stones which pricked our feet almost pleasurably, like spicy food; until when the water was up to Jenny's thighs she'd jump in and then I'd jump in and the water was cold and the sun was hot and Jenny would be laughing and calling to me, "Come on! Make big swims! Big swims!"

7

"Have you ever made watermelon punch?" said Marisa, and I said no, and she leaned forward confidingly and said, "All you've gotta do is take like a watermelon, remove the rind, and put it in a blender – not for very long, though, just because all it is is water. You don't want to chop up the seeds. And then you put it through a strainer to get the seeds out, and you can put as *much* alcohol in it as you want, and you'll *never* taste it. It's pretty cool."

"I'll have to try that," I said.

"You should *do* that!" growled Marisa with a hoarse friendly kind of toughness.

"On Jenny and her pretty roommates," I said, eating my scared eggs – and there was one of those transitional silences, as Bootwoman Marisa came to herself and remembered that I was not as pure and wholesome as I had pretended to be, because I stooped to racial shame with Jenny, and she turned to Thorn and said dryly, "Jenny is his girlfriend."

"Oh," said Thorn, knowing enough from Marisa's tone to

take on an air of distaste, although she did not yet know Jenny's sin.

"And," grinned Marisa, screwing her voice into a cheerful singsong, "she's going to look really *gross* by the time she's *forty*!"

I laughed, but as I recall my laugh now it seems to have been a somewhat insincere, wooden laugh, my empire of humor already riddled with termites, and Marisa moved in for the kill, saying, "I'm warning you, Bill, dump her while you've still got the chance!" – and to Thorn she explained my shameful secret, in the parentheses used by two people speaking of a third's terminal disease: "(She's Oriental.)"

"I'll pass that on to her," I said, still laughing in my loud insincere way, and Marisa said rapidly and coolly, "You do that, Bill. You just do that."

8

I had a party, for which Jenny made artichoke dip, kahlua cake, sweet-and-sour chicken and a variety of other foods, abetted by her housemate, Margaret; and Marisa and Thorn were invited. Most of the other guests were Jenny's Korean friends. When Marisa came in, she cried out, "Hey, Bill, I brought you a present. We were at the St. John's Grill, and we stole you this ashtray fair and square!", and I was touched and thanked Marisa with a big hug, but Jenny's friends contracted, and I took Marisa and Thorn into my bedroom, away from the drinks, and closed the door so that we could shoot my airgun, and the girls laughed at the target and yelled, "That's Cougar's head! – That's Rona's face! I'm going to *kill* that slut!", and Marisa shouted, "*KEE-lore!*" – meaning, "KILLER!" Thorn and Marisa mainly stayed in the kitchen after that, helping Margaret mix up drinks, since this affair was a little quieter than the skinhead parties which often started in early afternoon when you pulled your boots on and buttoned up your black jacket nice and tight and took the bus down to the Tenderloin or the Fillmore where you knocked on the door of a garage and two beefy Skinz looked you over and took a dollar for beer and one of them stamped your hand with a dinosaur stamp to verify that you had paid, allowing you to go on through the garage and up a passageway that took you into a barren courtyard of stamped-down dirt with rickety apartment buildings towering around you, and skinheads and bootwomen permeated this snakepit, some ascending the fire escape to the first-storey terrace, the second-storey terrace, the third-storey terrace where things were dark and rotten, and at any point a skinhead might block your way and you'd have to be awfully polite to get past him and keep climbing to the fourth-storey terrace where Bootwoman Dan-L yawned and scratched her new-shaven head, and Marisa sat on the stairs with other skinhead girls in a pool of beer, which trickled slowly down the stairs in a mad uncaring way, like Ice's piss, losing itself in Marisa's jacket and under Marisa's leg and behind Bootwoman Kim's shoulder and so on to the ocean. For the most part Marisa said nothing, because she was already very stoned.* She stared out across the world; you could see clouds here, and dirty windows, and laundry hanging from distant fire escapes, and at any time you could look down on the yard as if from a low-budget watchtower, to see the Skinz lined up at the beer keg to pump Bud into plastic cups for themselves, their buddies, their girls; and in the middle of

---

* This was not too long after Marisa lost her job at the bakery on Castro Street because the owner read an official government report that skinheads were racist and sexist. – What a surprise! – "I don't have anything to say about that," said Marisa defiantly. – "Well, I can't have someone working here with those opinions," said the owner, whose boyfriend was Jewish. Marisa told her to fuck off.

that grey sad space there was a grey sad tree that rose three storeys; and the Skinz tied a rope around a cupful of beer and threw the rope up around a branch of that tree and caught the free end and started raising the cup very slowly and carefully until it was about thirty feet high and then they began to swing the rope back and forth, back and forth as they raised it, the beery pendulum whizzing merrily over everyone's faces, and then the Skinz got excited and started really yanking with their big tattooed arms and the cup upended at about fifty feet and rained beer on everybody and some girls in black frowned and said, "*Fuck* you," and some Skinz laughed, and some individuals were not noticeably affected. Everybody was getting a little drunker and louder now. Some guy ambled up to Nazi Joe and asked him what his boot size was. Nazi Joe stopped talking to his friends and turned around very slowly and said, "Why, do you want to *steal my boots?*" He knocked the guy's head against the wall and punched it hard five times! Blood burst out of the guy's ears. After that, my friend Ken kept going up to Nazi Joe and asking him what his boot size was. Nazi Joe only laughed, I guess because it mattered who asked him. Later on, it got dark, and things *really* got going; Ken got drunk and took a girl whose face he never saw into the basement and porked her against the wall. – So Marisa and Thorn, in short, were not entirely at ease in the more ideologically flabby surroundings of my party where Jenny and her friends talked about Macy's and other topics which Jenny forgot about later, and everyone else stood around the living room table and sipped the Chivas Regal which Jenny had bought me down in L.A., or else they sat on the sofa and talked about new innovations in computer programming, such as the UNIX chip that was due on the market for micros, and with two of my favorite mechanical engineers I discussed the possibility of printing books on plastic paper, and I took my schoolmates Paul and Nancy into my room to show them the 1902

Tamerlane edition of Poe that Jenny had bought me for my birthday for a hundred and fifty dollars, and Jenny came over to make sure that I was eating the food that she had made for me, and Nancy and I discussed five books for five minutes, and then Paul and I each had another drink, and Jenny had another drink, and I went back to the kitchen to visit Thorn and Marisa and joke with them about the size of my dick. – "*That's* nice!" they chorused laughing. I leaned up against the refrigerator and they leaned up against the sink, and I drank tequila and beer and tequila and beer but Thorn drank lightly in order to make sure that Marisa drank lightly, because Marisa got violent when she drank too much. – "San Francisco used to be the skinhead capital of the world," sighed Marisa by the sink. "Now it's so pathetic, it makes me want to puke." – My flatmate Martin came in and grinned at us uncertainly. – Meanwhile my other guests drank margaritas and walked around the living room table and stood up and sat down and talked and avoided Marisa and Thorn, while Marisa and Thorn avoided *them*; and Jenny drank Old Bushmill's and got very dizzy. Thorn told me about her drawings (she has since been accepted by a fine art school), and Marisa told me about the time she had belonged to a ballet troupe in Australia (which I have never visited and therefore enjoy imagining), getting picked up on wherever she went, not that she cared since she knew she'd never see those men again; and at the Hotel King's Cross in Sydney she played strip poker in the boys' room until the Director came back, so freckled Marisa had to get her clothes back on real fast and crawl out on the window-ledge to get back into her room, and the Director saw her, so she bitched Marisa out for that and then Marisa had to be watched for days and days, until finally there was a free day when members of the troupe could go out in groups, but Marisa said *fuck* this shit; she was going to hitchhike, so she set out for a fleamarket to buy her San Francisco friends some stupid Australian T-shirts and the Director saw her sneaking back and wrote up a report on her for that, too, but Marisa, who at that time had greenish-red hair which was short in some places and long in other places (and in other places still it just went *tiiing!*), didn't care because at the fleamarket she'd gotten picked up by some guy who was *really* good looking; meanwhile everywhere they traveled around the circumference of this reddish-brown continent, a more faithful admirer still followed Marisa in a chocolate-brown Rolls-Royce, and she would always get mixed up and try to get in on the driver's side instead of the passenger side because the roads and cars were opposite from the ones in America, but Marisa's admirer just laughed; he was about forty, and the Director, who was seventy-two, had a *big* crush on him, not that it did the Director any good; and then the troupe danced at the Sydney Opera House and another man fell in love with Marisa and took her out to dinner, but the Director caught her sneaking back into the hotel late at night, totally fucked-up, so Marisa was barred from dancing for the next two performances, and in the next city the guy in the chocolate-brown Rolls-Royce gave Marisa enough pot to get the whole company completely stoned, which she did, so they had to call off the next performance, and Marisa got expelled from the company, although they couldn't send her home early because that would have cost too much, so she got to stay on and get into as much trouble as she wanted. Finally the company had to stop boarding her with families who had sons. The people were *cool* in Australia, except that they spread Vegemite on toast.

9

At the party, Jenny's blue wallet disappeared. She did not notice until the next day because she had drunk too much.

257

Jenny was very careless with her belongings, and had lost her wallet several times before. Once we were coming home from a movie, and just as we got out of the car Jenny realized that she did not have her wallet. We drove back to the theater and did not see it; we went to the bar where I had bought Jenny a drink and it was not there; then we saw it lying in the middle of the street, miraculously unrifled. Evidently Jenny had dropped it while unlocking the car. So I was now certain that the wallet would soon be found, but it wasn't. Jenny was in a frenzy of anger and panic. Her keys were gone, too. Evidently she had left her wallet and keys on the table all night, beside the drinks and potato chips.

"It was your friends!" shouted Jenny in my ear. "*You* invited them here! This is your fault! And they took my keys, so they can break in to your apartment and my apartment and my car! And they have my goddamn credit cards! You're responsible for this! I bet Marisa's down at Macy's right now, buying bluejean things. Oh! I got a headache that just won't go away. I told you not to invite those Nazi Skinz, 'cause they're delinquents!"

"Let's look for it downstairs," I said. "Maybe you left it there." At that time, still convinced that the wallet would turn up at any moment, I still did not understand how angry Jenny was. I preferred to be entertained with her ludicrous image of Bootwoman Marisa going to Macy's.

"In this instance, I just remember it so vividly," Jenny insisted, "'cause what I did, I left the wallet in the car, then I went to your room directly, thinking I had the wallet with me, but I didn't, so I went back and got it, and I sat down and I put the wallet there. As it is, the only places I could have put it is in the kitchen or in the living room. Who else would do it? It had to be your goddamn skinhead friends!"

"They wouldn't do anything like that," I said.

"They came in with a stolen ashtray!" Jenny screamed.

"Maybe they wouldn't steal from you, but they don't know me. Far as I'm concerned, you can forget about me if you ever see them again. Sometimes I hate you so much. I don't know why I ever hung around with you. You don't ever care about me. You think your criminal friends are more important. Top of everything else, I bet you're glad they stole my wallet and keys. I'm telling you, I don't ever want to see those bad girls again."

"Jenny," I began, but she hit me and said, "Don't say 'Jenny' like that to me! They have my wallet and my keys. What am I supposed to do now? I want you to look all over the house again. Look through the trash. Maybe somebody threw the stuff away by mistake. I'm not gonna be able to sleep tonight."

We did not find the blue wallet.

"I told you they were like that," Jenny said. "You better promise me right now that you're never gonna see those skinheads anymore."

"No," I said.

"Then you're not gonna see me anymore," Jenny said, tears rolling down her plump golden cheeks. Jenny did not mean exactly what she had said; she meant only the worst thing that she could think of.

10

"At first I thought they were really funny," said my flatmate Martin, preparing to embrace the views of his class. "But then I decided they were kind of frightening when I realized that they were serious."

"I don't think they did it," I said.

But Martin was certain that they had.

*

II

There are times when you know that something is not right anymore or that something is over, but with that knowledge comes a sick premonition of what it will mean to you, as if you suddenly realized that the ground was dissolving under you, and under *that* was darkness and dirt and crawling bugs, and you want the comfort of solid ground back so much that you will keep to the thing that is not right, willing it to be right for another day's journey, a few thousand more steps, because you want to not think about the dark hole waiting for you, and if you *can* delay the collapse of the ground you will certainly do it. I had felt this way toward my relationship with Jenny on many occasions, and I felt it now regarding distrusting my friends. I could not believe that Marisa had taken anything, and I could not believe that anyone else had taken anything.

Jenny hardly slept for two nights. – "These skinheads, these Bootwomen," she said, "I wonder if they disapprove of me. I wonder if they hate me 'cause I'm Asian girl. Maybe they want to hurt me. I mean, they're Nazis!" – I had not told her what the skinheads said about her, but even so she knew that one night a month or two from now, when we had forgotten the incident, Marisa would come sneaking up to the door and unlock it with the stolen keys, and then Dickie and Mark Dagger and Chuckles and Blue and Yama and Hunter and Dee and Spike and Nazi Joe and Ice and Dan-L would then come charging up the stairs and Dagger would shatter the banister with one kick of his Nazi boots and Yama would smash in the curtained glass door of Margaret's room and start hitting Margaret over the head with a chair and the rest of them would come back into Jenny's room and find Jenny and me sleeping on her waterbed and Dickie would slit the waterbed with a sharpened tin can and the skinheads would yell at us,

"All right, where's the money? Where's the money?" – and Marisa would tell me I had one minute to get out and leave Jenny to her fate, and then Yama would hit her in the face and say, "Shut up, bitch! We're gonna carve 'em all!", and Chuckles and Blue would piss into our faces and Ice would begin to dismantle the living room stereo with tender care.

12

After two weeks, Jenny became resigned. We took to locking her door and my door with the deadbolts, which had not been used before, and which Jenny had not had keys for. Her face was still puffy with tears. For Jenny, who loved clean things and neat things and organized things despite her own careless-ness, the loss of the wallet was an aesthetic disaster as well as a security risk. "I wish I misplaced it," she said mournfully, "though it really doesn't make any difference, 'cause I still have to go through all the hassle. It's been so many days now. Get me a new bank card. Call about my driver's license. I'll cancel Macy's card. Now, today I want you to eat a good lunch 'cause I'm gonna cook the Mom's meat for you. Promise me you'll eat a good lunch. Do you promise? And you want frozen chicken nuggets?" A little later she was humming a Korean song about barley fields.

13

Meanwhile, Jenny's other brother Adam came up for a visit. He was a slender self-confident young man who liked to wear polo shirts. Jenny adored him and was always calling him long-distance late at night to give him advice, which I am not certain that he consistently followed. The look of a baby brother still clung to him. He and his friends from Yale carried in a bucket of giant clams which they had gathered on the beach. Jenny dumped the clams into the sink at once and began scrubbing their shells with soapy steel wool to get rid of every subversive germ; in Jenny's world, as in Marisa's, every alien must be sterilized. She steamed the biggest ones, who sighed futilely through their excurrent siphons; the rest I popped into the freezer for five minutes to weaken them so that their numb adductor muscles would be unable to resist my knife; already sick from the long oceanless ride in the trunk of Adam's car, they cracked open in easy surrender to their sushi doom. I carried them out on a plate and set them before Adam, who sat at the dining room table loudly laughing with his friends, these boys evidently respecting him as their leader, much as Izutsu and Sagara respected Isao in Yukio Mishima's *Runaway Horses* because Isao was going to turn them into rightwing extremists and then become divine by cutting open his belly in a ritual rapture that would most likely make the sun explode behind his closed eyelids; I imagine that Adam's clams felt this way when I slit them open; but Adam accepted them without seeing either them or me and passed them to his disciples, who cried, "Adam! Adam!", and Adam gave one clam to Jenny and then ate one, and passed the clams to Izutsu and Sagara again, who doubtless were learning how to become divine with him at Yale. – "Well, Adam, do you need anything?" I said. He went on talking to his friends. But when he saw me in Jenny's bed, his jaw fell and he shook his head very slowly and went out, leaving the bedroom door ajar, and before driving home the next day he taped a note in Korean to Jenny's door. The note said "Elder Sister: I was very disappointed about your boyfriend. I was ashamed of you. Please think of Mother and Grandmother." – How to explain this revulsion that the colors of the rainbow feel for each other?

In her nightgown, biting a juicy peach, Jenny sat down on

her waterbed and called Adam. I had made her do it. "I'll be there late," she said. "Can you do me a favor? Tell Grandmother not to sleep in my room. Margaret and I will be sleeping there. Another thing. Rent me a couple movies. And tell Mom to take the big car to work. And tell Richard not to go out with the big car early."

She swaddled herself in blankets. "Now, I keep forgetting to tell you this, but you're really rude leaving that letter. What do you mean, honest opinion? And you were really rude. He kept trying to talk to you, be nice to you. You acted like a brat. – What do you mean? – Adam, you really have to behave. What is honest opinion? No. Listen to me. Listen. Bill's my boyfriend, and you have to – Adam! – Listen! *Listen!* LISTEN! You say you love me, but if you do, you have to respect. . . – *Listen!* LISTEN!

"Adam, I don't understand why you think things that way. I want to know why you came to that kind of opinions. You have to defend your opinions. – No, you have to provide a reasonable cause. You can't say, I just don't feel good. Adam. Adam. *Adam!* I know you're upset. But you cannot just act on first impressions. What do you think now? What do you think now? You see, you don't know him and you said things that really hurt me. I want to understand why you wrote that letter, why you behave that way. – Just because of appearance? In what way? What do you mean, you don't remember? I'm not criticizing you, I'm asking your opinion. Just because one's different? That note you wrote said you're ashamed of me. Why, why, why, *why*? What type? What type is he? He didn't do anything to you."

She made her little brother cry on the phone (which gave me satisfaction), but he still hated me.

14

If this had been a Chekhovian story, or a tale from de Maupassant, the blue wallet would have turned up eventually, proving by its determined refusal to be elsewhere that all suspicions had been reified to the point of logical and moral death, so that now, as all the thought-chains strained inside our brains, and the little homunculi downshifted the thought-gears to provide maximum mechanical advantage in their futile attempt to drag the blocks of leaden trust back to safety, those corrupted metal concepts hung upon the summit of that black waterfall that everything goes down eventually, and the homunculi did their dwarfish best but the chains snapped and the trust careened down the waterfall and fell into the spray below and we never saw it again, but the blue wallet remained to remind us of our limited beings.

In fact, I did find Jenny's wallet eventually. It had fallen into a paper bag under the living room desk, along with her keys.

We went to other movies, and Jenny sat with her knuckles pressed raptly against her cheeks, happily crying at the spectacle of a newly imagined romantic disintegration.

15

A month before Marisa's seventeenth birthday, Jenny and I met her at a party on Haight Street. In the doorway it said: S.F. BOOTWOMEN - THEY'LL ROB YOU OF YOUR MONEY, YOUR PRIDE AND YOUR MAN! Marisa did not have her bicycle messenger job anymore because she'd come riding into some Bank of America office tower with an urgent message, and a secretary or petticoat executive had looked her up and down in a sneering sort of way, so Marisa called her a bitch or possibly a fucking bitch, and the bitch had complained and the messenger service had lost the B. of A. account and so Marisa was fired. — Jenny and I were sitting together on the sofa listening to the Supremes going, "*Ba*-by, *ba*-by! Where did our

264

love go!", at a volume suitable for launching killing vibrations through our tympanic membranes and into our bony labyrinths and so into our membranous labyrinths to cause special damage; and Jenny was trying to get me to dance with her.

"Come and dance," she said.

"I don't feel like it," I said.

"Please dance with me," she said.

"No," I said.

Marisa came into the living room and started dancing by herself, looking very soft and furry with her sweater and the grey downy stubble on her head, and Marisa's eyes were closed, and she danced and danced on the rug, and Jenny said wryly, "Marisa! Pull him up and make him dance. I've never seen him dance" – and Marisa came over and stared expressionlessly into Jenny's face, and said coolly, "And you never will."

For Jacob Dickinson and Janis Kibe Dickinson

FOREVER OVERHEAD

David Foster Wallace

David Foster Wallace was born in 1962. He is the author of *The Broom of the System* (1987); of *Girl with Curious Hair* (1989), a collection of stories and novellas; and, with Mark Costello, of *Signifying Rappers* (1990), a book about music and U.S. culture. His next novel, *Infinite Jest*, will, with any luck, be published sometime in 1995.

FOREVER OVERHEAD

HAPPY BIRTHDAY. Your thirteenth is important. Maybe your first really public day. Your thirteenth birthday is the chance for people to recognize that important things are happening to you.

And things have been happening to you for the past half year. You have seven hairs in your left armpit now. Twelve in your right. Hard dangerous spirals of brittle black hair. Crunchy, animal hair. There are now more of the hard curled hairs around your privates than you can count without losing track. Other things. Your voice is rich and scratchy and moves between octaves without warning or pattern. Your face has begun to get shiny when you don't wash it. And two weeks of a deep and frightening ache this past spring left you with something dropped down from inside: your sack is now full and vulnerable, a commodity to be protected. Hefted and strapped in tight supporters that stripe your buttocks red. You have grown into a new fragility.

And dreams. For months past, there have been dreams like nothing before: moist and busy and distant, full of yielding curves, frantic pistons, soft warmths and great fallings; and you have awakened through fluttering lids to a rush and a gush and a toe-curling scalp-snapping jolt of feeling from an inside deeper than you knew you had, spasms of a deep sweet hurt, the streetlights through your window blinds cracking into sharp stars against the black bedroom ceiling, and on you a dense white jam that lisps between trembling legs, trickles and sticks, cools on you, hardens and clears until there is nothing but gnarled knots of pale solid animal hair in the morning shower, and in the wet tangle a clean sweet smell you can't believe comes from anything you made inside you.

The smell is, more than anything, like this swimming pool; a bleached sweet salt detergent, a flower with chemical petals. The pool has a strong clear blue smell, though you know the smell is never as strong when you are actually in the blue water, as you are now, all swum out, resting back along the shallow end, the hip-high water lapping at your locus of change.

Around the deck of this old public pool on the western edge of Tucson is a cyclone fence, the color of pewter, decorated with a bright tangle of locked bicycles. Beyond this a hot black parking lot full of white lines and glittering cars. A dull field of dry grass and hard weeds, old dandelions' downy heads exploding and snowing up in a rising wind. And past all this, reddened by a round slow September sun, are mountains, jagged, their tops' sharp angles darkening into definition against a deep red tired light. Against the retreating red their sharp connected tops form a spiked line, a graph, an electrocardiogram of a dying day.

The clouds are taking on color by the rim of the sky. The water is bright spangles off soft blue, five-o'clock warm, and the pool's smell, like the other smell, connects with a chemical haze inside you, an interior dimness that bends light to its own ends, softens the difference between what leaves off and what begins.

Your party is tonight. This afternoon, on your birthday, you have asked to come to the pool. You wanted to come alone, but a birthday is a family day, your family wants to be with you. This is nice, and you can't talk about why you wanted to come alone, and really truly maybe you didn't want to come alone, so they are here. Sunning. Both your parents sun. Their deck chairs have been marking time all afternoon, rotating, tracking the sun's curve across a desert sky heated to an eggy film. Your sister plays Marco Polo near you in the shallows with a group of loud thin girls from her grade. She is being blind now, her Marco's being Polo-ed. She is shut-eyed, twirling to calls, spinning at the hub of a wheel of shrill girls in bathing caps. Her cap has raised rubber flowers. There are limp old pink petals that shake as she lunges at blind sound.

There at the other end of the pool is the diving tank and the high board's tower. Back on the deck behind is the SN CK BAR, and on either side, bolted above the cement entrances to dark wet showers and lockers, are gray metal bullhorn speakers that send out the pool's radio music, the jangle flat and tinny thin.

Your family likes you. You are bright and quiet, respectful to elders – though you are not without spine. You are largely good. You look out for your little sister. You are her ally. You were six when she was zero and you had the mumps when they brought her home in a soft yellow blanket; you kissed her hello on her feet out of concern that she not catch your mumps and your pain. Your parents say that this augured well. That it set the tone. They now feel they were right. In all things they are proud of you, satisfied, and they have retreated to the warm distance from which pride and satisfaction travel. You all get along well.

Happy Birthday. It is a big day, big as the roof of a whole Southwest sky. You have thought it over. There is the high board. They will want to leave soon. Climb out and do the thing.

Shake off blue clean. You're half-bleached, loose and soft,

tender, pads of fingers gently wrinkled. The mist of the too-clean smell is in your eyes; it breaks light into gentle color. Knock your head with the heel of your hand. One side has a flabby echo. Cock your head to the side and hop: sudden heat in your ear, delicious, and brain-warmed water turns cold on the soft nautilus of your ear's outside. You can hear harder tinnier music, closer shouts, much movement in much water.

The pool is crowded late. Here are thin children. Hairy animal men. Disproportionate boys, all legs and necks and knobby joints, shallow-chested, vaguely birdlike. Like you. Here are old people moving tentatively through shallows on stick legs, feeling at the water with their hands, out of several elements at once.

And girl-women, women, evokers of wows, curved like fruit or instruments, skin burnished brown-bright as staircases of old wonder, suit tops held by delicate knots of fragile colored string against the pull of soft mysterious weights, suit bottoms riding low over the gentle juts of hips totally unlike your own, immoderate swells and swivels that melt in light into a sur-rounding space that cups and accommodates the soft curves as things precious. You almost understand.

The pool is a system of event. Here now there are: laps, splash fights, divings, corner tag, sharks and minnows, Marco Polo (your sister still the blind player, halfway to tears, the game teetering on the edge of cruelty, odd man out, not your business to save or embarrass). Two clean little bright-white boys, caped in cotton towels, run along the poolside with tiny steps until the guard stops them dead with a shout through his bullhorn. The guard is as brown as a tree, blond hair in a vertical line on his stomach, his head in a jungle explorer hat, his nose a white triangle of cream. A girl has an arm around a leg of his little tower. He's bored.

Get out now and go past your parents, who are sunning and reading, not looking. Forget your towel. Stopping for the towel means talking, and talking means thinking. You have decided that being scared is caused mostly by thinking. Go right by, toward the tank at the deep end. Over the tank is a great iron tower of dirty white. A board protrudes from the top of the tower like a tongue. The pool's concrete deck is rough and hot against your soft bleached feet. Each of your footprints is thinner and fainter. Each shrinks behind you on the hot stone and disappears.

Lines of plastic wieners bob around the tank, which is its own field, empty of the rest of the pool's convulsive ballet of heads and arms. The tank is as blue as energy, small and deep and perfectly square, flanked by lap lanes and SN CK BAR and rough hot deck and the bent late shadow of the tower and board. The tank is quiet and still and healed between fallings.

There is a rhythm to it. Like breathing. Like a machine. The line for the board curves back from the tower's ladder. The line moves in its curve, straightens as it nears the ladder. One by one, people reach the ladder and climb. One by one, spaced by the beats of hearts, they reach the tongue of the board at the top. And once on the board they pause, exactly the same tiny heartbeat pause. And their legs take them to the end, where they all give the same stomping hop, arms curving out as if to describe something circular, total; they come down heavy on the edge of the board and make it throw them up and off.

It's a swooping machine, lines of stuttered movement in a sweet late bleach mist. You can watch from the deck as they hit the cold blue sheet of the tank. Each falling makes a white that plumes and falls into itself and spreads and fizzes. Then blue clean comes up from the deep in the middle of the white and spreads like thick smooth pudding, making it all new. The tank heals itself. Three times as you go by.

You are in line. Look around. Look bored. Few talk in the

line. Everyone seems by himself. Most look at the ladder, look bored. You almost all have crossed arms, chilled by a late dry rising wind on the constellations of blue-clean chlorine beads that cover your backs and shoulders. Beside you is the edge of the tower's shadow, the tilted black tongue of the board's image. The system of shadow is huge, long, off to the side, joined to the tower's base at a sharp late angle.

Almost everyone in line for the board watches the ladder. Older boys watch older girls' bottoms as they go up. The bottoms are in soft thin cloth, tight nylon plastic stretch. The good bottoms move up the ladder like pendulums in soft liquid, a gentle uncrackable geometric code. The girls' legs make you think of deer. Look bored.

Look past it. Look across. You can see so well. Your mother is in her deck chair, reading, squinting, her face tilted up to get light on her cheeks. She hasn't looked to see where you are. She sips something sweet out of a bright can. Your father is on his big stomach, back like the hint of a hump of a whale, shoulders curling with animal spirals, skin oiled and soaked red-brown with too much sun. Your towel is hanging off your chair and a corner of the cloth now moves – your mother hit it as she waved away a sweat bee that likes what she has in the can. The bee is back right away, seeming to hang motionless over the can in a blurred sweet air. Your towel is one big face of Yogi Bear.

At some point there got to be more line behind you than in front of you. Now no one in front except three on the slender ladder. The woman right before you is on the low rungs, looking up, wearing a tight black nylon suit that is all one piece. She climbs. From above there is a falling, then a plume and a healing. Now two on the ladder. The pool rules say one on the ladder at a time, but the guard never shouts about it. The guard makes the rules by shouting or not shouting.

This woman above you should not wear a suit as tight as

the suit she is wearing. She is as old as your mother, and as big. She is too big and too white. Her suit is full of her. The backs of her thighs are squeezed by the suit and look like cheese. Her legs have abrupt little squiggles of cold blue shattered vein under the white skin, as if something were broken, hurt, in her legs. Her legs look like they hurt to be squeezed, full of curled Arabic lines of cold broken blue. Her legs make you feel like your legs hurt.

The rungs are very thin. It's unexpected. Thin round iron rungs laced in slick wet Safe-T felt. You taste metal from the smell of wet iron in shadow. Each rung presses into the bottoms of your feet and dents them. The dents feel deep and they hurt. You feel heavy. How the big woman over you must feel. The hand bars along the ladder's sides are also so thin. It's like you might not hold on. You've got to hope the woman holds on, too. And of course it looked like fewer rungs from far away. You are not stupid.

Get halfway up, in the open, big woman placed above you, and a solid bald muscular man on the ladder underneath your feet. The board is still high overhead, invisible from here. But it rumbles, and flaps, and a boy you can see for a few contained feet through the thin rungs falls in a flash of a line, a knee held to his chest, doing a splasher. There is a huge exclamation point of foam into your field of sight, then scattered claps into a great fizzing. Then the silent sound of the tank healing to new blue.

More thin rungs. Hold on tight. The radio is loudest here, one speaker at ear level over a concrete locker room entrance. Grab the thin bars tight and twist and look down behind you and you can see people buying snacks below. You can see down into it: the clean white top of the vendor's billed cap, tubs of ice cream, steaming brass freezers, scuba tanks of soft drink syrup, snakes of soda hose, bulging boxes of salty

275

popcorn kept hot in the sun. Now that you're overhead you can see the whole thing.

There's wind. It's windier the higher you get on the ladder. The wind is thin; through the shadow it's cold on your wet white skin. It makes a shivered whistle in your ears. Four more rungs to the top of the white tower. The rungs hurt your feet very much. They are thin and let you know just how much you weigh. You have real weight on the ladder. The ground wants you back.

Now you can see just over the top of the ladder. You can see the board. The woman is there. There are two ridges of red, hurt-looking callused skin on the backs of her ankles. She stands at the beginning of the board, your eyes on her ankles. The solid man under you is looking through the rungs into the contained space the woman's fall will pass through.

She pauses for just that beat of a pause. There's nothing slow about it at all. It makes you cold. In no time she's at the end of the board, up, down on it, it bends low like it doesn't want her. Then it flaps and throws her up and out, away, her arms opening out to inscribe that circle, and gone. She disappears in a dark blink. And there's time before you hear the hit below.

Listen. It does not seem good, the way she disappears into a time that passes before she sounds. Like a stone down a well. But you think she did not think so. She was part of a rhythm that excludes thinking. And you have made yourself part of it, too. The rhythm seems blind. Like ants. Like a machine.

You decide this needs to be thought about. It may, after all, be all right to do something scary without thinking, but not when the scariness is the not thinking itself. Not when not thinking turns out to be wrong. Here wrongnesses have piled up blind: affected boredom, weight, thin rungs, hurt feet, space cut into laddered parts that melt together only in a disappearance that takes time. The wind on the ladder not what anyone would expect. When it all turns out to be different you should get to think. It should be required.

The ladder is full behind you. It is fed by a solid line that stretches away and curves into the dark of the tower's skewed shadow. People's arms are crossed. It is a machine that moves only forward.

You climb up onto the thing's tongue. The board turns out to be long. As long as the time you stand. Time slows. It thickens around you as your heart gets more and more beats out of every second, every movement in the system below you.

The board is long. From where you stand it stretches into a nothing. It is a flatness covered with a rough white plastic stuff. The rough white surface is freckled and lined with pale watered red: drops of pool water that are catching low light over sharp mountains. The rough white stuff of the board is wet. And cold. Your feet are hurt from the thin rungs and have a great ability to feel. They feel your weight. There are handrails running above the beginning of the board. They are set low, and you almost have to bend over to hold on to them. They are just for show, no one holds them. Holding on shakes the rhythm of the machine.

It is a long cold rough white plastic fiberglass board, veined with the sad pink color of old candy.

But at the end of the white board, the edge, where you go off, there are two areas of darkness. Two flat shadows in the broad light. Two vague black ovals. The end of the board has two dirty spots.

They are from people before you. Your feet as you stand here are tender and soft and dented, hurt by the rough wet surface, and you see that the two dark spots are from people's skin. They are skin, abraded from feet by the violence of the disappearance of people with weight. More people than you could count without losing track. The suddenness of their disappearing leaves little bits of soft tender feet behind, bits and shards and curls of skin that dirty and darken and tan as they lie tiny and smeared in the sun at the end of the board. They pile up and get smeared and mixed together. They get dark in circles.

No time is passing outside you at all. It is amazing. The late ballet below is slow motion, the broad movements of mimes in blue jelly. If you wanted you could really stay here forever, vibrating so fast you float still and magic in time, like a bee over something sweet.

But they should clean the board. Anybody who thought about if for even a second would think that they should clean the board of people's skin, of two black collections of what's left of before, spots that look like eyes, like blind cross-eyed eyes.

Where you are now is still and quiet. Wind radio shouting splashing not here. No time and no real sound but your blood squeaking wild in your head.

Overhead here means sight and smell. The smells are intimate, newly clear. The smell of bleach's special flower, but out of it other things rise to you like a weed's seeded snow. You smell deep yellow popcorn. Sweet tan oil, hot coconut, a shiny sugared memory. Either hot dogs or corn dogs. A thin, cruel hint of dark Pepsi in paper cups. And the unique smell of tons of water off tons of heated skin, rising like steam off a new bath. Animal heat. From overhead it is more real than anything.

See it all. You can see the whole thing, blue and white and brown and white, soaked in a watery spangle of deepening red. Everyone. This is a view. And you knew that from below you wouldn't look nearly so high overhead. You know now how high you are. You knew from underneath no one could tell.

He says it behind you, his eyes around your ankles, the solid bald man, Hey kid. They want to know. Do your plans up here involve the whole day or what exactly is the story. Hey kid are you okay.

There's been time this whole time. You can't kill time with your heart. Everything takes time. Bees have to move to stay still.

Hey kid he says Hey kid are you okay.

Metal flowers bloom on your tongue. No more time for thinking. Now that there is time you don't have time.

Hey.

Slowly now, across everything, there's a watching that spreads like silent energy pudding. Watch it. Your sighted sister and her thin white pack, pointing. Your mother looks to the shallows where you used to be, then makes a visor of her hand. The whale stirs and jiggles. The guard looks up, the girl around his leg looks up, he reaches for his horn.

Forever below is rough deck, snacks, thin metal music, where you used to be; the line is solid and has no reverse gear; and the water, of course, is only soft when you're inside it. Look. Now it moves in sun, full of hard coins of light that shimmer red as they stretch away into a mist that is your own sweet salt. The coins crack into early moons, long pins of light from the hearts of sad stars. The square tank is a cold blue sheet. Cold is just a kind of hard. A kind of blind. You have been taken off guard. Happy Birthday. Did you think it over. Yes and no. Hey kid.

Two black spots, violence, and disappear into a well of time. Height is not the problem. It all changes when you get back down. With your weight.

But so which is the lie? Hard or soft? Silence or time?

The lie is that it's one or the other. A still, floating bee is moving faster than it can think. From overhead the sweet drives it crazy.

The board will nod and you will go, and black eyes of skin can cross blind into a cloud-blotched sky, punctured light emptying behind sharp stone that is forever. That is forever. Step into the skin and disappear.

Hello.